Magpie

An Avian Shifters Novel

By Kim Dare

Magpie (Avian Shifter Series, Book 2)
ISBN # 978-1-910081-16-7

Published by Kim Dare
Edited by Christine Allen-Riley and Shannon Leeper
Cover Art by Kris Norris

First Edition – October 2012
Second Edition – November 2015

Dedication

To everyone who encouraged me to write another avian shifters book.

I really hope you like the way it turned out.

Chapter One

"They've cornered the little bastard in the back room."

Everet nodded, but he hadn't really needed the bouncer's help to work that out. The sound of fists slamming into flesh travelled clearly through the otherwise silent nightclub, and Everet had no doubt who was playing the part of the punch bag tonight.

With the establishment already closed for the evening, there were no dancers or drinkers to get in Everet's way as he strode quickly toward the door at the far end of a long, curved bar. On the other side of the sleek metallic counter, a man stopped restocking the shelves with bottles and tracked Everet's progress. If a human's senses were acute enough to hear the beating taking place on the other side of the door, the bartender betrayed no sign of it.

The hairs on the back of Everet's neck prickled as he felt the man run an assessing eye over him. He tensed, automatically trying to work out if the guy should be considered a threat. It was the kind of nightclub where the bartenders probably doubled up as extra dumb-muscle when required, and the man was as big as a bloody albatross.

Everet's brain whirled. His survival instincts screamed at him to get out of there, but he didn't let that slow his progress across the room. He reached the door and pushed it open, knowing that any sign of weakness or hesitation might sign two death warrants.

In a split second, Everet took in every detail of the scene before him.

Four humans. One avian.

Four attackers. One poor sod curled up on the floor taking a pounding from them all.

"That's enough." Everet's words cut cleanly through the sound of one of the human's boots meeting the prone avian's ribs.

Just as he expected, the men were shocked enough to stop what they were doing. The boy on the floor temporarily forgotten, all four guys turned toward Everet. They had the look of men who did as they were told—who were used to delivering a beating in the

1

dispassionate manner of those who simply had a job to do.

Everet's eyes narrowed. He looked past the men who'd been throwing their fists around. His suspicions were quickly proved correct. There was one more human in the room. A man sat slightly removed from the action; distant enough to make sure he wouldn't get any nasty blood stains on his expensive suit, but still close enough to watch every blow land.

He appeared to be in his late forties or maybe his early fifties. He flicked ash off the end of his cigarette as he studied Everet in return. It didn't take a genius to place him as Crenshaw, the owner of the club and the man who'd demanded someone come there to retrieve an avian who'd disgraced his kind.

"I assume you're from the *nest*?" Crenshaw bit out.

"Yes."

Silence descended upon the room and demanded to be filled, but Everet already knew what kind of human he was dealing with. He wasn't worth wasting words on.

Crenshaw blinked first. "You're not the same class of shifter as that thing was."

Crenshaw didn't glance toward the avian on the floor, and neither did Everet. The hush was good for something. Everet could just about make out the sound of the boy's laboured breathing. He'd made it there in time. It wasn't appropriate to apply the past tense to the boy's life, not yet.

Crenshaw's lips thinned when Everet failed to offer him any information.

The bodyguards, or bouncers, or whatever the hell they were, seemed to be well attuned to their employer's moods. Each one altered his stance and figuratively rolled up his sleeves, ready to make Everet their new target the moment the order hit the air.

Four in here, plus the guy on the door. Add in the one behind the bar. There was no way Everet could guess how many other men were in the building. They were probably all humans. Still, at least six guys against one shifter. If nothing else, they'd be able to make Everet hurt.

"Species?" Crenshaw snapped.

"Raven."

A slight moan from the huddled figure in the middle of the room pulled everyone's attention toward it. Everet could only risk being distracted for the briefest moment, but that was more than enough time for him to take in the pair of tiny silver shorts the boy wore. The rest of him was bare—all the better to display his bruises.

Some of his injuries had obviously been inflicted long before the present beating had begun. Everet's hand ached to form a fist at his side, but he pushed the instinct away. Six against one, and the boy might get hurt even further. That was unacceptable.

"Tell me, raven, is your breed as stupid as his?" More ash landed on the floor at Crenshaw's feet.

"I don't know what species he is, but ravens aren't known for being fools," Everet said, his voice completely emotionless. That much was true. For one thing, he was easily smart enough to know when to act like the same kind of dumb muscle Crenshaw employed. "My orders said you want to be rid of him as soon as possible."

"Yes." Crenshaw took a deep pull on his cigarette, making the tip glow brightly in the gloomy room. "I wonder, how do you bird-boys punish slutty little thieves?"

Everet didn't even blink. "Decisions like that would be made by avians far higher up the pecking order than—"

"Guess!" Crenshaw ordered. "I want to know what will happen to him." He leaned forward in his chair as he spoke.

Everet quickly scanned the other men in the room as he considered his options. They stood around like men who were used to standing around waiting for orders rather than thoughts to arrive. They didn't look like the type to question a command to beat the hell out of anyone, but at the same time, Everet doubted they'd do it for fun.

Crenshaw, however…yes, Everet saw the gleam in his eye. He was exactly the kind of man who wouldn't see the fun in hurting anyone masochistic enough to enjoy it. He'd do anything it took to make a man writhe in agony. Seeing genuine fear on his victim's face would be like an expert blowjob to him.

"He'll be punished for bringing avians as a whole into disrepute," Everet said. "It's a matter that every nest takes very seriously."

"How?"

Everet swallowed down a bitter taste that filled the back of his mouth and folded his arms across his chest. He'd be damned if he'd feed the bastard's fantasies. "There is no set punishment. Species is taken into account."

"Oh?"

3

"All species have their talents and their weaknesses," Everet said, speaking on something close to automatic pilot as he weighed up the chances of either Kane or himself getting out of there alive.

"He's a magpie."

Everet failed to feel the least bit shocked. "Magpies have always loved anything that glitters and sparkles. Did what he stole from you fit that description?"

Crenshaw paused to take a deep drag on his cigarette, obviously debating if he should tell the truth or lie just to make things worse for the boy.

Everet didn't bother to wait for his answer. He had no interest in an unreliable witness. "The elders will decide what's to be done with him," he said again.

Crenshaw slumped back in his chair. Everet held his gaze for what felt like several minutes. Finally, Crenshaw turned away. He waved a hand toward the curled up figure in the centre of the room as he apparently realised that he wasn't going to get anything interesting out of Everet.

Crenshaw appeared bored. The gesture seemed dismissive. Everet still held his breath, tensed and ready for anything.

Suddenly, Crenshaw jerked to his feet. "He's all yours. Get rid of him however you see fit."

Two of the guys who'd been delivering the beating filed out of the room ahead of Crenshaw, and the other two followed in his wake. Bodyguards rather than bouncers then, not that it really mattered.

Everet watched them go. He listened to their footsteps fade away. Finally, he sensed that he and his charge were alone in that part of the building.

The boy had curled himself into the foetal position. He hadn't moved in several minutes. Everet approached, making sure his footsteps were loud enough to alert the boy to his presence. He dropped to one knee alongside him.

"They've all gone. It's just you and me."

No response. If it weren't for the shallow, shaky breaths, the boy might have succeeded in playing dead.

"Uncurl yourself," Everet ordered. "I need to check your injuries."

While he waited for the boy to obey, Everet assessed what he could already see. There were scars on the boy's back. Some looked like they had been made by a whip; others were small and round—the same size and shape as the tip of Crenshaw's cigarette.

Everet ground his teeth together, but he kept his thoughts on that to himself. Bruises seemed to cover almost every inch of the magpie's body, but it was hard to tell where the bruises ended and the dirt began. The floor hadn't been cleaned in a long time, and there was now a circle of less grubby tiles where the magpie had rolled around trying to evade his attackers.

The boy remained curled into a ball and showed no sign of having heard Everet.

Everet resisted the temptation to look over his shoulder toward the door, or point out that the longer they stayed where they were the more likely it was someone would join them. He wanted the boy co-operative, not more scared than ever.

"I won't hurt you," he tried.

Nothing.

Everet pushed a hand through his own hair, disordering the thick black strands. It was impossible to tell how much damage he might cause if he simply picked the boy up and carried him out of there, but giving him any more time would be too big a risk.

Everet placed a hand on his bare shoulder.

The boy twisted away from him, scrambling back on the floor. He kept his head down, making it impossible for Everet to see his face, but Everet didn't need to see his expression to know how afraid he had to be.

"No touching without paying!"

Everet mentally raised one eyebrow at the huddled figure, but at least the boy was conscious and able to talk. "What's your name?"

"You said you were sent to fetch me."

Everet looked toward the door for a moment, wondering how much cash he'd have to hand over to make the boy come quietly out to his car; probably far more than he had on him. The guy was a magpie after all...

"Names aren't my specialty."

The boy lifted his head a fraction. His hair was dirty. Some of the strands were stained with what had to be blood; they hung down in front of the boy's eyes and obscured Everet's view of his face.

Finally, the magpie blinked. "Kane."

"Everet. Raven." He held his wrist out so Kane could see that

5

he was indeed a raven shifter, even if he happened to be in his human form.

Kane glanced at the tattoo on the inside of Everet's wrist, but he didn't seem to care what symbol was there.

"You're a magpie?" Everet prompted.

Kane didn't take the hint.

Everet frowned. Kane couldn't have lived among humans for so long he'd forgotten even that basic a piece of avian etiquette, could he?

Everet peered more deeply into the shadows below the hunched figure. He could just make out the way Kane kept his right arm huddled tightly against his body. That explained that.

"Are you going to come with me quietly?" His orders were to take Kane back to the nest, and that's where Kane would go. Quietly or not—that was his only choice at this point. Everet didn't even consider pretending otherwise.

Kane lifted his left hand and pushed his hair out of his eyes. He knew the score. He might not like it, but he seemed to be too sensible to fight it—or, at least, too exhausted.

Kane finally uncurled his body. He tried to stand. A startled cry left his lips before he was even halfway up. Everet's reactions were only just quick enough to let him catch Kane before he hit the floor.

Wrapping his arms around Kane's torso, Everet brought them both to their full height. Kane pushed against Everet's chest, but even if he hadn't been injured, a magpie would never have been any match for a raven's strength. Within seconds he stumbled and collapsed against Everet.

Everet frowned. Forget being a magpie, it was consisting of little more than skin and bone that was Kane's problem. Everet scooped Kane's fragile form up into his arms. He weighed next to nothing.

"What the hell do you think you're—?" A pain-filled gasp made Kane stop short.

Everet stepped forward. Doing his best not to jostle Kane any more than necessary, he made his way out of the back room. Checking in every direction, he found the bar empty. The exit wasn't far away. He took his chance.

Kane squirmed in his arms, but it was just the fussing of a child who didn't understand what was going on, or that the adults

6

around him were there to help him.

"Put me down."

Everet ignored the petulant demand.

By the time they reached the other side of the bar, Kane's head had dropped to rest on Everet's shoulder. His breathing remained steady, but any sign of consciousness seeped away.

The same bouncer that had let Everet in stood by the exit. It was closed and bolted. Everet tilted his chin up. "I have permission to take him back to our nest."

"Good riddance. He was a nasty little sod." The guy didn't seem to be in any rush to unlock the door. "Always sucking up to the boss. Never hesitated to play the cock tease with one of the boys then throw him under the bus when the boss caught them."

Everet waited with outward patience until they were finally ushered out into the darkness of a grubby back alley.

Briefly regaining consciousness, Kane shuddered when the chill air caressed his skin. He curled in closer to the only available source of warmth—Everet's body.

Marching down the alley, Everet had all his senses on high alert. Were they being watched? It felt like it. He strained his hearing, but nothing other than the normal sounds of a human city reached his ears.

His whole body ached with the desire to simply forgo all the human bull shit, take to his wings and soar high above the mess and confusion of the human world. As a raven flew, it wouldn't have taken him any time at all to be back among his own kind, back to where no one would have beaten the hell out of someone like Kane just for being a thief. Hell, even the most stupid avian would know not to expect any better from a magpie.

A whimper made Everet look down. Kane stirred and pushed weakly against Everet's chest.

Damn. Everet looked along the alley. There were far too many shadows, far too many places where a threat could lurk.

"Hush," he hazarded, in a half whisper.

Kane only squirmed more.

"It won't be long. I'll soon have you back at the nest." Everet frowned, aware that his voice sounded loud and rough in the otherwise silent alley. Damn, but he wished the alley had been wide enough for him to drive down.

Kane fell still as he passed out again.

Everet walked more quickly. He was acutely aware that, for the first time in almost as long as he could remember, he wasn't in a position to deal with any threat a human could pose.

His custody of Kane made him vulnerable in a way he hadn't been since he'd reached his avian maturity, and Everet didn't like that feeling at all.

Turning a corner and spotting the car he'd driven there from the nest was a blessed relief. Luck was on their side. It hadn't been stolen. As far as Everet could tell as he approached it from the rear, it hadn't even had its tires slashed. Considering the neighbourhood, that alone was little short of a miracle.

Hurrying to the passenger side, Everet carefully wedged Kane against the side of the car and opened the door. The boy didn't stir as Everet awkwardly manoeuvred him into the passenger seat and fastened the seatbelt around him. It was probably just as well. Consciousness could only have made the process painful for him.

Everet jogged around to the other side of the car and got behind the wheel. The dashboard displays lit up, casting a strange light across Kane's face and body. Or, perhaps, they just made the colour of his bruises more noticeable.

Shaking his head, Everet put the car into gear and pulled away. The sooner he got the boy back to his own kind, the better it would be for him. Seeking out any kind of humanity among the human population obviously hadn't done him any good at all.

* * * * *

Bastard.

As Kane stubbornly fought his way back toward consciousness, the only thing he was aware of was the whole-body ache that came from being denied his fix. Crenshaw must be holding out on him again. There wasn't a single part of Kane's body that didn't hurt.

His lips were dry. Opening his mouth far enough to lick them set off an explosion in his jaw. Wincing caused a shaft of rusting metal to stab him in his left eye. Other thoughts and realisations gradually made their way into his mind. There'd obviously been a beating—a bad one if he was able to feel any of it through what was left of his last high.

His face...

8

Crenshaw must have really had enough of him if he hadn't told his guys to avoid messing up his looks. No point going back there then. He'd have to get what he needed elsewhere.

His face...

Kane mentally cursed. That would cost him over the coming days. No one would pay top money to screw a guy whose features were a mass of bruises. Frowning with the effort, Kane managed to lift one hand from where it had rested at his side.

"No."

The voice didn't sound especially angry with him. That was good. It probably wasn't one of the guys who'd delivered the beating. It might even be someone who could get him a fix.

Kane brought his hand a little closer to his face, ignoring both the ache in his shoulder and the man's words.

"No."

A hand came to rest on Kane's forearm. It pushed Kane's arm down to rest at his side. The voice sounded stubborn. At any other time, that might have made it a challenge. Right then, Kane couldn't summon up the energy to show some jumped up prat that there was only one man in the room who'd get his own way in the long run.

First a fix, then some money, then Kane would show him.

Kane finally managed to pry open one eye. A bright light shining straight down on him made sure he knew that it was a mistake. He tried to lift his hand and protect his eyes.

"I said no."

That same touch returned and trapped Kane's arm at his side.

Kane turned his head toward the voice. A blurry outline gradually resolved itself into a man. A young, attractive man with black hair slicked back from his face and serious brown eyes. Kane forced both his eyes open and struggled to focus in on the details a little more quickly.

It had been a long time since he got a pay-out from anyone within a decade of his own age, even longer since he'd been screwed by anyone as hot as this guy. The man staring down at him didn't look like the kind who'd have to pay for it. That alone made him a customer worth having.

Mr. Tall, Dark and Sexy also looked mildly pissed off with the world. Kane smiled as much as what felt like a severely split lip would allow. In his experience, a poor worldview was nothing a good blowjob wouldn't fix.

The guy had said no to Kane three times now, but that could easily change.

"What do I need to do to make you say yes?" Kane asked. The words came out slightly slurred.

"Stay still, I need to finish checking your injuries now that you're awake."

Kane knew then that, despite appearances, the man sitting alongside him had to be exceptionally short. How could a hint that obvious have gone straight over his head otherwise?

"I've heard that one before," Kane said. "Let me guess, I just have to get naked and bend over for the *exam*, right?"

"You just have to stay still," the guy repeated.

Seriously? There was no way anyone, of any height, could miss flirting that blatant! Kane grunted his disapproval and squirmed irritably on the—

He squinted at his surroundings. He lay on a sofa in a room he didn't recognise. "Where am I?"

"You're in a nest. You passed out on the way to the car."

Kane did a quick assessment of the room. It was richly furnished with lots of deep red velvet and gold brocade. Very promising. "This is your room?"

"Part of a guest suite," the guy said, running his hands over Kane's body in a dispassionate way that hinted that he really did want to check for injuries rather than simply check him out.

Kane nodded slightly. The room still looked encouraging. This particular nest had obviously done very well for itself. "You said a nest. Which one?"

"Anderson. We're on the northern edge of the city centre, in Jameson Court. The leader of the nest is Hamilton, an eagle."

Kane filed it all away for future reference. "I haven't heard anything about there being a breeding colony around here," he said. "What species live here?"

"It's not a breeding colony. It's a male-only nest, and it's open to all species. Is that a problem for you?"

Problem? Hell, no! If it was true, it was bloody well perfect! There was bound to be someone high up the pecking order that would like a pretty little boy-toy to hang on his arm and suck on his cock.

"What's your position here?" Kane demanded.

Everet's expression remained impassive. "I'm part of the nest's security flock."

"You're a cop?" Kane didn't even try to hide his horror. Everet could obviously be crossed off his list of possible sugar-daddies. Cops weren't just trouble; they were usually broke, too.

"Something like that," Everet said, absentmindedly. "I don't think anything is broken."

Sod bones. "I want to look in a mirror."

Everet took a brief break from his inspection and met Kane's gaze. "You're not going anywhere until I've checked your injuries. You're in no condition to wander around—"

"Then bring one to me," Kane snapped. Really, ravens weren't half as clever as they thought they were. The solution should have been obvious.

Everet looked down, as if in submission. Kane smiled, but his expression quickly soured as he realised that Everet had only dropped his gaze to resume his examination.

"I said—"

"I heard you," Everet cut in.

"Then why aren't you doing what I said?" Kane demanded.

"Because your priorities are screwed up." Everet didn't even look away from his study of Kane's right wrist as he spoke.

"I can cause a lot of trouble for you."

That convinced Everet to look up. He held Kane's gaze very steadily for several seconds, his expression serious, the emotions in his eyes unreadable. Finally, he looked away.

"You appear to have more scrapes and bruises than anything else. Probably some sprains. Maybe a few cracked ribs as well."

Kane pursed his lips, annoyance bubbling up inside him.

"Do you think you'll be able to clean yourself up on your own, or will you need help?" Everet asked.

"I'm fine."

Kane levered himself up, swung his legs over the side of the sofa and stood up. At least, that's what he intended to do. His knees trembled; his ankles buckled. Suddenly, he found himself scooped up in Everet's arms. It was almost like being lifted by a high, except—

"Don't even bother arguing with me," Everet snapped.

He carried Kane across the room and through an open doorway. A big, elaborate bathtub stood on the far side of a marble tiled room. One wall housed a toilet and bidet; opposite it stood a huge vanity containing a pair of matching sinks. And, most importantly of all, above the sinks hung a large, gilt-framed mirror.

Kane twisted around in Everet's arms. "I want to look in the mirror!"

Everet played deaf, walked straight past the sinks, and set him down on a chair next to the bath.

Kane instantly tried to stand up.

"No."

"Who the hell do you think you are?" Kane demanded, glaring up at him.

"Take your shorts off."

"Dream on," Kane sneered. "You can't afford me."

Everet reached across the bath and turned on the gold taps. "Take off your shorts so I can clean you up," he specified.

Steam quickly filled the air. The water looked hot and tempting. It couldn't hurt to be clean and pretty when he was finally introduced to someone who it could be worth making a play for.

Kane had to struggle to get out of his shorts. Crenshaw had specifically chosen them to be so tight Kane couldn't conceal any stolen items on his person. As if that would stop him!

Sore joints and bruised muscles protested at his squirming, but Kane finally managed to toss the shorts aside. Everet held out a hand and helped him into the bath.

The plug hadn't been put in. All the hot water ran straight out. Before Kane had time to call him an idiot, Everet diverted the hot water so it ran through a shower hose. Holding the shower head in his hand rather than putting it up on the gilt stand alongside the bath, Everet maintained complete control over the spray. He moved it slowly over Kane's body, washing away the worst of the dust and dirt.

Kane hesitated. It seemed pointless to complain that all the dirty water hadn't been trapped in the tub with him. He tipped back his head as Everet let the water pour down over his hair.

Being clean felt good, and it could only improve his chances with the richer avians at the nest. And, for a few minutes, while there was no one worth impressing looking on, Kane was free to simply enjoy a moment's peace. That felt good, too.

There was no one he needed to flirt with, no one he needed to throw himself at. Kane just sat.

Shampoo and soap were offered and accepted. Kane remained silent as he washed himself all over several times in an effort to get rid of dried blood and accumulated dirt. He glanced up through his lashes as Everet patiently moved the shower hose over him, rinsing off the suds each time.

In a way, it was a pity that Everet had no chance of raising the kind of money it took to keep Kane happy. He might have found lying face down on the bed while some guy shoved his cock up his arse mildly enjoyable, if the guy was someone like Everet.

Chapter Two

Everet turned off the water and handed Kane a towel. It was hard to tell if the droplets that hung from the magpie's lashes were tears or spray from the shower. Kane had seemed to be in a world of his own for the last half an hour. That didn't change as he began to dry his body.

The shower might have made Kane cleaner, but it hadn't given him back his balance. As soon as he tried to stand, he swayed. Everet caught him by his shoulders and ended up taking most of his weight as he guided him onto the chair alongside the bath.

Everet ran his eyes over Kane, checking to see if any new injuries had become visible. "While you were out-cold, I sent one of the wrens to fetch some clothes for you."

Kane's eyes narrowed. Wherever his mind had wandered off to before, he was suddenly back in the here and now, and apparently as suspicious as hell. "What kind of clothes?"

"The kind that will stop you from having to walk around the nest naked."

Right on cue, someone knocked on the guest suite door.

"Stay where you are." Everet didn't wait for a response. He strode out of the bathroom, trying not to make it obvious just how eager he was to get away from Kane for a while. Being trapped in such close proximity to the naked magpie wasn't helping him feel either detached or professional. Pushing his fingers through his hair, Everet tried to force his mind back onto the job at hand.

Fetch the boy, clean him up, and take him to the elders. His orders were simple. They did not involve getting all hot and bothered while helping Kane take a bath. An erection was not going to be required in order to fulfil his duties. Now, if he could just convince his cock to believe that.

He jerked the suite door open with far more force than he'd intended and glared down at the wren standing on the threshold. The servant lifted up the clothes, as if they were some sort of talisman that could ward off evil spirits—especially those which came in the form of a very pissed off raven.

"Thanks." Everet snatched the clothes from the wren and slammed the door in his face.

There was no time for polite, little niceties. Everet's faith in Kane's ability to obey his order and remain safely on his chair was severely limited. As he reached the bathroom doorway, Everet half expected to find Kane sprawled across the floor, quite possibly with a gash to his temple, after hitting his head when he collapsed.

Kane's chair was empty. So was the floor. Kane stood in front of the sink, staring into a section of mirror he'd wiped clear of steam.

"I look like I was hit by a steamroller."

"I told you to stay where you were."

Kane ran his fingers over his face. One side of it was a mass of bruises. It was a wonder he could stand to touch it at all. Or, perhaps it would have been, if certain other facts hadn't become apparent while Kane was in the bath.

Everet's mood turned more serious than ever as he set the clothes on the counter alongside the sink. "What are you on?"

Kane continued to stare into the mirror. "Nothing. I don't do drugs."

Everet caught hold of Kane's wrist and turned his arm so the inside of his elbow was clearly visible to them both. With all the dust from Crenshaw's floor washed away, the track marks were obvious.

"They're old. I used to have a problem, I don't anymore." Kane didn't even blink as he said it. In a way, it was quite impressive.

Everet was used to being lied to. It was practically part of his new job description at the nest, but he'd come across relatively few men who lied as seamlessly or as shamelessly as Kane. "I know what fresh track marks look like," Everet bit out.

"Apparently, you're not as well informed as you think you are." Kane tried to pull his wrist out of Everet's grip and failed.

"If you weren't high, you'd be in so much pain you'd barely be able to remain conscious, let alone move around the room."

"I have a high pain tolerance. Spend a few years getting whipped just so some old fool can get his rocks off, and you'd barely notice a few bumps and bruises either."

15

"Tell me what you've taken over the last few days," Everet ordered once more, keeping his voice emotionless through sheer force of will.

Kane rolled his eyes. "Nothing! Are you deaf or something?"

"If I have to, I can order a blood test and—"

"I don't belong to you." Kane turned to face Everet. Tilting his head back, he glared up at him, real anger burning in his gaze. "If you want to order me around, you can drop your money on the end of the bed, just like everyone else. I don't do freebies—not even for cops."

"I'm acting on orders from the elders. While you're in this nest—"

"You want to screw me, don't you?"

Everet said nothing. There was no point trying to deny it while his erection was straining against the inside of his jeans.

"I can always tell when a man wants to pin me against the wall and screw me, quick and rough," Kane sneered. "You're gagging for it."

Everet remained silent for several seconds, while Kane grinned in triumph.

"Finished?" Everet asked, when Kane failed to add another taunt to his list.

"Only because I've obviously won!" Kane's laughter was brittle and harsh—an ugly sound to come from such a pretty boy.

"Tell me what you've taken."

Kane tried to snatch his hand out of Everet's grip again. This time, Everet let him.

Kane pushed against Everet's chest. There was little strength in him, and even less weight. Everet remained exactly where he was; Kane didn't.

It was only Everet's quick reactions that stopped Kane crashing to the floor as he stumbled backward.

"Let me go!"

Everet gritted his teeth as he held back a sigh. The elders were expecting them; he had no time to question Kane further.

"Get dressed." Everet released Kane, allowing him just enough room to follow the order.

Kane glanced at the clothes. "No way. I'm not wearing this crap!" He picked disdainfully at the neat little pile, causing the shoes balanced on the top to tumble on to the floor.

"You're going to see the elders in a few minutes," Everet said. "You can do that dressed or naked, your choice."

Kane parted his lips. He was about to say naked, Everet knew it. Then Kane apparently caught sight of his blurry reflection in one of the steam-covered mirrors. Even in the distorted reflection, his injuries were obvious.

It wasn't just his face that looked like it had been through several rounds with a heavyweight-boxer. Kane looked down and ran his hand over some of the more interestingly coloured marks on his torso. He glanced at the clothes again, weighing his options. Finally, he turned to Everet.

"I want something else to wear."

"Depending on what the elders decide should be done with you, other clothes may be provided. For now, your choice is between those and nothing."

Everet glanced at the little pile of garments as he waited for Kane to make his decision. He'd be dammed if he could work out what the boy was making so much fuss about. They were clothes. Jeans, a long-sleeve T-shirt and trainers.

They weren't all black, which would have made them perfect in Everet's eyes, but they looked like they were about the right size for Kane—or as close as could be expected until the boy ate something that didn't include a chemical high.

Kane gave a theatrical sigh and picked up the jeans. He turned to Everet. "What? You want to watch everything I do in here? Did the elders order you not to give me room to take a piss on my own, or do you just get off on that sort of thing?"

Everet ran an assessing eye over Kane. He looked a little steadier on his feet than he had been. The request was reasonable. "I'll be just outside the door if you need me."

Having closed the bathroom door carefully behind him, Everet leant against the wall alongside it, shut his eyes, and let his head bang back against the paintwork. No man who was that beaten up should have been able to exude so much raw sex appeal. No man who was that much of a brat should have made Everet want to do anything other than throttle him.

Everet adjusted himself within his now uncomfortably tight jeans. He needed to get out more, or at least stay in with another man, rather than on his own.

Minutes ticked past; no plea for assistance came through the door. Everet waited. Another few minutes. Kane was just taking the piss now.

Everet glanced at the clock on the opposite wall and rapped pointedly on the door. "Kane?"

Nothing.

Everet was just about to reach for the handle when the door swung inward.

If Everet had been inclined to think about it, it might have occurred to him that the supply of toiletries in the guest suite bathroom may extend past mere soap and shampoo.

Kane had obviously thought about it. He'd transformed his hair into a fashionably messed up style that made it look as if a lover had run his fingers through the golden-blond strands all night.

The fact that the bruises on his face appeared to have undergone an entire week's worth of healing, hinted that he'd found whatever makeup had been placed in there for guests to use, too.

Everet might have assumed there was a shaving kit in there somewhere. But, it would never have occurred to him that a man would take the razor out of said kit and use it to slice through his jeans in several places. One knee was cut open, so was a pocket, and a point so high up on the inside of one thigh that, if Kane had dressed to the right, a lucky man might glimpse far more than mere leg.

What had been a perfectly normal long sleeve T-shirt had also been sliced and restyled while Everet had cooled his heels outside the bathroom door. Somehow, Kane had managed to keep the fabric covering up the worst of his injuries and had only exposed healthy looking patches of skin.

Everet finished his assessment of Kane's wardrobe and returned his attention to his face. It had obviously never occurred to Kane that the man they'd borrowed those clothes from might expect to get them back in one piece. Mentioning the possibility now seemed pointless.

Everet turned toward the door leading out of the suite. "The elders are waiting for us."

"What?"

Everet stopped and glanced back toward Kane. "The nest's elders, they're—"

"That's all you're going to say—" Kane stopped as suddenly as he started. He pursed his lips. "Whatever." He strode past Everet, his steps now strong and confident.

Easily keeping up with him, Everet made no attempt to take the lead until Kane stopped at a crossroads, obviously realising he had no idea which corridor to take.

Everet pointed to the left. He'd put Kane in the guest suite closest to the elders' meeting room, so they were already in the more formal part of the nest that was usually only used by the higher-ranking shifters. It was all expensively carpeted hallways, lined with portraits of past elders of the nest, in this section of the building.

As they walked, Everet kept a careful eye on his charge. If Kane was overawed by his surroundings, he didn't show it. In fact, he did a damn good impression of someone who had been born to roam around corridors like this. There wasn't a hint of nerves in him. Poor sod, he was probably too high to realise how large an effect the forthcoming meeting might have on his life.

Stopping outside an overly tall door surrounded by ornate carving, Everet rapped on one of the flatter bits of woodwork. He kept his expression blank, but his mind worked overtime. The appropriate thing to do would be to simply deliver Kane to the elders and let them get on with it. So why didn't it feel like the *right* thing to do?

"Enter." Hamilton's voice carried a thick undercurrent of displeasure that didn't bode well for Kane. Everet opened the door and stepped back for Kane to go in first.

Following in Kane's wake, Everet pulled the door closed and took up position to one side of it. He'd just wait to see if anything else would be required of him before he went back to his regular duties, nothing unprofessional about that.

Kane approached the long table where the elders held their meetings. Only six men sat on the other side of the table that day, although there was room for more than a dozen of them.

"You're the magpie the humans required us to retrieve?" Hamilton snapped.

Kane stopped directly in front of him, about a yard away from the table.

As the leader of the nest, Hamilton occupied the central seat, but Everet sent up thanks that Hamilton wouldn't be making any decision regarding Kane's fate alone. The only man in the nest capable of really influencing Hamilton was there too.

Ori, the nest's swan, smiled shyly at Everet as their eyes met.

Everet dipped his head in due deference and took a slow, deep breath. For some stupid reason, he found himself incredibly relieved that there was someone at the meeting who might be inclined to be merciful toward Kane—not that the little brat had shown any sign of deserving it.

On Ori's right, just as Everet expected, sat a hawk, sat Ori's...

Everet faltered. Over a year and a half after Ori and Raynard had come to some sort of arrangement, Everet was damned if he could work out how any of them were supposed to refer to Ori and Raynard's relationship.

"I asked you a question," Hamilton said, his words more clipped than ever.

"I heard you," Kane said. "And yes, I am. Who the hell are you?"

Everet glared at the back of Kane's neck. If Kane thought that kind of attitude would get him anywhere with Hamilton, he really hadn't read the man well.

Damn it, even Ori wouldn't be able to help Kane, if someone didn't give the elders the full facts.

Everet stepped forward. "I believe he is still under the influence of the drugs he took while among the humans, sir."

Kane glared over his shoulder at Everet. "No, I'm not!"

Everet held his ground. It all came down to who the elders would choose to believe now—a raven or a magpie.

* * * * *

Kane turned away from Everet and glared at the guys sitting along the other side of the table.

"I see," said the oldest man, who was occupying the biggest chair in the centre. He sounded even more prissy now than he had at the start.

Kane saw too. He saw very well indeed, and he didn't like it one little bit. He ran his eyes over all the men on the opposite side of the table. There was only one guy who looked like an attractive prospect as a potential sugar-daddy. One out of six. If that was the best the nest could offer then Kane was going to be screwed—or worse still, that he might have to put up with being screwed by someone like the stuck-up bastard in the middle.

"Perhaps if you both sit down and join us at the table, we can work something out?"

Kane glanced at the youngest of the so-called elders. In spite of the white hair, he looked like he was in his early twenties. The guy dropped his gaze when their eyes met, but there was no hint of flirtation in the gesture.

"He said sit." That was the prospective sugar-daddy, speaking from the right of the guy with the white hair. "You too, Everet."

A hand came to rest on Kane's shoulder. The bloody raven. Kane shrugged irritably. The hand remained firmly in position.

Rolling his eyes and doing his damnedest to make it look like he was humouring them rather than giving in because he knew he was beaten, Kane slumped into one of the rather less impressive chairs lined up on his side of the table. He pulled one foot up in front of him on the cushioned seat and wrapped his hands around his bent leg.

The chair wasn't built to accommodate bad posture. The small of Kane's back protested almost immediately, but he stuck with it. Just like the pain he'd felt from his bruises a little while ago, his discomfort soon slipped away.

Only the buzzing in his ears reminded him that he'd need to get another shot of something good into his veins soon if he wanted to remain impassive to anything the world and its heavy leather boots could kick out of him.

Kane was vaguely aware of the raven sitting down alongside him, but he made a point of not looking in his direction.

"You're marked, of course?" That was the grumpy old git again.

"Of course," Kane sneered, in what was a bloody good impersonation of the old man's tone, if he did say so himself.

"It is customary for avians to address those of a higher rank as sir."

"Shall I tell you what you can do with your customs, *sir*?"

"Display your wrist." Ice dripped off the words.

Kane didn't move. A few seconds passed. The guy with the white hair broke first. Kane watched impassively as he placed his right forearm on the table, his palm up and his wrist exposed.

A tattoo covered the skin directly over his vein. The swirls and curves proclaimed a species but it wasn't one Kane recognised.

Mr. White-Hair's actions seemed to be a signal for everyone else to do the same. All the men around the table followed his lead.

That was wrong. Kane felt it in every cell in his body. The guy wasn't someone that other men naturally followed. Every other man in the room gave off a greater instinct toward dominance than little Mr. White-Hair.

Kane glanced at the other men's wrists. He recognised the head of the nest as an eagle. The man with sugar-daddy potential was a hawk. He didn't study the rest of the men's marks for long enough to know if he'd recognise them or not.

"My name is Ori," Mr. White-Hair said. "I'm a swan. Mr. Hamilton," he indicated the grumpy sod in the big chair. "Is an eagle. Mr. Raynard is a hawk."

Kane was more than happy to turn his attention toward the hawk. Yes, there were very real possibilities there. Raynard's eyebrows drew closer together as he frowned. He looked like the kind of man who'd get off on spanking his lover for being a naughty little boy. There was a shed-load of money to be made from that sort of stuff.

"This is the point where you give your name and confirm your species." Raynard sounded just as pissed off as he looked, but it suited him far better than Hamilton.

Kane held Raynard's gaze as he slowly unfurled his arm. He pushed his sleeve back just far enough to show his tattoo. "And my name is Kane."

"It's nice to meet you."

The words came from Ori, but Kane kept his attention on Raynard. Ori wasn't the kind of man who'd pay to screw him; there was no reason to glance in his direction.

"There can be no doubt about your species?" That was Hamilton, and it was a strange enough question to make Kane turn away from Raynard for a moment.

"What?"

"There are no doubts regarding your species? You were born into an established nest, you can trace your parentage and you've successfully completed your first shift?"

"Looks like someone's a bit past his prime." Kane smirked. "Job getting too much for you, *sir*? Not quite able to keep up with what's going on?"

Hamilton straightened up in his chair. "In that case, there

seems very little for us to do here." He turned to Everet. "I trust there is an empty cage available?"

Kane glanced at Everet, just in time to see him tense.

"There is," Everet said.

"What are you talking about?" Kane demanded. "What cages?"

A moment of silence drew out, as everyone seemed to wait for another man to offer an answer.

Kane grabbed hold of Everet's arm.

Everet's voice was unemotional. "There are traditional bird-cages built into one of the basements. They extend up a column in the centre of the nest. Avians who don't conduct themselves in an acceptable manner, can be housed in them until they're behaviour improves."

"You're winding me up. We stopped using them back when we stopped building nests out of twigs!"

No one laughed. No one said a word.

Even as he sat in the middle of the huge meeting room, Kane felt the walls closing in on him. "Who the hell uses that sort of shit these days?" he demanded, growing more anxious by the moment.

"We do," Hamilton snapped. "We reinstituted them earlier this year. They're perfectly humane."

Kane launched himself to his feet. He'd had enough of humanity and its kicking, punching, human-ness. He was fed up with them flittering around the issue. "You're talking about putting me in prison!"

"What did you expect when you were brought here?" Hamilton said.

Rough sex from a man who was rich enough to pay for the privilege. Some deep survival instinct kicked in, and stopped Kane saying that aloud.

Kane was aware that he was very much the centre of attention. At any other time that would have been fun, but being locked away in a cage...

That couldn't happen.

The time for messing around and kicking the chairs out from beneath stuffy old gits was over. Kane's mind raced as he quickly weighed his options. He'd been right in his first instinct. There was only one man worth approaching. He caught Raynard's gaze and held it.

"Surely there's something you can do." Kane let his voice soften as he spoke, until blatant invitation dripped from each syllable.

"Perhaps we should hear Kane's side of the story before we come to any firm decisions?"

The words should have come from Raynard, but they came from Ori.

Kane continued to stare at Raynard until it became obvious that the hawk had no intention of uttering a damn word to help him. Kane glanced toward Ori and saw the way that Ori looked toward Raynard for approval.

"It's well within your remit to ask him any questions you wish him to answer," Raynard said.

Kane's gaze flicked quickly from hawk to swan, and back. They were screwing each other. Bloody brilliant. The one man worth renting himself to by the hour, and Kane would have to get rid of the resident boy-toy before he could make any sort of use of the hawk.

"Kane?" That was Ori again. "Please, sit down. Tell us what happened. You've been accused of stealing from the owner of a club, a human club," he specified. "And of bringing avians into disrepute among the human population. This is your chance to explain yourself."

Rapidly calculating a new strategy, Kane lowered himself onto the edge of his seat. Ori would believe anything he was told. Kane knew the type. He was obviously out to "do good". He'd go for any sob story a guy threw at him. Anyone with half a brain could wrap him around a finger, a toe, or any other part of his body.

However, Ori was only one man on the committee sitting before him. Damn, but Kane knew he'd probably need some sort of majority vote.

Hamilton would see him swing if he had half a chance. Raynard wasn't fool enough to believe any line of bull. The rest would probably follow the birds of prey unless he made a *really* good show of it.

Kane nodded slowly. "Crenshaw. Yes, I'll admit it. I did steal from him."

"Then there is nothing else to be said," Hamilton snapped.

"You were asked to tell us what happened," Raynard said to Kane, before the last of Hamilton's words had faded from the air. "Finish your story."

24

Story.

Kane looked up. Raynard knew he was lying, but he wanted to hear it anyway. Maybe he was ready to play with a new toy after all.

"I—" Kane let his voice crack. He'd become good at feigning emotion over the years. Now, he dragged his A-game to the fore. "I was just so hungry, sir. Mr. Crenshaw was furious with me because one of his friends told him I'd been disrespectful to him. And Mr. Crenshaw said I wouldn't be allowed to have anything to eat until I...until I did what his friend wanted and—" He bowed his head, but not so low that he couldn't assess the company through his lashes and adapt his performance to suit.

Ori was already on the edge of his seat, stupidly quick in his sympathy. Swans were obviously suckers.

Kane pushed his sleeves back and displayed his forearms, only stopping just short of revealing his track marks. The bruises there were impressive, even by Kane's standards, and he'd seen plenty of them over the years. "I wasn't even sure if you'd be able to make out my species mark."

Hamilton didn't look the least bit impressed. Bastard.

Kane dropped his voice to a whisper. "I thought they were going to kill me, sir. I think they nearly did. If you hadn't sent someone to rescue me... If he hadn't arrived when he did..."

"You're safe now." Ori reached across the table and took hold of Kane's hand.

Kane glanced toward Raynard. It was impossible to tell if he bought it or not. More than half his attention still seemed to be on the bloody swan.

Kane snatched his hand back, too pissed off to consider how it would suit his performance. Ori blinked in surprise. Kane hurriedly wrapped his arms around his torso, as if that had been his intent the whole time.

"If that's all you have to say," Hamilton began.

"Does he really have to go to the cages, sir?" Ori cut in. "I thought we agreed that they'd only be used for a few days at a time, and as a last resort?"

Hamilton seemed to hesitate. He might be sitting in the biggest chair but Kane realised in that moment that Hamilton's leadership of the nest wasn't as complete as he might like to pretend it was.

"If he's left to roam freely at this time, he'll cause trouble, sire," Hamilton said. "However, he'll be allowed out as soon as he can be trusted; either to behave well in the nest, or not to bring avians to disrepute among the humans. We've lived discreetly among the non-shifters for far too long to risk upsetting the balance just because one magpie can't control his base instincts."

Ori looked toward Raynard. The hawk didn't say a word, but Kane thought something seemed to pass silently between them. "How long do you think it will be before he could be trusted, sir?" Ori asked Hamilton.

Hamilton altered his position in his chair, like a schoolboy who'd been caught lying to his teacher. "It is not an inhumane punishment, sire. He'll have plenty of room to shift and stretch his wings whenever he wishes. He'll be well fed and warm. He'll even be given suitable employment if he wishes it."

Ori dropped his gaze, but Kane had no doubt that the question still stood, Hamilton was still obliged to answer.

"It's a well-established fact that magpies cannot be rehabilitated," Hamilton finally admitted. "They're not capable of any sort of self-control, sire. That's probably what led to him being cast out of his original nest and into the human world in the first place."

"He'd have to be kept in a cage forever?" Ori blurted out, his eyes round with shock.

Hamilton didn't say anything; he didn't need to. The answer was obvious.

Kane tensed, his fingers clawing at the shirt on either side of his torso. There was no such thing as a cage that could keep him forever. Eventually, he'd be able to screw a guard into letting him out, or perhaps one of the other elders would hear about the pretty little prisoner and come to visit him. Either way, it was a chore Kane could do without. He needed his fix *now*.

"There's no alternative?" Ori asked, with what sounded like an insane amount of compassion for someone he hadn't set eyes on two minutes ago. He couldn't actually give a damn about Kane, but he put on a good show of it.

"He cannot be trusted if he is free," Hamilton said again, each word clipped and brittlely polite. "He'd have to be guarded twenty-four hours a day."

Ori nibbled at his bottom lip in concern. "Maybe we could

find someone who would take him on as a…a submissive of sorts?" he offered, tentatively.

Submissive? Kane raised a mental eyebrow. He knew how that game went. He could look pretty in leather twenty-four hours a day if he needed to. Twisting a kinky old man around his little finger couldn't be that much harder than manipulating a vanilla sugar-daddy.

"I'll do it."

All eyes turned toward Everet, including Kane's. The raven had been still and silent for so long, Kane had almost forgotten he was there. Apparently, so had everyone else in the room.

"You'll take charge of him?" Hamilton asked. "You'll take complete responsibility for him?"

"Yes."

Kane studied Everet very carefully. The raven showed no emotion. There were no obvious signs of sympathy. On the other hand, he didn't look angry because he knew damn well that everything Kane said was a lie, either. Everet didn't seem to care about any of that.

Sex. That had to be at the root of it. Well, that made everything simple. Everet was offering to take charge of him so he could screw him.

Kane mentally played out his future in his mind's eye. Everet was far lower down the pecking order than he'd have liked, but he was hot. He'd do until Kane got the chance to upgrade to a wealthier model.

"If you take him under your wing, you'll be responsible for *anything* he does," Hamilton said, not even trying to hide the fact that he wanted to talk Everet out of it. "The only way we could ever agree to this kind of proposal would be if he accepted you as his master and you took *complete* ownership of him. You could punish him however you wanted. But in the eyes of the nest you'd still be guilty of every crime he committed and eligible to receive any punishments he earned. As far as the rules of the nest are concerned, you'd be one person."

"I understand."

"You believe Kane can be rehabilitated?" Ori asked, eagerly, leaning forward in his seat.

"Yes," Everet said.

Poor, delusional sod. Kane only just kept back a burst of

laughter.

"What do you think, sir?" Ori asked Raynard.

"If Everet thinks he can reform him, I see no reason why he shouldn't be allowed to try." He studied Everet for a moment. "It can't be an irreversible decision. Submission doesn't work like that—neither does mastery. Each man needs to be allowed to back out of the arrangement at any time, in favour of Kane being sent to the cages. If each of them can call it off whenever they want, I don't see any harm in it."

Ori smiled, as if he'd been given permission for a huge treat. Without warning, he turned to Kane.

"Do you understand what this would mean, Kane? You'd belong to him in every way." Ori looked down for a moment. "Everet is a good man, but submitting to another man's will can't always be easy. He'll be allowed to set any rules he wishes you to follow. If you do something wrong, he'll be allowed to punish you in whatever ways he sees fit."

Yeah, right. Kane was sure they all thought that was the way things would be between them. More fool them. "I understand," he said. He understood far more than any of them ever would.

Silence filled the room for several seconds.

"So, what do you think, Kane?" Ori eventually asked. "Will you accept Everet as your master and agree to do your best to be a good submissive for him?"

Kane smiled, all his faith in his ability to find a nice safe perch to land upon very nicely confirmed. "Of course, sir."

If he'd given a damn about being honest with any of the men in the room, he might have crossed his fingers when he said that last bit. As it was, he didn't even bother.

Chapter Three

Everet closed the door leading into his apartment at the nest carefully behind him. It was important that he pay attention to every single thing he did. Monitoring his actions was essential now in a way it had never been before. Now, he was aware that, if he didn't keep a careful watch on himself, he might let another insane act slip through all the barriers that common sense should have erected in its path.

Everet still didn't know what the hell he'd been thinking when he'd agreed to take the damn magpie under his wing. He was reasonably sure that it would always remain a mystery—possibly because he'd lost his mind.

Holding back a curse, Everet turned away from the door. He was just in time to see Kane stride into the middle of the small sitting area that took up most of his accommodation at the nest.

Kane ran his gaze over the space with obvious distaste. "The guest quarters were much nicer."

"I'm not a guest," Everet said. "I work here. Once you've healed, you'll be working here too."

Kane made no comment on that. Selective deafness seemed to be one of his current specialties. Everet added it to the end of the ever-increasing list of behaviours he'd have to try to modify if Kane could ever be allowed any kind of freedom in the future.

Everet stepped away from the door as he watched Kane examine his surroundings.

Sofa, armchair, shelves, coffee table—Kane didn't miss a thing.

Whatever drug Kane had taken, it was obviously doing a sterling job of keeping him oblivious to his pain. Every movement he made was fluid and easy. It was almost possible to believe the bruises were just colours painted onto his skin.

The boy was going to get a hell of a shock once his high wore off.

"Are you hungry?"

Kane shook his head, not even bothering to look over his shoulder.

Everet, however, was hungry enough to eat whatever anyone would put in front of him. Stepping over to the fireplace, he took the internal phone from its holder on the wall and called down to the kitchens.

Kane glanced into the bathroom before drifting into the apartment's only bedroom.

Everet listened for a thud, just in case Kane's high was about to end with a bang, but no sound emerged from the bedroom. No comment regarding the fact Everet's apartment only contained one bed floated out of the room either.

It was a big enough double that it would easily hold two men who had no intention of touching during the night. If Kane hadn't exuded sex through every pore in his body, then that might have actually been a possibility.

Order placed, Everet hung up the phone, and made his way into the bedroom. He half expected to find Kane crashed out, asleep on the bed.

He was partially right. Kane was certainly on the bed, but he wasn't curled up and sleeping off his high.

Kane lay in the centre of the mattress, propped up by several pillows. His lips curled into a smile; an invitation shone in his eyes.

"Well?" Kane asked.

Everet couldn't help but run his gaze down Kane's body. Even though Kane was dressed, the memory of him naked was right in the forefront of Everet's mind. God, he was gorgeous. But, he bloody well knew it too.

"Well what?" Everet said.

Kane laughed. "Well, now that you've got me, what are you going to do with me?"

Everet remained just inside the bedroom door. A good three yards of dark blue carpet stretched out between him and the other man, and that was the way it would stay.

"Now, I'm going to break you of all your bad habits and make you a credit to the nest," Everet said, very simply.

This time, Kane's laugh contained less flirtation and far more real mirth. "Of course you are. And I'll bet stage one of that plan involves you sticking your cock up my arse, right?"

When Kane smiled, it was so easy to focus on his expression and forget everything else. Everet folded his arms across his chest and held his ground through sheer force of will. The bruises—those were the important things to remember. The bruises, and the track marks, and the fact that Kane had probably spent so much of his life either whoring himself out or stealing from those who screwed him, he couldn't remember how to do anything else.

"No," Everet said. There would be no sex. "The first stage is to get you clean and sober. It shouldn't take long for all the drugs to leave your system, but it probably won't be pleasant for you."

Kane's eyes narrowed. He seemed to remain deep in thought for a few seconds. Then, the smile came back. He trailed one hand down his body, teasing the tears he'd slashed into his clothes and caressing the skin visible through them.

"The second stage will involve finding a role in the nest that suits your abilities," Everet went on, doing his damnedest to pretend the little show wasn't having any effect on him.

Kane's hand reached his crotch. He caressed the line of his shaft through the denim. He had indeed dressed to the right. The tip of his cock became visible through the rip in his jeans as he hardened.

Everet had seen Kane naked in the bath. It should have been easy to ignore the glimpse of his cock, but it wasn't.

"Abilities." Kane grinned as he looked down at his hand. "Yeah, I've got lots of those. You wouldn't believe the tricks I've learned over the years. There's this thing I can do with my tongue that—"

Everet took several quick steps back and slammed the bedroom door—sealing Kane in the bedroom and himself outside it.

"Get some sleep," he yelled through the door. "We're making an early start in the morning."

Kane's laughter was muffled by the door, but there was no doubt the cheeky little bastard thought he'd won round one of their little war of wills.

Everet pressed the heel of his hand against his straining fly. Kane had certainly done a wonderful job of getting him all hot and bothered. On the other hand, Everet hadn't given in to temptation.

Everet frowned. At best, that could only be counted as a draw.

A knock fell upon a door. For a second, Everet thought Kane

wanted permission to leave the bedroom, but no, it came from the door to his apartment.

A distraction! Yes! That was exactly what Everet needed.

He jerked open the door, willing to invite in whoever was there.

Ambrose stood on the threshold, his huge form practically filling the entire doorway. "Your food was delivered to my apartment by mistake." He proffered a plate. The sandwich was huge, just as Everet had requested, but in Ambrose's hand, it looked dainty.

"Thanks." Everet took the plate and stepped back to let his friend in.

"You've had a busy day," Ambrose said. "The rumour mill is working overtime."

Everet grunted. Well now, wasn't that great? "What is it saying?"

"A hundred different things about you and a magpie," Ambrose said, folding himself carefully onto one end of the sofa. Just like every other piece of furniture, the sofa seemed to be the wrong scale for him. No matter how small he tried to make himself, he was still too big for the rest of the world.

Everet slumped onto the other end of the sofa, rested his elbow on the back of it, and let his temple fall against his fist. "His name's Kane, he's in the bedroom."

Ambrose glanced across at the bedroom door. "Seriously?"

Everet nodded.

"That's…nice?" Ambrose hazarded.

"It's bloody insane—that's what it is," Everet said with a half-sigh, picking at his sandwich as his appetite deserted him. "I told the elders I can rehabilitate him and make him a credit to the nest."

"Perhaps the magpie side of him isn't as strong as—"

"I brought him here from a human club," Everet recounted, without the slightest hint of emotion. "He serviced the owner, and probably half the other men there. They wanted to get rid of him because they couldn't stop him stealing from them."

"Oh."

Everet smiled wryly, knowing there was nothing anyone could say that would make the situation any better than it was. The light at the end of the tunnel wasn't an oncoming train; it was a serial killer shining a torch as he searched for victims. "I'm screwed."

"Maybe..." Ambrose frowned. "No, you're right," he finally admitted a minute later. "You are screwed."

But Kane hadn't been—not by Everet. That was important. Everet kept that fact to himself, but that didn't mean it was any less vital to his sanity.

"What are you going to do?" Ambrose asked.

"I'm going to do my damnedest to follow through with my promise and sort him out. It's not as if I can—"

The bedroom door swung open. Everet and Ambrose both turned to stare as Kane stepped into the living room, completely naked. He strolled past them and disappeared into the bathroom. The door clicked closed behind him.

Everet felt Ambrose's attention swing back to him, but his own gaze never wavered from the bathroom door. A minute passed and Kane emerged, just as naked as before.

All his movements leisurely and graceful, he walked past the sofa and draped himself across the armchair opposite them. His legs fell open, putting his crotch on display; he was half-hard. "What are we talking about?" he asked, his voice a veritable purr of pure seduction.

Everet's eyes narrowed. "Ambrose, meet Kane. He's going to be under my protection for the foreseeable future. Kane, this is Ambrose. He works with me on the nest's security team."

"Pleased to meet you," Ambrose said, politely.

Kane's eyes sparkled. In one erotic little movement he was off his chair and kneeling at Ambrose's feet.

He turned his hand up to show the mark on the inside of his wrist, which was all good and proper, Everet supposed. It was just a pity that Kane chose to rest the back of his fingers against Ambrose's fly when he did it.

"I'm a magpie."

Ambrose squirmed in his seat, as if there was any way he could retreat from Kane without dismantling the back of the sofa en route.

"Albatross." He turned his hand over to display his mark. "It's nice to meet you."

"You said that already." Kane caught hold of Ambrose's hand before Ambrose had a chance to move it away. He held it between both of his smaller hands, bringing both sets of his knuckles to rest on Ambrose's crotch. "Everet wants to find a position for me in the nest—one that suits my talents," Kane went on. "What do you think my talents are, Ambrose?"

Somehow, he managed to make the question sound like an invitation to do a million different depraved things with his body. His tone completely overwhelmed his words. His body language was all seduction.

"Um..."

"Kane," Everet cut in. "Go back to the chair."

Kane turned his head toward Everet, but he made no attempt to rise from his current position.

"I only asked him a question," he said. The fake innocence was the last straw. Everet stood up, stepped behind Kane, caught hold of his arms and pulled him bodily to his feet before dumping him unceremoniously in the chair.

"That hurt!"

"You're still too high to feel anything," Everet snapped, well aware that he'd made damn sure his actions hadn't hurt the boy in the least. "Quit playing the sympathy card; it won't do you any good with me."

Kane glared at Everet before turning back to Ambrose. His expression changed. The smile spread across his face like the sun rising on a cold winter's day. Suddenly, he was all warmth and charm.

"Before we were so rudely interrupted, you were going to tell me what talents you thought I might have," he said.

Ambrose was so far out of his depth he needed a stepladder, and probably a couple of levels of scaffolding, just to help him back to ground level.

"Throwing yourself at my friends won't get you anywhere either," Everet warned, re-taking his seat on the sofa.

"Yes, it will," Kane said. "For one, it may well get me transferred to the protection of a far superior avian."

"To a far more easily manipulated man, you mean," Everet translated.

Ambrose made no objection to the description. He knew it was the truth, just as well as Everet did.

Kane sighed and stretched lethargically in his chair, until he settled upon a different, although equally suggestive, pose. His cock was completely hard now, curving up toward his stomach. He stroked it a few times, before letting his hand drop away to better display his merits.

"I think I'd better leave," Ambrose said, shuffling to the edge of his seat.

"I'll see you tomorrow." Everet didn't take his eyes off Kane as he listened to his friend hurry out of the apartment, closing the door softly in his wake.

*

"What is it with the big ones?" Kane asked the world in general, as he found himself once more alone with Everet. "It's as if they all went around the muscle queue twice and forgot to visit the brain one at all." He spread his legs wider as he relaxed more comfortably into his seat. He'd found that soft, fuzzy place where nothing hurt and, god, it felt good.

"Leave him be."

Kane turned his head and smirked at Everet.

The raven leaned forward in his seat, but his posture and expression were both very different to Ambrose's just before he made his escape. "Let me be perfectly clear about this," Everet said. "You are under my protection. I'm responsible for you, and you will obey the rules I set for you."

Kane raised an eyebrow. His temple throbbed for a moment, then the sensation faded into the pretty pink mist that occupied all the other corners of his mind.

"The first rule is no sex—with anyone."

"You mean anyone apart from you," Kane said, knowingly.

"I mean anyone, me included." He actually sounded serious.

Kane bit back a grin. "Whatever you say." It wouldn't be long before Everet broke the rule himself; Kane would see to that. And, once Everet had fallen off his self-appointed pedestal of virtue, Kane would never let the sanctimonious bastard forget it. "Anything else?"

"That will do for tonight. Go and get some sleep." Everet nodded toward the bedroom.

"And when do you intend to join me?" Kane asked, pulling himself to his feet and stretching in a way he knew showed off all his best assets.

"I'll sleep out here."

"Don't you trust yourself to share a bed with me?" Kane teased. He dropped his gaze pointedly to where Everet's erection strained against his trousers. "It seems my talents haven't deserted me after all. I've always been a brilliant cock-tease."

Everet just glowered at him.

On his way into the bedroom, Kane made sure Everet got a good look at every inch of his body. At the door, he looked over his shoulder. "Oh, Everet?"

Everet looked toward him, and the wonderful view of his arse that Kane took care to present. "What?"

"You know the best cure for a cock-tease, don't you?"

"Go to bed." Everet ground the words out from between clenched teeth. Kane laughed as he slipped into the bedroom. This was going to be fun.

* * * * *

"Wake up."

Someone grabbed hold of Kane's shoulder and shook him. Kane had no idea who it was; he knew that the guy deserved to die a slow and excruciating death. Every part of Kane's body ached. His fingernails, his toes, even his eyelashes seemed to pound with pain unlike anything he'd ever felt. He lay on his stomach, but his back hurt just as much as the front of his body. Crenshaw's cigarette burns were bright stars of anguish, hot as any supernova.

"Kane?"

"Hurts," Kane managed to croak out. Opening his eyes was out of the question, so was shaking off the hand on his shoulder—no matter how many waves of rolling misery it sent through him.

"Your high's worn off?"

Kane didn't try to answer. He wasn't sure his vocal cords would survive another attempt at speech. All the pretty coloured clouds that had filled his mind for the last two years were gone. All that remained was blackness and pain—so much pain.

"Have you ever gone cold turkey before?" That was Everet's voice. Kane recognised it now. He also recognised the complete lack of sympathy in his tone.

Kane pushed against the mattress in an attempt to lever himself up off his stomach and get out of bed. Every muscle and joint screamed at him. He couldn't make it an inch off the mattress.

Kane's stomach turned over. If he'd eaten anything in the last few days, he'd have thrown it up. He swallowed his queasiness down as best he could. Something was more important than that— even more important than his pain.

Quicksilver.

A little bit of quicksilver and Kane would be fine. All he had to do was get up and find someone with a stash. There was bound to be someone in the nest who bought and sold the stuff. There had to be a dealer who'd take payment in kind.

Kane tried to get up again, but quickly collapsed back onto the mattress, incapable of lifting his own weight.

"Kane, can you hear me?"

The words seemed to come from a long way off, but Everet's hand still rested on Kane's shoulder. That meant the raven had to be close enough to provide Kane with what he needed. If he couldn't get to drugs, he'd just have to get someone to bring them to him.

"Quicksilver," Kane whispered, his voice as raw as it would have been if he'd screamed in torment all night.

Everet cursed. "Quicksilver, that's what you were on?"

"Need."

Everet slammed his hand against Kane's forehead, hard enough to make his mind spin. "Bloody hell, you're burning up."

Through super-avian effort, Kane managed to lift a hand and blindly grab Everet's wrist just when he would have taken his hand away. "I'll do whatever you want."

Everet pried Kane's fingers from his skin and retrieved his wrist. The next moment, all the blankets that had covered Kane were gone.

Yes. That was good. Still face down on the sheet, Kane dutifully shuffled his legs apart. "Quicksilver," he repeated. That was what he was trading his arse for. It was important they were both clear on that.

Everet's hands pulled at Kane's limbs, forcing him to turn over. Flames screeched through Kane's veins. His usual inclination to say the man with the drugs could have him any way he wanted was completely absent. The fire that filled his muscles was too much to bear. He tried to scream, but his throat closed up around the sound.

Suddenly, Kane felt Everet's arms push their way beneath him and lift him off the bed. Kane couldn't raise the energy to grapple for a hold on Everet. He couldn't even demand to be told where Everet was taking him. He managed to open his eyes, but the whole world was a blur.

The sound of hurried footsteps competed with the buzzing in Kane's ears. The world bobbed and weaved around him. A sound that Kane couldn't place filled the void left by Everet's footsteps when they came to a halt. Kane was vaguely aware of being lowered down. Then, blessedly, wonderfully, he felt the flames fade a little.

There had been no scratch against the inside of his arm; no searching for a vein healthy enough to take the needle. There was just relief and it poured over his skin like...

Kane blinked as his vision slowly came back to him.

Bright white light surrounded him on all sides. For a second, he thought he'd died and, against all the odds, he'd been given the chance to float off toward some wonderful paradise. Then, lines appeared in the whiteness, dividing the blur into neat little squares— the bathroom in Everet's apartment at the nest.

In infinitesimally small increments, Kane lifted his hand. He stared blankly at it as he turned it over. Droplets clung to it.

Kane felt Everet's fingers sliding through his hair, stroking it back from his face. Everet's palm was cool and blissful against Kane's skin. It was also wet. Kane lifted his head from whatever it had been resting on. He was in the bath. The shower was on above him.

Everet was in there too, kneeling behind Kane's back, supporting him and keeping him half-upright.

Shower sex?

Thoughts plodded sluggishly through his brain.

No, that didn't make sense.

"You're dressed," Kane mumbled.

"I didn't have time to strip off."

"Oh..." Kane let his head drop back against Everet's shoulder. The explanation seemed reasonable enough to him. He closed his eyes. He'd thought that the last shower he'd had at the nest was good, but this one was bloody amazing.

Nothing but the sound of dripping water filled the air for several minutes.

Kane groaned as instincts reared up. He couldn't just lay there. He had to think, had to make his brain work. That was how a man stayed one step ahead of everyone else—how he stayed safe.

Everet hadn't had time to get undressed. Okay, Kane could work around that.

"You'll have to take the time to at least undo your zipper," he said. The words came out slurred, but that wasn't because he'd had too much to drink. Kane was sure of that. Lifting one hand, he scratched clumsily at the inside of his other elbow. No, he hadn't had his shot of quicksilver either.

Everet caught hold of his hand and made him stop trying to find an injection site. "You're going to be fine."

It had never occurred to Kane that he'd be anything else until Everet tried to reassure him. "What's...going...on?" he managed to ask.

"You're coming down off your high."

"Hurts."

"I know it does. But it will get easier soon." Everet stroked Kane's hair again. It felt nice.

Kane smiled. Everet sounded nice too. That was new. Kane liked it.

"Are you hot or cold?" Everet asked.

Kane mentally checked in with various parts of his body. "Wet."

"A hot kind of wet or a cold kind of wet?" Everet pushed.

Kane frowned. Men who just wanted him to bend over were so much easier to deal with than men who wanted him to think. "Hot." He finally settled on.

"That's fine," Everet said. "You need to tell me if you start to feel cold. Can you do that?"

"'Kay," Kane mumbled, sleepy now that some of the pain seemed to have faded away. He tried to turn over. His knee hit something hard. Everet's arms tightened around him.

Kane frowned. He remembered they were in the bath, but he wasn't sure why they were in there. He blinked open his eyes and peered at the bright white tiles.

"Shower sex?" Had they fallen down?

"Hush. Just relax. I'll let you know if I want anything from you."

Kane nodded. The darkness that crept up on him wasn't nearly as soothing as the rainbow of clouds that he was used to seeing while on quicksilver, but that didn't matter. There was no way he could stop the blackness rising around him and covering his head.

Chapter Four

Everet had never been so relieved to hear someone knock on his apartment door in his life. "Come in!" he yelled.

"Everet? Are you okay? You said you'd be at the meeting this morning..."

Ambrose—thank God! "We're in the bathroom," Everet yelled, desperately trying not to let his shivering make him stutter.

"Sorry, Ev. I didn't realize you and Kane were, um... I'll meet you down—"

"No! Get in here." If Everet had been able to leap out of the tub, run out of the room and grab Ambrose, he would have taken a death grip on him. But, hell, if he could have done all that, he wouldn't have needed his friend's help.

Ambrose peeked around the bathroom door, as cautious as someone approaching a rattle snake. When he saw Everet in the tub fully dressed and supporting Kane's unconscious form, he finally seemed willing to believe he wasn't interrupting shower sex. He stepped into the room. "What happened?"

"Do you know what coming off quicksilver cold turkey does to someone?"

Ambrose shook his head. "I'll try and find someone who does." He took a step back.

"No. Help me out of here first." It took all of Everet's strength of will to keep his teeth from chattering as he gave the order.

Ambrose approached the side of the bath, only to hesitate.

"Just support him for a minute," Everet commanded.

Ambrose was so wary, it would have been easy to believe that was his first time touching a naked man, but he finally did what he was told. With all the gentleness of a guy who knew he was too big and too strong to risk being careless, Ambrose slid his arm behind Kane's back and let Everet clamber to his feet within the cramped confines of the tub.

Everet's knees sent symmetrical spikes of pain shooting up his thighs. He made a mental note never to ask any sub to kneel in a bathtub for more than two minutes in a row. Damn, but the bottom of the tub was bloody hard. All future shower time blowjobs were definitely going to feature high quality kneepads.

Gingerly stretching out his limbs, Everet clumsily hauled himself onto the mat beside the bath. His clothes were sodden. Shivers racked his entire body.

"Does he still feel hot to you?" Everet demanded, grabbing a towel from the rail and rubbing it against his hair and face.

Ambrose placed the back of his fingers against Kane's forehead. "He's still got a hellish fever. How long have you had him under the cold water?"

Everet pulled his T-shirt over his head and dropped the sodden fabric in the sink. "How late am I for the meeting?"

"Bloody hell," Ambrose muttered. His forehead furrowed with unease as he peered down at Kane. "The meeting finished ten minutes ago."

Everet scrambled out of his jeans as quickly as his numb legs would allow. Everything he took off followed his shirt into the sink. Rubbing roughly at his skin with a towel gradually coaxed a little bit of warm blood into his extremities.

"Can you keep an eye on him while I grab some dry clothes?"

Ambrose nodded, just as Everet knew he would. Ambrose was good at obeying orders. But, the idea of letting

Kane out of his sight still sent a barb of horror through Everet's mind.

Kane was his responsibility. The idea of anything happening to him made it impossible for Everet to take a deep breath, let alone walk back into the bedroom and do anything as practical as get dressed.

Kane was his. The magpie should be at his side, tracking his every step. And, if Kane wasn't well enough to follow him, then Everet sure as hell shouldn't leave him behind.

"I won't let anything happen to him," Ambrose promised.

The realisation that his stupidity was so blatant that even Ambrose could spot it, finally kicked Everet into action. Rushing into his bedroom, he snatched clothes out of his wardrobe and fought his way into them, his skin still damp, his movements ham-fisted.

His fingers were numb. His whole body shook. Damn it, he didn't have time for any of this bull. The moment his clothes were in roughly the right place, he raced back to the bathroom.

"I checked his pulse," Ambrose informed him. "It's strong and steady. If it wasn't for his temperature, anyone would think he's sleeping peacefully."

Everet sat down heavily on the closed toilet lid, his mind racing so fast he couldn't catch hold of any sensible thought.

"You said he was on quicksilver?" Ambrose asked. His tone was wary, as if he was unsure how Everet would react.

Everet simply stared at Kane. "That was what he asked for when I found him this morning. He wouldn't even admit he was on anything until…" He waved a hand at Kane's slumped form. "Until this happened."

Magpies obviously healed quickly—at least from simple, physical wounds. Kane's bruises were already a little less vivid. As he lay naked in the bath, it was easy to believe that he would lift his head at any moment, open his eyes and, in all probability, come out with some smart arse remark. But, the only thing keeping him upright was Ambrose's arm behind his back.

"Can you think of anyone who might know what to do for him?" Everet asked.

"Shall I go ask around and see who I can find?" Ambrose suggested.

Everet knelt down alongside the bath and took Ambrose's place, sliding his arm behind Kane. When Ambrose straightened up, Everet noticed that half of Ambrose's shirt was saturated by spray from the shower. Ambrose made no complaint. Everet couldn't bring himself to take his attention away from Kane for long enough to mention it either.

A few seconds later, Ambrose closed the bathroom door softly in his wake.

"Everything's going to be fine." Everet wasn't sure who he wanted to reassure. It had all seemed so bloody simple when he woke up that morning. He'd keep Kane under his protection for a few weeks. A little bit of discipline, some practical instructions, and some firm rules from someone who wouldn't screw him. If it worked, he'd release him back into the world and probably never set eyes on him again. If it didn't work, Kane would go down to the cages, and Everet would at least know he'd tried his best.

Everet stared down at Kane. It wasn't obvious if he was sleeping, passed out or somewhere in between.

"Everything will be fine," Everet repeated, just in case Kane could hear him. "All you need to do is push through this, and we'll have you back on your feet in no time. We'll have you back on your wings as well. I bet it's been a hell of a long time since you flew, hasn't it?"

Kane failed to answer, but it was impossible for Everet to let silence settle over them. That would have meant facing the idea that Kane was too ill to speak. Everet shook his head.

Who the hell would have thought he'd be praying for a sarcastic word from the boy after only one day?

"You'll enjoy spreading your wings again," Everet babbled. "And you'll enjoy living in the nest once you settle in. I'll make sure everything goes fine for you. You just need to get through this. Okay? You can do it."

Behind Everet, someone politely cleared his throat.

Everet jerked his head around to face him. He glared over his shoulder. A small, delicate looking man with dark skin and black hair cropped close to his head, stepped forward. "Your friend said you need a doctor-bird?" His accent hinted that he was the genuine thing, from a nest that actually originated in the West Indies, rather than someone who'd just been trained by a doctor-bird.

For a few seconds, Everet was too relieved to say anything. It didn't matter. The guy didn't wait for a response. He strode purposefully to the side of the bath and pressed his fingers against Kane's throat, checking his pulse.

Everet automatically checked the guy's wrist. Yes. It was a hummingbird mark—and specifically one that marked him out as a doctor-bird.

Everet knew he should have breathed easier, knowing Kane was in safe hands. So, why the hell was he feeling jealous, just because the doctor's fingers rested against Kane's skin?

"When did his fever strike?"

Everet moved his gaze to Kane's face in an effort to stop glaring at the doctor's hand. "In the night. I'm not sure what time. I found him six o'clock this morning."

The doctor took a digital ear thermometer from his medical bag and placed it in Kane's ear.

"You did right to bring down his temperature this way."

Everet glanced up at the doctor. "He's been taking quicksilver. I'm not sure how long for."

The doctor frowned as he inspected the insides of

Kane's elbows. "At least a couple of years, I should think."

Everet gritted his teeth and kept his curses to himself.

"How long have you known him?" The doctor took the thermometer from Kane's ear, inspected it and returned it to his bag without sharing the reading.

"Since yesterday," Everet admitted. "But he's my responsibility now. He's my submissive."

The doctor nodded, as if that explained everything. For a few seconds, he stared down at Kane in silence, as if considering his options.

Everet's eyes narrowed. "Do you know how to treat someone coming off quicksilver or not?"

"Yes, I do." The doctor tapped one delicate fingertip against his chin. "It's no rare thing. More and more cases are popping up all the time—especially in the magpies. Once humans realised how easy they are to control when they're hooked..." There was no need for him to finish the sentence.

Everet tightened his hold on Kane, as if that would do the poor little sod any good now.

"Not that they've ever been that difficult for a man with money to manipulate..." the doctor murmured, apparently to himself.

Everet clenched his jaw. A medical opinion was one thing, but when it came to anything else, Kane was his, and no one had the right to say anything against him.

The doctor seemed to notice the sudden change of atmosphere. He cleared his throat and took a notebook from his bag. "There are three stages of withdrawal from quicksilver," he said, suddenly all professional.

As he listened to the doctor, Everet used his hand to scoop up some of the cold water still pouring from the shower head and used it to cool Kane's brow.

"His fever should break before nightfall. He should come back to himself a little at that point. In the meantime, just keep him as cool as you can."

Everet nodded. He could do that.

"After that, put him to bed. He should sleep for quite some time." The doctor's tone turned sharper. "It's probably for the best considering his other injuries—"

Everet jerked his head up. "I wasn't the one who beat him."

While Everet had had all his attention on Kane, the doctor had produced a pair of reading glasses from somewhere. He stared at Everet over the top of them for several seconds but made no comment on what Everet had said.

The doctor cleared his throat again, obviously drawing a line under that part of the conversation and making it clear he was moving on to a new topic. "In the second stage of withdrawal, he'll almost certainly complain of being in a great deal of pain." The doctor paused his explanation as he made a note on the pad.

Still on his knees beside the bath, Everet silently glared up at him until he resumed speaking.

"You'll have to watch him carefully. His cravings will be…intense. He'll do whatever he can to get his next fix. In his mind, the only thing that will help will be quicksilver. You'll have to be strong and prevent him taking anything, no matter how distressing you find it."

"That won't be a problem." Cruel to be kind—Everet could do that. He could do whatever Kane needed him to do—he had to be able to.

"If he reaches the third stage of—"

"When," Everet corrected.

"When that happens," the doctor said, barely skipping a beat. "Things should get easier. His body will adapt relatively quickly. He won't need quicksilver, but he'll want it. Strict supervision will be required. Addicts can get very adept at finding their fix."

"I'm not going to let him out of my sight," Everet said, coolly, and not just because the arm behind Kane was once more frigidly cold.

The doctor made a few more notes and put his things in his bag. With a brief promise to return and check on Kane later that day, he left.

Everet bowed his head against the edge of the bath as he found himself once more alone with Kane.

"When they said you'd be trouble, this wasn't quite what I expected." He muttered as he lifted his head and brushed Kane's dripping-wet hair back from his face. The water had washed away whatever makeup he'd used to cover his bruises.

His skin was pale between the patches of fading purples and blues.

"I was right," Everet informed Kane, just in case the magpie hadn't been paying attention to the doctor's words. "You're going to be fine."

Once more, a cough let Everet know that someone was in his bathroom doorway.

"Did Dr. Jenson help?" Ambrose asked as he joined them in the small room.

Everet relayed the scant information the doctor had been able to provide, skipping over the bits that implied magpies' flaws couldn't be tamed or that Everet would ever be so sloppy in his care of Kane that he wouldn't be able to get him clean.

He shook his head as he fell silent. *Wait it out* wasn't the miracle cure he'd hoped for.

"Dr. Jenson seemed like a nice guy," Ambrose said, as he fidgeted with the tube of toothpaste propped up alongside the washbasin.

Everet glanced over his shoulder. In spite of everything he should have been worrying about, or maybe because he desperately needed something, anything, to distract him from those things, he found himself smiling. "Really?"

Ambrose squinted at the perfectly acceptable toothbrush that lived alongside the toothpaste as if it had personally offended him. "It can't be fun, having to rush away from your breakfast every time anyone in the nest you're visiting is taken ill."

"Good point," Everet murmured, bathing Kane's face with another handful of water. Despite his best efforts, his fingers shook slightly. The water was so cold it was a wonder that a layer of ice hadn't formed over Kane's skin.

"He didn't even hesitate to come and help."

Everet made a vaguely approving noise in the back of his throat. Part of him had always wondered what kind of man would eventually be the one to catch Ambrose's attention. Now, he apparently knew.

Everet's annoyance with the doctor eased a little. It was hardly the guy's fault he didn't know anything other than petty rumours about magpies — most people fell into the same category. If Dr. Jenson made Ambrose happy, Everet was willing to forgive the doctor's uneducated comments about Kane. On the other hand, if he didn't treat Ambrose the way the gentle giant deserved...

"His breakfast probably went cold when he was up here," Ambrose added.

Everet glanced up at him. "Maybe you should go down and make sure he gets a fresh plate. He'd probably appreciate some company."

Ambrose shook his head vehemently. "No way!" From his tone, Everet might as well have asked Ambrose to throw himself at the doctor's feet and beg to be screwed right there in the middle of the dining room.

"Are you sure?" Everet asked, just a touch of teasing in his voice.

Ambrose's cheeks flushed as he met Everet's gaze for a moment. "I'll stay and help you here. I mean, I can wait around in case I can help, or..." He took a deep breath. "I'll get us both some coffee." He nodded to himself as if he really believed that everything would be better once there was coffee. "You could probably use something hot."

Everet turned his attention back to Kane as the

albatross scurried from the room. "If you heard any of that, you're not going to use it against him. I'll throttle you if you do."

Kane made no response.

Everet tried his best not to be disappointed. At that moment, he'd have relished hearing even the brattiest comment from him.

* * * * *

"Wha hap-ed?" Kane frowned. He had a vague memory of slurring his words before, but that just made the fact that his tongue still wasn't under his control even more annoying. A man couldn't stay that drunk forever, could he?

"You're coming off quicksilver."

Kane squinted up at a figure looming over him; it was probably the same guy who'd just spoken. A hand came to rest on his forehead — the same man or someone else?

No, it was the same guy. A name floated into Kane's mind.

"'Ret?"

"Close enough," the guy allowed.

Yes. That was definitely Everet's voice. For some stupid reason, Kane felt a bit better now that he knew it was Everet who stood alongside him.

"Where?" Kane managed to say.

"You're in my room at the nest."

"Nest…" Yes. Kane remembered now. Everet had taken him to a nest. And Everet had told Kane that he had to tell him when he stopped feeling like he was being boiled alive from the inside out.

"Cold," Kane managed to whisper.

"Your fever broke."

Kane bullied his eyes into focus just in time to see Everet spread another blanket over him. From the weight pressing down on every part of his body below his neck, there were already more than a few layered on top of him.

Kane cleared his throat. "You look...like hell," he croaked out.

Everet made no comment. Kane peered up at him. The only colour in the raven's face came from the dark circles beneath his eyes.

One brain cell finally fired up and sparked its neighbours into action. Kane's first clear thought since waking appeared inside his head. If Everet looked bad, how did *he* look?

Everet must have a mirror in the room somewhere. Kane tried to sit up.

"Whoa. No, you don't." Everet put his hand on Kane's shoulder and pushed him back.

It didn't take much pressure to make Kane collapse against the soft pillows. He tried to glare at Everet, but he wasn't sure if his facial muscles co-operated.

"You're allowed to get up if you need to take a leak. Apart from that, you're staying right where you are," Everet informed him, as if someone had died and made him king of the whole damn world while Kane was asleep.

Kane squirmed as much as the weight of the blankets allowed. Every bit of him ached.

"You said..." Damn, even talking made his whole body hurt. "You said you'd get me something for the pain," Kane whispered.

"No, I didn't."

Kane huffed. It had been worth a shot. "Say it now," he ordered. "I need something. I'm in so much pain. Please?"

"You're going through withdrawal." Everet stated that fact as if it was one he'd said a great many times before.

Kane scrolled through his recent memories. Nothing. "Wh-what day is it?"

"You were in and out for three days."

"What?" Kane tried to sit up again. Once more, Everet's hand came to rest on his shoulder. He didn't even need to push this time. Kane fell back, his body filled with a writhing mass of poisonous snakes that forced more and more agony into his body every time he tried to so much as take a deep breath.

Everet sat down on the edge of the bed. "Do you remember a doctor visiting you?"

"What doctor?"

Everet started talking and didn't seem to be able to stop. He babbled on about all the reasons why Kane needed to rest and take things easy. In amongst that were several lines of bull about why Kane shouldn't take any more drugs.

When Everet said the pain was all in Kane's mind, Kane didn't bother to disagree. It was already obvious that Everet wouldn't be willing to provide what Kane needed. Kane would have to find someone else.

"The doctor," Kane whispered, already feeling too exhausted to attempt anything louder. "I want to see him."

Everet frowned. "You shouldn't be in that much real pain anymore..."

"Doctor," Kane repeated. Doctors had drugs. That was pretty much the whole point of doctors — to provide people with drugs that made them feel better — and Kane knew exactly what would make him feel really fantastic.

Everet stepped away from the side of the bed for just long enough to ring down to the servants' hall and ask someone to find the doctor. Kane would have breathed a sigh of relief, but even that was beyond him. His whole body pulsated with need. The inner part of his elbows itched with the desire for the reassuring sharp scratch that would lead to such perfect bliss.

"Are you up to eating anything?"

"No." The only thing he needed went straight into his veins. If he put anything in his stomach, Kane knew he'd throw it up.

Everet fell silent.

Kane tried to turn his back on him. He failed.

"Do you need help getting comfortable?" Everet asked.

Kane ignored him and settled on turning his head away from him.

His forehead tingled. Kane frowned, wondering why some random little part of his body should expect a gentle touch at that particular moment.

It took an age for the doctor to turn up, but, eventually, a stranger arrived. He walked into the room as if he had every right to be there. He had a doctor's bag with him—a bag that was easily big enough to carry more drugs than an avian could survive in one sitting.

Kane managed a small smile, but it died as Everet greeted the doctor and completely failed to leave the room.

"Private," Kane whispered.

"No."

Kane tried to frown. Everet showed no facial reaction whatsoever. "You belong to me, Kane. I'm responsible for you. Whatever is said between you and the doctor, I need to hear it."

He had that look in his eyes. There would be no moving him. With a grunt of displeasure, Kane turned his head toward the doctor. "I need something for the pain."

"Anything I give you will only prolong your pain in the long run," the doctor began.

Kane shook his head. "Before, when I felt like this, a doctor gave me an injection. It helped a lot."

"Let me guess. An injection of a sparkly, silver substance?" the doctor asked.

"Yes!"

"No." That was Everet.

Pointedly ignoring him, Kane kept his eyes on the doctor.

"It would hurt you more in the long run," the doc repeated.

"No, it wouldn't. It helps," Kane snapped, anger bubbling up inside him, demanding to be released, even when he felt as if he could barely lift his head from his pillow.

"It's not going to happen, Kane." Everet sounded so bloody certain about that.

Kane dragged himself up into a sitting position through sheer force of will. Everet's hand came to rest on his shoulder, but pure desperation fuelled Kane now. "If you won't help me, I'll find someone who will!"

Catching Everet off guard, he swung his legs over the side of the bed and lurched to his feet. Pushing past the doctor, Kane staggered toward the door, his blankets trailing behind him.

He managed to get halfway across the bedroom before Everet caught hold of him and pulled him back toward the bed.

"No!"

The next moment, Everet's embrace encircled Kane, trapping his arms down against his sides.

Kane screamed. He had no idea what he yelled out. Words were complicated things, and there was no room for them inside his head. The only thing that existed was need. He needed his fix. The sound that echoed around the room was wild, feral, unlike anything Kane ever remembered hearing, let alone making himself.

His arms were trapped and useless, but Kane could still kick. He delivered several good blows to Everet's knees and shins. Kane flung back his head, but curses failed to fill the air. He hadn't managed to break Everet's nose.

Kane squirmed and bucked, but Everet didn't let go. His grip around Kane remained unchanged, as if he intended to keep hold of him no matter what.

Kane struggled on, now completely demented with need. Thoughts, even those that were all about getting free, or why he needed to do that, began to get lost in the confusion. No other thoughts arose to take their place. Kane couldn't think about anything any more, all he could do was panic.

Everet twisted and leant back as Kane tossed his head. Unless Everet was very much mistaken, that was the third time Kane had tried to break his nose.

Pain shot through Everet's knee as Kane delivered a particularly hard kick to the sensitive spot just below the kneecap. Everet's grip faltered. Kane took his chance. He jerked his elbow back catching Everet just below his ribs.

Everet grunted, but managed to regain his hold on Kane. Despite Everet's best efforts, they staggered closer to the bedroom wall.

Kane's legs went up. Planting his feet on the paintwork, he kicked out, pushing them both backward. Everet stumbled. All the air rushed out of his lungs as they landed heavily on the bed, his arms still encircling Kane.

Whatever was powering Kane gave him more strength than any man his size should have been able to possess. There was no weight to him, and little enough muscle. Hell, he hadn't even managed to eat anything for over three days. But somehow, he had the strength of a damn albatross.

And the only one who could save him from himself was Everet.

The doctor couldn't have done anything, and he'd already left at Everet's command, closing the door behind him. No doubt Ambrose had left Everet's apartment too, trailing after the doctor like a duckling trailed after its mother.

There was no one except Everet there to help Kane. The responsibility fell to him alone. Kane was his and no one else's.

Better able to use his extra weight to his advantage now they were horizontal, Everet finally managed to pin Kane down against the mattress. Time passed. There seemed to be no end to Kane's struggles, no limit to his energy.

"Bastard! Let me go!" Kane's speech was muffled against the bed sheets. That didn't take any of the venom out of his words, but at least they were words. He was capable of forming syllables now. Perhaps the worst of it had passed.

"I hate you. Let me go." Kane squirmed and bucked. Lifting his head, he yelled at the top of his voice. "Help!"

Everet used every part of his body to hold him down, but Kane seemed to have more limbs than any avian should, and he wasn't above fighting dirty. Everet only just pulled his hand away from Kane's mouth in time to avoid a vicious bite.

"Calm down!"

Kane didn't seem to hear him.

Everet's heart raced even faster as Kane kicked and writhed beneath him. His brain understood that the way he and Kane were rolling around on the bed had nothing to do with sex. His body didn't give a damn what his brain thought about the situation.

Every time Kane struggled to get free, his arse pressed back against Everet's crotch. Friction was still friction no matter how it was obtained. When it was produced by a naked man as beautiful as Kane, thinking of it as asexual was impossible.

Suddenly, Kane stilled.

For several minutes, neither of them moved except to gasp for breath.

"I'll let you screw me," Kane finally whispered. "I'll do whatever you want."

Everet closed his eyes.

Kane arched his back. There was nothing accidental about the way he pressed his buttocks against Everet's erection now.

"You can whip me. You can do me in front of your friends. They can watch while I beg you to screw me. I'll let them take turns with me afterward, if you want."

"Kane," Everet whispered, shaking his head.

"You have no idea what a magpie can earn in one hour with another man," Kane rushed out. "I can bring in far more in a day than you'd have to spend on quicksilver for me in a week, and — "

"No."

Kane whimpered, squirming underneath Everet like a man in more pain than he could physically contain. "Please?" He gasped. "Yes! Begging! Is that what does it for you. You want me to get on my knees and plead. I will. I'll — "

"No!" It was all Everet could do to keep the word anything less than a yell. "There is nothing you can do or say that will convince me to put you back on that stuff."

From their respective positions, it was just possible for Everet to see Kane's profile. He watched as Kane closed his eyes very tightly.

A tear beaded in the corner of Kane's left eye and ran across the bridge of his nose.

"Kane?"

Half of Everet was furious at what was almost certainly another attempt at manipulation. But the other half of him tensed at the sight of Kane's tears, simply wanting to do whatever it took to make him feel better.

Kane turned his face into the blankets as if trying to hide the moisture gathering on his lashes. A really good attempt at manipulation, or was he ashamed of genuine tears?

Everet couldn't tell. It didn't matter. Either way, he couldn't give in. He closed his eyes too, but permitted no frustrated tears to gather on his lashes, not even when he felt Kane finally fall into an exhausted sleep beneath him.

Wincing each time he put too much weight on his sore knee, Everet slowly rearranged Kane in his bed and tucked him beneath his blankets. There was no telling how long he'd remain asleep this time.

Everet slumped back into the chair by the side of the bed. He felt like he hadn't slept in years. In truth, it hadn't been more than a few days, but that didn't make his eyeballs itch any less.

He closed his eyes for a moment. The moment stretched out into a minute, then an hour. Everet's eyes remained closed.

* * * * *

A sudden bang jerked Everet out of a deep sleep. He lurched forward so quickly, he almost threw himself out of his chair. He looked around, frantically trying to get his bearings. The chair. Yes, he was well acquainted with the chair by the side of his bed. It wasn't the first time he'd dozed there since meeting Kane.

Everet rubbed at his eyes and blinked toward the bed. Kane was…not there.

Kane wasn't there!

Suddenly wide awake, Everet quickly took in several details about the room. The most important one was that Kane wasn't in it; everything else could wait.

Everet rushed out of the bedroom. One of those less important details from the bedroom was repeated in his living room—every item Everet owned had been emptied out of the drawers and cupboards.

Carelessly trampling his possessions, Everet strode toward the door leading into the bathroom, hoping against hope that Kane might still be in the apartment.

He was almost to the other side of the room when a movement caught his attention.

Kane. He was hunched down, almost entirely hidden from view, as he rooted through the back of a low cabinet. Relief almost made Everet light-headed. Several items cracked beneath Everet's feet as he rushed across the room, but Kane seemed so absorbed in whatever the hell he was doing, he didn't even hear Everet's noisy approach.

Everet put his hand on Kane's shoulder. Jerking as if he'd been struck by lightning, Kane spun away from Everet. He opened his eyes very wide, staring up at Everet as if he had never seen him before.

Shuffling back on his heels and palms, Kane only

stopped when his elbow hit the cabinet. Everet's wallet tumbled from Kane's fingers, so did several folds of notes. Lose coins scattered across the floor.

Everet held his hands up. "I'm not going to hurt you."

Kane wasn't listening. He was too busy scrabbling at the fallen money to care about anything else.

Everet tried to put a hand on his shoulder again. "Kane. Kane, look at me."

Kane had already gathered up most of what looked like every penny Everet possessed. He still didn't seem to have heard a damn word.

Everet reached out to capture the magpie's hands.

"No! Mine! It's mine, you can't have it." Kane lurched for the remaining coins, keeping a fearful watch on Everet as he hunched over the money, but never once looking Everet in the eye.

"Kane," Everet said again, as calmly and as patiently as he knew how. "You need to look at me."

Kane shook his head, pressing himself against the cabinet in an attempt to get away now he'd scooped up all the money. His hair fell over his eyes, hiding his expression, making it harder than ever for Everet to read the situation.

Everet's heart raced faster and faster, but somehow he kept his voice level. "It's going to be okay, Kane, but it's important that you look at me."

Finally, Kane obeyed. Their eyes met for the briefest of moments. Kane's gaze was completely unfocused. His attention darted from one place to another before finally returning to Everet, just for a fraction of a second.

"Hurts."

Pain overwhelmed the word. No one was that good an actor. Everet swallowed down his own emotions. "Yes, sweetheart, I know it hurts."

Kane hesitated before slowly shuffling away from the cabinet.

Everet held his breath and remained perfectly still,

simply letting Kane come to him. Kane's movements were jerky and damn near the least graceful thing Everet had ever seen, but he'd also never witnessed anything more beautiful.

Kane put his fingertips on the back of Everet's hand and stroked them slowly up his arm. "Anything you want?" he whispered, repeating the offering he'd made hundreds of times now.

Everet turned his hand over and offered it to Kane. Empires rose and fell in the time it took Kane to put his hand in Everet's grasp, but eventually, he did. Everet slowly stood up and helped Kane to his feet.

He gently led Kane back into the bedroom, ignoring the fact that Kane still held handfuls of his money.

"Anything you want," Kane repeated, again. He paused by the side of the bed. "What—what do you want me to do?"

Everet turned to face him.

Kane's hair was a mess after all the time he'd spent in bed. His skin was pale. Most of his bruises had healed, but he was so weak, he swayed with fatigue.

"I want you to get back into bed and try to get some sleep."

"Then you'll give me the quicksilver?" Kane asked, a frown marring his forehead.

"No."

Kane looked down.

Everet tensed, ready to block any attempt by Kane to run for the door.

The magpie cradled the stolen cash against his chest. When he let go of Everet's hand, he stumbled, barely able to remain on his feet.

He was so out of it, it was impossible to know what he understood about the situation. But, to Everet's relief, Kane remained outwardly calm as Everet nudged him back into the bed.

He was asleep the moment his head hit the pillow.

Pushing his hand through his hair, Everet took a deep breath and let it out very slowly. It was only then he had time to take in the havoc Kane had wreaked on his apartment while he'd been asleep.

The floor was covered in clothes that the magpie had tossed aside as he searched the back of each drawer for cash. Either Kane had been aware enough of his actions to be incredibly quiet, or Everet had been more exhausted than he'd thought.

Very slowly, Everet's panic subsided. His knee reminded him that he really shouldn't have rushed around like that, but he ignored the ache in the joint as he began to clean up.

His whole body was heavy with exhaustion, but there was a part of Everet that didn't give a damn. The man under his care had needed him, and he'd looked after him. That felt good. No, in fact, it felt fantastic—better than anything Everet ever remembered experiencing in his whole life.

Within half an hour, the floor was clear. Then, there was only one job Everet needed to do before he could go back to sleep. Picking up the chair from beside the bed, Everet carried it to the bedroom door and placed it directly in front of Kane's only exit route.

Job done, he dropped heavily onto the chair and stretched his legs out toward the foot of the bed. Sleep claimed him the moment his eyelids dropped closed.

Chapter Five

"You look like hell."

Everet reluctantly tore his eyes away from Kane's sleeping form. It was an hour since he'd moved the chair back alongside the bed, temporarily leaving the bedroom door open and unobstructed. Now Raynard and Ori stood on the threshold, blocking the exit just as effectively as the chair ever had.

"That's exactly what Kane said last time he woke up," Everet replied. He gave his best attempt at a smile. Then, he remembered who he was addressing.

Pulling himself to his feet, Everet dipped his head politely toward both the hawk and the swan. "Sir, sire, good morning. Is there anything I can do to serve you?"

"Yes, you can stop fussing over the boy like a mother hen for a few seconds. I want to speak to you. Ori will sit with Kane and make sure he's not abducted by aliens while you're gone."

Everet glanced from Raynard to Ori and back again. He'd thought he'd succeeded in keeping his expression blank, but some hint of his concerns must have been visible because Raynard's eyes narrowed.

"Is he violent?" Raynard demanded.

Everet glanced down at Kane—he looked so bloody innocent when he was asleep. It was hard to believe how strong or how sneaky he could be while awake. "He's going through withdrawal," Everet explained, carefully. "He can be very…excitable when he wakes up."

Raynard nodded. "We won't go any further than your

living room. Ori will call us the moment Kane shows any sign of waking." He caught Ori's eye as he said the last bit, obviously making damn sure that Ori knew the matter wasn't up for debate whatever their respective ranks might technically be.

"Yes, sir." Ori turned to Everet. "He'll be fine, sir. I won't take my eyes off him."

Everet hesitated, but it wasn't as if he could refuse to obey either of them. He studied Kane for a moment. His breaths were slow and even. There was no sign of him waking any time soon. He was fine, and Everet would only be in the next room.

"Of course, sire," Everet managed to say. Through sheer force of will, he made himself step away from the side of the bed and walk out of the room.

Raynard closed the door firmly behind them, putting a solid barrier between Everet and Kane for the first time in days.

"Just this once, I'm willing to agree with your charge. You look like hell," Raynard repeated. "Anyone would think you hadn't slept for a month." He crossed the room and folded his tall frame onto the sole armchair, leaving Everet to sink down onto one end of the sofa.

Sometimes appearances weren't at all deceiving. Everet felt like he hadn't slept for half a lifetime. The sofa was wonderfully comfortable after the wooden chair he'd been perched on next to the bed. The moment he leant back against the cushions, sleep tried to creep into the corners of his mind.

"You're taking your duties toward Kane very seriously, aren't you?"

Everet had no idea how to answer that. He managed to keep his eyes open, but talking when he didn't have anything important to say wasn't his strongest point, even when he was at his best; and even if he wouldn't willingly admit it out loud, he hadn't been at his best for days.

"He won't remember half of what you've done for him,

and he'll be bloody ungrateful for whatever he can recall."

That wasn't the point. Even more annoying was the fact that Everet was certain Raynard bloody well knew that. Silence still seemed like Everet's best option.

"If a better prospect came along, he'd be off in a flash," Raynard went on.

"He's mine." And silence could go to hell.

Everet met Raynard's eyes. It didn't matter if he knew Raynard was goading him on purpose. The instinct to protect what was his, and see off anyone who threatened to take it away, was far too strong to deny.

"Your what?" Raynard asked. "Your servant? Your lover? Your submissive? In what way is he yours?"

Everet frowned. Leaning forward, he abandoned the comfortable cushions behind him in favour of resting his elbows on his knees. He tapped his knuckles together. His thoughts about Kane had never made it as far as those kinds of specifics.

Kane was his, and it was Everet's job to make sure nothing happened to him. At first, that had simply meant making sure Kane didn't die from a fever less than twenty-four hours after coming under his control.

Now that Kane's life wasn't in danger, it was about getting Kane through each stage of his withdrawal. When Everet had cleared that hurdle, then...

"While you've been watching over him, some of the elders have been keeping an eye on you. Concerns have been raised," Raynard announced.

An invisible fist punched straight through Everet's ribs and caught hold of his heart. "Raised by Ori?" Everet asked.

Raynard tipped his head once in acknowledgement. "Yes."

Everet glanced toward the bedroom door. If Ori decreed that he wasn't a fit guardian for Kane then—

"Ravens have always had a strong bonding instinct," Raynard said. "And a strong protective instinct. You didn't end up working security by chance. And, when Ori decided that there was a need for some avians to be protected from others within the nest, you were the natural choice. Ravens protect their nests; they protect those who live around them, and they protect what is theirs."

Everet went back to staring as his knuckles. At some point, they'd turned white. "If there's a point you intend to make, sir?" he prompted.

"Don't mistake a natural instinct toward wanting *a* submissive for a desire for this particular submissive."

Very slowly, Everet looked up. "Meaning?"

Raynard didn't even blink. Everet wasn't surprised. There was no way in hell Raynard would back down from anyone.

"Meaning that the first man you take under your protection doesn't have to be the man you spend the rest of your life with." His tone hinted that he was trying to be kind, but that didn't make his actual words any less insulting.

"Because no magpie is worth that much effort?" Everet demanded. The man he'd looked after for the last two weeks was worth it. Kane's species didn't stop him from being lost and helpless; it didn't stop him needing someone.

"Because, until you've formed a pair bond with someone, it's easy to mistake a temporary, albeit obsessive, interest in someone for a true mating bond."

Everet straightened up. "I haven't told you that I—"

Raynard huffed. "This isn't about what you're *telling* people. It's about what's going on inside your head."

Everet retreated into silence.

"I won't bother trying to give you any orders right now; you'd only ignore them. But, I will say this—if you insist on sitting up with him at all hours and looking after him entirely by yourself, then you should use some of the time while he's asleep to decide what it is you'll expect of him when he returns to full health. Get it clear in your own mind that you can't expect him to have any sort of bond with you when he recovers — he won't even have been conscious most of the time you'll have known each other."

Everet nodded.

Raynard pulled himself to his feet.

For once, Everet found a string of completely unnecessary words leaving his mouth. Still in his seat, he tilted back his head. "I don't think I'm in love with him or anything like that, sir. I'm not a fool."

"No, you're not," Raynard said, with a half-smile. "You're a raven — even when it would probably be far easier for you to deal with the situation if you weren't. It's not only magpies that have their weaknesses."

Everet said nothing. It was hard to talk when a ball of air had lodged in his throat, and he couldn't even breathe.

"For example, I've been told that a hawk's greatest weakness is a tendency not to give a damn about anyone except those who they love. Or those to whom they feel they owe a debt."

Their eyes met. Everet didn't nod in agreement. Neither Raynard nor Ori owed him anything. Even if they had, they'd repaid it a hundred times over by having faith in his ability to run the in-nest security flock.

Raynard turned away without saying anything else. He strode across to the bedroom door and opened it without bothering to knock.

"Come along, fledgling. Visiting time is over."

Raynard marched out of Everet's apartment. With a quick smile to Everet in passing, the highest ranking avian in their nest scurried after him, more than happy to follow wherever Raynard led.

Everet went back into his bedroom and closed the door behind him. Moving the chair so it once more blocked the door, Everet went back to silently watching Kane sleep.

* * * * *

"Do you feel dizzy?"

Kane scowled at Everet. "I'm not a bloody invalid!"

Everet didn't take the least bit of notice. He continued to hover next to Kane, his arms held slightly away from his body, as if to catch Kane when he fell.

Doing his damnedest to prove he didn't need anyone's help, Kane managed one slow step forward, then another. Everet never took his eyes off him. Kane might only have been thinking clearly for two days, and he might have slept through most of those forty-eight hours, but he felt as if Everet hadn't glanced away from him in months.

It was like being a bug under a microscope, or perhaps like a prisoner on death row—where there was always a guard on watch, just to make sure the poor sod didn't deprive the hangman of his moment in the spotlight by taking matters into his own hands.

"I'm fine," Kane said through gritted teeth. Admitting he still felt like he was about to pass out wasn't going to do him any good—it would just get him sent back to bed, only to be permitted to get up for brief visits to the bathroom.

Faking feeling fine—that was his best chance of getting away from his jailer and getting something nice and shiny into his veins.

Making his way out of the bedroom, Kane forced himself to keep putting one foot forward until he had crossed the small living room and was within sight of the door leading out of the apartment.

He had to get out of there. He needed his high and, almost as importantly, he needed to be completely surrounded by guys who were, well...guys who weren't Everet. Being in the raven's company twenty-four hours a day was messing with Kane's mind.

Kane lifted his hand and rubbed at his temple as if that might help straighten out his thoughts. Everet was hot. Fair enough. He had nice muscles. He might even have a very pleasant face if he was a bit more willing to smile. But that didn't mean Everet was the be all and end all of Kane's world — it didn't.

Everet didn't have a big enough wallet to keep Kane content for more than a day or two. For the first time he could remember, Kane had to keep nudging that fact to keep it at the forefront of his mind.

Kane stepped outside Everet's apartment.

Freedom!

Kane frowned. Freedom...and miles and miles of ugly green carpet.

The corridor looked ridiculously long, but with Everet standing right behind him, just waiting to swoop down on any excuse to send him back to bed, showing any sign of weakness was out of the question.

He turned right and set off.

"Go the other way."

Kane glanced over his shoulder.

Everet nodded toward an equally long length of corridor heading off in the opposite direction. "The only thing you'll find if you keep going your way are apartments for the other avians who live here as well as work here."

"What's that way?" Kane demanded, glancing suspiciously in the direction Everet suggested.

"The main part of the nest."

That did sound more promising. Kane huffed and grudgingly set off along that route. Everet quickly fell into step behind him.

Kane pushed one hand into the back pocket of his jeans. The time he'd spent in Everet's bed had given someone time to find him some better clothes. At least these looked like they'd been chosen by someone who understood what would make him look his best.

Running the fingers of his other hand through his hair, Kane thought back to his reflection in the mirror that morning. All his bruises were gone. He no longer looked like a zombie in need of a nice long nap. He was back on form and looking good enough to earn whatever he needed.

It wouldn't take him long to find a rich bird of prey who'd be happy to take him under his wing in return for having access to a nice tight backside that he could screw any time he wanted.

Two long flights of stairs led down to a busy lobby. Kane kept a tight grip on the handrail, trying to look like he wasn't knackered even after just a short stroll.

He stopped with six steps left to go and ran his eyes slowly over the people bustling back and forth in the lobby. There wasn't a woman in sight.

"It really is a male-only nest," Kane said.

"Didn't you believe me?" Everet said, from one stair above and behind him.

Kane glanced over his shoulder. The raven had a good enough height advantage over him when they were on level ground. There was no need for him to stand up there and loom.

"Have you visited a male-only nest before?" Everet asked.

Kane shrugged, as if it was no big deal, but he couldn't help but be fascinated. Had his parents known this kind of nest existed? Why hadn't they told him? If there were this many avian men who liked men, why the hell had they allowed his older sister to give him so much hell about taking it from guys?

Kane looked heavenward, as if there would be any answers coming from that direction! He blinked several times in quick succession as his gaze came to rest on a truly wonderful sight.

A huge chandelier sparkled right above them. Kane stared up at it, admiring the way the gilt arms that held the lights shone with a deep golden lustre. The crystals were magnificent; every one of them cut so it would refract the light and make each ray dance and shimmer.

It was a work of art, far more beautiful than any of the

69

boring paintings of stuffy old men who stared down at them from the high, wood-panelled walls. Kane's neck protested as he tilted his head back even further in an effort to see every bit of sparkle.

Maybe one day he'd get screwed by a man who had something like that hanging in his house. Then, every moment that his arse or his mouth wasn't required, Kane would lie on the floor beneath the glorious combination of shiny metal and sparkling glass and just stare at it.

Kane smiled. The very thought of it pulled at something deep within his magpie side. He wanted it. If he could have leapt from the stairs and caught hold of it, he'd have clambered into the centre and had himself completely surrounded by the lights and lustre.

No. It was no good. It had been years since he took to the wing. Kane wasn't even sure if he'd be able to if he tried. Maybe it would be worth it, though. If he could build a nest up there surrounded by sparkle and —

"Kane?"

Everet gently prodded Kane's shoulder. Kane jerked out of his daydream. Willing to let Everet think he was in charge, for now, at least, Kane made his way down the remaining steps.

He was halfway across the lobby before he realised that, while he'd stood on the stairs, he'd missed the perfect opportunity to scope out a rich man to latch on to, or even a dealer he could approach directly. Kane frowned. He obviously wasn't completely himself yet.

"This way." Everet didn't walk on ahead. He stayed beside Kane, apparently unwilling to let him out of his sight.

Kane gave a mental shrug and allowed Everet to have his way, just this once. A tour guide could be useful until he got his bearings. Kane lifted himself up onto his toes and stretched his neck in an effort to see as much as possible. He ran his eyes over the men around him, looking for a man who looked rich enough to own a chandelier — or at least some other shiny things.

Being in the midst of the crowd soon got Kane's adrenaline pumping. His eyes darted from one object to another as he took in his surroundings. Fancy carving surrounded every door. Another, far smaller and less impressive, chandelier glittered above them as they made their way down a wide corridor. Even the tiles beneath their feet screamed out their high-quality status. Everything must have cost a fortune.

Kane smiled to himself. The humans could keep their seedy little clubs. This was much more his kind of world. This was where he'd really thrive.

Kane frowned as Everet placed a hand on the small of his back and tried to steer him toward what looked to be a much quieter part of the nest. "Where are we going?"

"We're going to get something to eat. Then, if you feel up to it, we're going to talk about what you're going to do with your time now that you're up and about."

Kane made no comment about that. It didn't sound like the kind of chat he'd enjoy, but food—Kane could easily declare himself in favour of food. At the end of another corridor, they stepped into a high, beam-topped space that seemed to be a cross between a really high-end restaurant and the food hall of a huge human shopping centre.

It was all mahogany and glittering silverware, but if Kane had thought that nothing other than a murmuring of polite voices would grace that kind of establishment, he was soon proved wrong. Bustle and noise filled every inch of the place.

Everet put his hand on the small of Kane's back and tried to guide him to an empty table near the middle of the room.

Kane stopped short and pointed toward the right-hand side of the room, where the men looked far more capable of supporting a magpie in the way to which he'd really love to become accustomed. "I want to sit over there."

"No. We're sitting here," Everet calmly corrected. He had a way of stating stupid things like they were facts that couldn't be disagreed with. It was a bloody annoying habit. Kane folded his arms across his chest.

If Everet thought that a magpie wouldn't throw a tantrum just because they were in a public place, he really didn't have a clue what sort of avian he was dealing with. As far as Kane was concerned, making himself the centre of attention would just ensure the richer restaurant patrons noticed him more quickly.

"If you try to sit over there, one of the men who serve here will simply ask you to move."

"Why?"

"Because rank has its privileges, and neither of us have that sort of rank," Everet said, still in that annoyingly calm voice. He put his hand on Kane's shoulder and coaxed him down onto a seat.

Kane glared across the table as Everet took the chair opposite him. "It doesn't bother you that you can't sit wherever you want?"

For a second, Everet's habitually blank mask slipped. He actually looked surprised. "Why would it?"

Kane folded his arms and looked pointedly away from him. If Everet was going to be stupid about it, he could talk to himself.

"Kane—"

Whatever Everet was about to say, he stopped short when a man wearing nothing but a pair of very skimpy black shorts stopped at their table.

Kane's eyes narrowed. Just because he had no interest in remaining under Everet's protection, that didn't mean Everet could turn his attention elsewhere. Kane leaned forward in his seat. "Who the hell are you?"

The guy looked like he was barely out of his teens, but he was more than old enough to be a threat. At that age, Kane had been screwing cash out of men for years, and had already moved onto his third sugar-daddy.

The guy took a quick step back when he saw the pure hatred in Kane's eyes, but he didn't fly off completely.

"I'll be serving you this morning, sir. If you have no objection." He proffered several menus.

Kane snatched one from him. Everet took another.

"You can go now," Kane snapped.

The waiter looked to Everet for confirmation, as if Kane's words didn't mean a damn thing without the raven's approval.

Before Kane could make his feelings about that very clear, Everet nodded his endorsement. "Thank you. We'll let you know when we're ready to order."

The waiter hurried away, shaking his arse far more than he needed to, in Kane's opinion.

"There was no reason for you to be rude to him."

Kane pursed his lips and turned his attention pointedly toward his menu. Flicking open the leather cover, he peered intently at the list of options.

"Did you check the waiter's wrist?" Everet asked.

"No."

"You should have. His mark would have told you that he's a pigeon."

"So?" Kane snapped.

"So, in case you've forgotten everything you were taught before you left avian society, you and he are of a very similar social rank."

Kane lost all interest in his menu. He turned his complete attention to Everet.

*

Everet bit back a smile. If looks could have killed, Kane's expression would have had him hung, drawn and quartered, then buried at the crossroads for good measure. It seemed very possible that Kane's glare would have even

73

added a stake through Everet's heart, just in case everything else hadn't made his annoyance clear enough.

Kane threw down his menu, almost knocking over his glass. "He and I are nothing alike."

Everet had lived at the nest long enough that he didn't need to check the breakfast menu. He set it down, leant back in his chair and studied Kane. For the first time in an eternity, his primary concern was no longer about the boy being close to death. The novelty was almost dizzying. "You're not the same species," he granted. "But you are —"

"I have nothing in common with some pathetic little idiot, who's content to waste his life waiting on other people," Kane bit out.

"Pigeons do take to service far more easily than magpies," Everet allowed, very calmly. That was the important thing now. He needed to be calm and in control, or everything would quickly descend into insanity.

"They're stupid!" Kane snapped, apparently still completely focused on the pigeon.

"They don't have the reputation for being the brightest of breeds," Everet admitted. "Magpies are smarter."

"Smart enough not to stay at the bottom of the pecking order for a second longer than we have to!" Kane cut in triumphantly.

"But, at the same time, magpies aren't always shrewd enough to know what sort of role would suit them best," Everet continued, in an even, measured tone.

Kane's eyes narrowed. "You think *you* know what's best for me?"

"Yes."

"Bollocks."

Everet lifted a hand and summoned the pigeon to their table. "We'll both have the classic breakfast, please." He dismissed the waiter before Kane had a chance to try to change the order.

"That wasn't what I wanted!"

"You're under no obligation to eat it when it arrives," Everet said. "If you tell me, calmly and politely, that you don't like what's put before you, then we can order something else for you. But any decisions you make for yourself will be made quietly and with consideration for those around you, or you won't make any at all."

Kane put both his hands on the edge of the table. It looked as if he might bolt. Everet tensed, ready to spring up and chase him down.

"So this is why you agreed to keep me out of the cages?" Kane demanded. "So you'll have someone to bully and boss around? Do you think I'm going to wait on you twenty-four hours a day? Well, I've got a news flash for you—"

"I have no use for a personal servant."

Kane stopped short "What?"

"I said, I've no use for a servant. When you've finished acting like a brat, one of the things we'll be discussing is what kind of job you'll be doing at the nest."

Kane remained very still for a moment, but Everet had no doubt that inside the magpie's mind, thoughts were racing around at a truly frantic pace. "I want to look around before I make any decisions, get a feel for the place," Kane said.

"And find a rich old fool who'll take you under his wing and spoil you, rather than make damn sure you learn how to work for a living?" Everet asked, knowing that the subject had to be dealt with, and the sooner the better. His tone was polite, but there was no way he could make the subject palatable.

"You don't think pandering to a rich man's whims is hard work?" Kane shot back.

You're better than that.

Everet bit back the words, judging it best to keep that particular opinion to himself for now.

I didn't get you this far through withdrawal just so you could go back to getting high and whoring yourself out.

There was no need to make Kane aware of that fact either — far better for Kane to learn both things as time passed. Everet took a deep breath. All his carefully laid plans and promises to himself regarding how he'd deal with Kane, once Kane was through the worst of his withdrawal, seemed so unbelievably naïve, now that Everet faced an avian capable of talking back.

All the jobs he'd thought might suit Kane ran in the opposite direction at the sight of his current attitude.

Their food arrived.

Kane folded his arms and stared mutinously at the plate.

"If you're going to look for a wealthy new master, you're going to need your strength," Everet pointed out. "Unless you've already seen sense and abandoned that plan, of course."

Either Kane fell for it, or he was willing to use it as an acceptable excuse for giving in without a fight. He ate with far more appetite than he had shown before. He really was through the second stage of his withdrawal. That job could be ticked off Everet's list once and for all.

Everet's anxiety level decreased a notch. Everything would be fine. They were two thirds of the way there. If he could just convince Kane's *mind* to believe he didn't need the stuff.

"I take it you haven't had any training in a particular profession?" Everet asked as they each pushed their empty plates aside.

Obviously, he'd been right to keep the question back until Kane had finished his breakfast, because as soon as the question hit the air, Kane leant back in his chair and pointedly turned his attention away from Everet, in a complete and instant sulk.

"In that case, we'll start you off with something that you don't need any training for. It will give you a bit of structure while you're settling in and — "

"I'm tired. I need to rest now."

Everet didn't even miss a beat. "The avian in charge of the day to day maintenance of the nest is a barn owl. His name is Mr. Johnson. He'll know what jobs are available."

"Didn't you hear me?" Kane demanded.

"Yes. You're tired." Everet held Kane's gaze, almost daring the magpie to look away first. "If you really can't manage to join me, I suppose I can ask Ambrose to take you back to my apartment. You can rest there while Mr. Johnson and I decide how you'll be spending your time for the next few weeks."

"Like hell you will." Kane launched himself to his feet. His cutlery clattered to the floor as he carelessly pushed it off the table.

Everet remained in his seat, tilting back his head so he never needed to break eye contact. "You said you were too tired to speak to Mr. Johnson yourself."

"Where is he?" Kane demanded.

Everet raised an eyebrow.

"This Mr. Johnson," Kane snapped. "Where is he? I want to speak to him, right now."

"Sit down."

"I said—"

"I heard you, so did most of the men in the room. Sit down. Pick up your knife and fork, and put them back on the table. Then, when you're calm, I'll take you to see Mr. Johnson."

"No." From the way he said it, Kane seemed to expect some sort of dramatic reaction to the pronouncement.

Everet merely settled himself a little more comfortably in his seat. He had plenty to think about to pass his time. At some point, he'd have to get back to his own duties at the nest. No doubt everything had gone to hell when he'd been distracted by Kane's illness.

He'd have to sort out the mess the other members of the security flock would have made of his attempts to set up a

77

system to record and monitor those avians who, while not exactly breaking any of the nest's laws, had mistreated or taken advantage of lower ranking men.

"Are you just going to sit there?" Kane demanded, his voice still a dozen decibels louder than it needed to be.

"Yes, until you're ready to leave, that's exactly what I intend to do."

"I'm ready now!" Kane actually stamped his foot. He was obviously used to getting his own way whenever he threw that kind of a fit. It would have been amusing if it hadn't reduced a man with Kane's potential to something so far beneath what he should have been.

"The way to show me you're ready is to sit quietly in your chair, with your knife and fork back on the table."

"Seriously? *This* is what you want to make a stand over?"

Everet shrugged. It might as well be. The point that he wouldn't be influenced by hysterics would have to be made sometime. "No time like the present."

Kane dragged his chair back several inches, making the legs screech against the floorboards. He snatched up the cutlery and tossed it on the plate with a clatter. Shoving one hand into his pocket, he dumped himself into his seat as if the chair had personally offended him. Although why Kane should think anything in its right mind wouldn't love to be pressed up against his arse —

Everet cut that line of thought off very sharply. If he went down that route, they'd never get anything done. He stood up. "Good. Well done. Mr. Johnson's office is this way." He held his arm out, letting Kane precede him between the rows of tables.

Kane still didn't have much weight to him, but he stomped far better than most men twice his size. Every man in the room was staring at Kane by the time he'd gone a dozen steps; some gazed with disapproval or amusement, but most of them with straightforward lust.

Everet automatically quickened his pace, making sure he walked so closely behind Kane no one could miss the fact they were together. Kane was his, and Everet needed every man who even thought about screwing Kane to realise that it wasn't an option. Kane had already been claimed.

Everet's hands itched with an unaccustomed desire to lash out at any man who went near his magpie. He'd never felt anything like it, never felt so out of control inside his own skin.

Damn, but he'd have loved to be able to put a collar around Kane's neck—and to attach a lead to it. The idea of Kane being marked and kept at his side appealed like nothing Everet had ever known.

As his mind raced, Everet forced himself to keep his expression neutral and his fingers relaxed, no matter how badly they wanted to furl themselves into fists.

It only took them a few minutes to descend the stairs into an administrative part of the building. The elaborate décor of the public rooms morphed into a more business-like space that made up a middle ground between the grandeur of the most opulent areas of the nest and the more spartan servants' areas.

Mr. Johnson's office stood halfway along a corridor housing the entrances to a dozen different offices. Searching for something to keep his mind off thoughts of killing anyone who tried to steal Kane away from him, Everet read the brass plate on each door they passed.

Owls, pelicans, penguins, gulls—no ravens' names were etched there. But the species weren't that far away from him in the pecking order. They weren't so much above him as different from him.

A line of chairs stood in the corridor directly outside Mr. Johnson's doorway, but they were all unoccupied. The door stood open.

Everet tapped on the doorframe to catch the attention of the portly old gentleman sitting behind the large paper-strewn desk.

"Everet, always a pleasure!" Mr. Johnson stood up and extended a hand across the table.

Everet shook the barn owl's hand.

"And who have we here?" Mr. Johnson asked, as jovially as ever, as he turned to Kane.

"You don't *have me*, darling," Kane drawled. "And if you had ever *had me*, you'd remember who I was. Some of us aren't forgettable." He ran his eyes up and down Mr. Johnson in a way that made it quite clear which side of the memorable-unmemorable divide Kane thought the nest's household administrator fell onto.

"Ah, yes, Everet," Mr. Johnson said. "Your new charge. There has been more than a touch of gossip surrounding your little endeavour." He took his seat and indicated the chairs on the opposite side of the desk.

Everet sat down. Kane didn't. Everet nudged his chair back slightly so he could keep Kane in his field of vision, but he didn't try to force him into the seat.

"We all can but hope you are successful," Mr. Johnson went on, absentmindedly shuffling some of the papers on his desk. "It would be a fine day indeed if someone were to find a way to rehabilitate any of the less savoury species in our – "

"I am still here, you know," Kane snapped.

Mr. Johnson glanced up at him. "Yes, so you are!" He completely dismissed him as he turned back to Everet. Amusement danced in his eyes as their gazes met. "What can I do for you today, Everet?"

Everet's unease at Kane's behaviour gradually dissipated as he realised that Mr. Johnson had no intention of taking offense at anything Kane said. He put Everet in mind of a female owl who'd taught him when he was a fledgling in school. She'd had far more sense than to reward naughty children with attention as well.

"Kane would like a job at the nest. Preferably nothing too strenuous, but definitely something which will be supervised and which will give him structure," Everet said.

"Kane can speak for himself!" Kane cut in.

"You could," Everet allowed. "But you gave me the right to speak for you in certain matters when you agreed to submit to me. Until you can speak politely on your own behalf, I'll do the talking." He turned back to Mr. Johnson.

The older man bowed his head over a ledger. "Does he have any special skills that might be of use to the nest?"

"I give excellent blowjobs," Kane said, before Everet had a chance.

Mr. Johnson ran a finger down a column. "Unfortunately, we don't appear to have anything that requires that particular skill..." he murmured. "However, there's a position on one of the cleaning flocks that—"

"No way in hell am I—!"

"He'll take it."

Both statements hit the air at the same time.

Mr. Johnson's lips twitched. "Fantastic!"

Kane lurched forward and planted his hands on Mr. Johnson's desk. "I said—"

"You said you would defer to my decisions," Everet quickly cut in.

Damn, but he wished there was a way to turn down the volume on Kane. His head ached like he'd been punched by an albatross. And, god help him, he'd thought looking after the mute and motionless version of Kane had been exhausting!

Kane glanced over his shoulder at Everet. His eyes narrowed. "Whatever."

He was plotting something. Everet had no doubt about that. Kane wasn't simply giving in. Even after such a brief acquaintance, it was obvious that wasn't Kane's style.

Mr. Johnson looked at the clock on the wall opposite his desk. "As it happens, one of the cleaning flocks is due to congregate in an upper hallway in just a few minutes."

"Perfect. Thank you. We'll go straight up and meet

them there." Everet stood and offered Mr. Johnson his hand. The barn owl extended a hand toward him in return and told him exactly which corridor he needed to take.

Kane shoved his own hands deep into his pockets, as if making a point that he didn't want to shake hands with anyone. He turned and stormed out of the room before Everet had time to take a truly polite leave of Mr. Johnson.

Everet rushed out a brief thank you and good bye and hurried after Kane. He caught up with him at the end of the row of chairs in the corridor. Grabbing hold of Kane's arm, Everet turned him toward a flight of service stairs leading up to the top floor.

"Me. A cleaner?" Kane demanded as they reached the third floor. "Seriously?"

"There's nothing wrong with cleaning."

"Fine, then you can do it!" As they stepped into the hallway, Kane planted his feet firmly in the deep pile of the maroon carpet. "I'll do your job." Kane's frown deepened. "What do you do?"

"Nest security," Everet told him, not for the first time. "You wouldn't like it."

"I don't like this, either. I'm not going to be a bloody cleaner!"

Everet didn't bother to answer. He'd already seen the group of men milling around at the other end of the corridor. He strode forward. He still had hold of Kane's arm and he pointedly ignored any of his attempts to slow them down.

The group caught sight of them when they were just a few yards away. One man nudged his neighbour in the ribs. By the time Everet brought them both to a halt, all the men in the group were staring at them expectantly.

"Good morning, gentlemen," Everet said. "This is Kane. He'll be joining your crew today. He's new to the nest. He's also restricted to light duties for the time being."

One of the men stepped forward. His stance and attitude made it clear that he was the highest-ranking avian there, and had therefore taken charge of the group. "Yes, sir." He tipped his head respectfully to Everet.

The man looked to be somewhere in his forties, short, and dressed with a neatness that hinted he was fanatical in his attention to detail. Everet glanced down at the man's wrist. His species mark proclaimed him to be a partridge.

All in all, the guy looked like a fine choice to lead the mini-flock—and no match at all for Kane's current standard of behaviour.

"I'll be staying and following your progress today," Everet went on. "Just to make sure Kane settles in and that everything goes well on his first day."

"You're very welcome, sir." The partridge nodded to him again. When repeated so often, the gesture made him look a little like a puppet with a faulty string.

Everet acknowledged him with a very slight dip of his own head and took three steps back, leaving Kane to be part of the group while he removed himself from their immediate sphere.

*

Kane glared at the collection of drab little men standing before him. He could already sense how thoroughly they resented his presence. Well, screw them. Kane pursed his lips, not bothering to hide his distaste at the company he was temporarily being forced to keep.

Everet's gaze bored into the back of Kane's neck so fiercely the bastard might as well have put him in a permanent choke hold. If he'd just have buggered off and left him to it, it would have been so easy.

The fussy looking guy who'd been so deferential to Everet handed Kane a yellow duster and a canister of spray polish. Damn. With Everet there, he'd at least have to pretend to play along for a while. Kane snatched both items from the fussy little man.

"My name's Mr. Edwards. I'll be showing you what your duties will be today." He turned his palm up, showing Kane the inside of his wrist. There was a mark there, but Kane didn't recognise it.

"You're a magpie?" Edwards asked. Tilting his head back in an effort to peer down his nose at a man who was actually taller than him.

"Yeah." *What about it?*

Edwards glanced toward Everet. His decision not to answer the unspoken question was obviously based entirely upon the raven's presence.

Kane huffed his disgust. What a coward...

Edwards cleared his throat in that prissy manner self-important men always adopted. "You'll work on the left-hand side of the hallway. Make sure you get all the wooden surfaces. One of the other men will take care of the glass and the soft furnishings. Until we know what sort of standard you work to, I'll be making regular checks on your progress."

Kane rolled his eyes. Didn't that just make everything perfect?

The other members of the group picked up various bits of equipment from a wheeled trolley in the middle of the hall and spread out to do their jobs without any orders hitting the air. Apparently, they were all well-trained.

Kane tilted his chin up. He'd *never* be like them.

They all worked in silence—just to make the task that little bit more boring than it would have been anyway. Kane sighed and half-heartedly squirted some of the spray polish on a side table set between two doors.

Perhaps the job would have been slightly more tolerable if the thing had looked like it was worth keeping clean, but it was the most boring thing in creation. No sparkle or glitter, just drab brown wood. Kane gave it a quick rub with the cloth since Everet still lurked nearby, and then moved on to the next one.

"Kane."

Rolling his eyes, Kane returned to the table and tapped his toe against the floor as Edwards gave him an in-depth lecture about making sure he moved things and cleaned beneath them rather than just around them. He went on and on about how it was important to work the duster over the carving on the sides of the table as well. Apparently, it was also vital to make sure no dust clung to the rail underneath the table. As if anyone could possibly give a damn about what was down there.

"Any questions?"

Kane let his face go carefully blank. "Maybe you could show me on the next table? I'm sure I could get the hang of it then."

He offered Edwards a carefully calculated smile and saw colour rush to the partridge's cheeks in response.

Gotcha!

This one would be so easy to wrap around his finger. It would be—

"No."

Kane looked over his shoulder and there was Everet, well within eavesdropping range.

The head of the work party blinked as if he had completely forgotten about the bloody raven's presence.

"He knows what to do," Everet said, coldly. "He just wants to con you into doing it for him. Every table you demonstrate on is one less that he has to do himself. If you're not careful, he'll flirt his way into getting you to do them all for him."

Kane glared over his shoulder at Everet.

Bastard.

There was no point trying to get out of doing it now, at least not straight away. Kane snatched the cleaning supplies from the still-blushing Edwards and stomped along to the next table.

Everet silently took up position barely a yard away from him, arms folded across his chest, as still as a statue. If

Kane didn't do the job right, he had a horrible feeling that Everet would make him re-do it over and over again until he was satisfied.

Quick to spot the route of least resistance, Kane did exactly as he'd been shown. He even remembered the bar beneath the damn big lump of oak.

The only way to reach beneath the table was to get down on his knees. Kane turned to Everet the moment his knees hit the hall carpet. "You know, there are far more interesting things I could be doing in this position."

The raven wasn't an idiot; he knew exactly what Kane was offering him. Kane still licked his lips, just to make things that little bit more obvious.

"You've used sex to manipulate men for too long. It's time to stop," Everet said. His face remained expressionless, but the way his shoulders tensed made it clear that he wasn't half as unaffected as he'd like to appear.

"You think that's the only reason I'd want to suck your cock?" Kane asked. "I didn't realise you were so modest!" He turned and ran the cloth over the carved wood stretching between the table legs. There wasn't even any damn dust to be wiped away — talk about bloody pointless.

"Flattery won't get you out of doing your fair share of work," Everet snapped.

A few of the other men had vacuum cleaners going as they attacked the carpet with what had to be fake delight in their work. The machines were oversized and noisy as hell.

Despite the fact a dozen men were working in the hallway, Kane realised that no one was actually within earshot of them. "It's only flattery if I'm lying," Kane said, softly.

Everet's face remained impassive. He even managed to relax his shoulders and look stress-free. It was only the way his trousers tented over his growing erection that let Kane know that all his kneeling and flirting wasn't going to waste.

"You're not an idiot," Kane said. "You have to know you're hot, in a grumpy sort of way. After spending the last couple of years bending over for rich old men who'd never have a chance of getting laid if they weren't paying for it, you'd actually make a nice change for me."

Everet stepped forward, giving another member of the work party room to open a door behind him and step through it. The door swung closed, but Everet didn't retreat.

He was now less than half a yard away from Kane.

"More subtle attempts at manipulation aren't going to get you anywhere either."

Kane laughed. "Do you want to screw me just because you think it will make me more likely to obey you the next time you try to order me around?"

"Of course not!" Everet snapped. "That has nothing to do with—"

"So why can't I just want to screw you because I think it might be fun?" Kane stood up. "If I'm going to spend all day doing this," he brandished a duster, "I could use something hot to look forward to when I'm done. Sometimes sex is just sex."

Everet's gaze narrowed. He didn't trust him.

Kane smiled. He'd been right to say Everet was no idiot.

"You're neglecting your work," Everet finally said.

That wasn't a no. As Kane made his way to the next table, he had no doubt he'd be able to make the answer a very firm yes by the time they went back to Everet's rooms that night. Leaning over to wipe all the way to the back of a particularly deep table top, Kane made sure that his arse faced Everet and the fabric of his jeans stretched very nicely over his buttocks.

Against all his expectations when he'd first decided to make the offer, Kane found himself looking forward to exchanging something other than cross words with the raven. His own cock pressed against the inside of his fly just as firmly as Everet's did.

Chapter Six

"Well?" Kane demanded, before Everet had even had a chance to close the apartment door behind them.

Everet took a deep breath.

"I did the damn housework. What do I get in exchange?" Kane pushed.

"The nest will pay for your food and lodging here, and you'll be given a salary at the end of the month." Everet decided it was best not to mention that, as Kane's master, the salary would be paid to him. There was no need to invite another temper tantrum, especially since Everet was going to pass on every penny to Kane anyway.

Unable to stop himself fidgeting in an effort to expel some of the energy that coursed through his veins, Everet pushed his hand through his hair and strode across to the far side of his living room.

"You know that's not what I'm talking about," Kane snapped.

"Sex shouldn't be about exchanging anything other than pleasure," Everet said. "You can't *earn* sex any more than you can sell it—not anymore."

Kane scowled across the room at him. "You said we could have sex."

"No," Everet corrected. "I didn't." He'd been very careful about that. He hadn't promised anything. He hadn't guaranteed that anything would happen between them that night.

No matter how many times Everet turned the conundrum over in his head, he was damned if he could work out what decision he should make if he really wanted to do his best by Kane.

If he gave in, everything could fall apart. Kane would probably think he was the same as every other man who'd used him that way.

But if he avoided sex entirely, it would always be the issue hanging over their heads. Kane would always think he'd be able to get around him if he just flirted well enough.

Everet ran his hand down his face.

"We might not even get that much pleasure from it." The words were part of the conversation he was having with himself inside his head. He hadn't intended to share them with anyone else, but they were out of his mouth before he could stop them. The worst of it was, the words were true. Fantasy was one thing, but reality would probably be something else — for both of them.

"If you don't have the balls to follow through, then admit it," Kane ordered. "Don't lie to me. We have enough chemistry to start a meth lab, and you know it."

Everet huffed. If chemistry was all they needed, perhaps it would have been that simple. "You think I bossed you around a lot when you were dusting tables? You have no idea how much control I like to have over my lovers."

Kane leaned against the back of Everet's sofa. Everet wasn't sure why he should be surprised at that. The little sod had found a million different things to bend over during the day. God, but his arse was amazing.

"Ravens have a reputation for being kinky," Kane said, as if it were no big deal.

"And magpies don't," Everet countered.

Kane shrugged. Pushing himself away from the sofa, he walked slowly around it. He stopped directly in front of Everet, his hands hooked into the belt loops on his jeans, his crotch thrust forward, and his erection clearly visible against the fabric of his pants. "Think you can come up with anything I haven't tried before?"

"Tried when payment wasn't involved?" Everet asked. "Yes." He had no doubt about that.

Kane glared up at him, sudden anger burning bright in his expression.

Everet didn't flinch from it; he welcomed it. "We're talking about pleasure, not payment," he repeated. "You're not going to get anything out of this except a good time; and if you're not into my kind of sex, you probably won't even get that from me."

Kane turned and walked away from him, his steps slow and lazy. On the other side of the room, he glanced over his shoulder. "You'd best tell me what you're into then."

"I like to be in control."

Kane's eyes opened wide as he looked over his other shoulder and favoured Everet with another glimpse of his face. "I'm shocked."

If Everet wanted the truth from Kane, he knew he had no option but to offer it in return. "I like to play rough," he added.

"How rough?" There was nothing coy about that question. Kane turned back to face him head on.

"The kind of rough that doesn't leave painful bruises," Everet said. "The kind both guys can enjoy."

For once, Kane didn't rush to interrupt. He let Everet continue in peace.

"I like to pin a man down, but only if I know he enjoys the game as much as I do. I've reddened a few arses, but only when the guy getting spanked begged for more." Everet forced himself not to close the gap between them, but it was the hardest thing he'd ever done. "I like to feel a man squirm beneath me, but only when I know he's just testing my control over him instead of actually trying to get away."

Kane's lips twisted into a smile. "I think I'll survive."

"We're not talking about survival anymore."

Kane was suddenly six inches away from Everet's face. "You want permission to pin me down? You've got it. But, you know, if you want me to play hard to get just so you can have the pleasure of catching me, you don't need to try and press my buttons. I'm more than happy to run away if that's what turns you on."

And suddenly, Kane was in the bedroom. The door slammed shut in his wake. Pure predatory instinct kicked in. No raven would have been able to stand still.

Every thought of the nice civilized discussions Everet had intended to have before they so much as brushed against each other fled from his mind. He lurched forward. Long before his brain had caught up with his body, Everet was through the bedroom door.

It wasn't a huge room. There wasn't far for Kane to run. He stood on the opposite side of the room, eyes sparkling with mischief.

Alive.

He looked so damn alive. Just a few days before, Everet had been sure the only version of Kane he'd ever see in that room would be deathly pale, his breathing unreliable, and his temperature sky high.

Someone would have to have been a complete bastard to want to screw the magpie who'd been feverish and delirious, but *this* version of Kane was something different. This version was perfect; strong and bratty, and he certainly wouldn't let anyone do anything to him that he didn't want—not for free.

As Everet admired this new version of Kane, he stepped forward, closing the gap between them in careful, measured paces.

Kane grinned. There was no hint of fear in him, no sign of illness or weakness. He was cornered, but he didn't seem to know it. There was no way he could possibly escape while Everet stood—

Without any warning, Kane was gone.

Jumping up onto the mattress, he made the most of the energy in the bedsprings and leapt onto the floor on the other side of the bed. Damn, but he was quick. Everet spun around to face him again.

"Too slow, sweetheart," Kane chided.

Yes, Everet was exactly that—slow. He remained slow as he rounded the bed. He didn't rush or leap; every step he took was very deliberate.

For a few seconds, Kane managed to remain motionless and studied Everet in return, but he didn't have Everet's patience. Kane was all about movement. He shuffled his feet against the bedroom carpet as he fought against his instinct for action. His self-restraint lasted less than a millisecond. He leapt again.

This time Everet was ready. His slow progress meant he hadn't even moved past the bottom corner of the bed. He dived, just a split second after Kane. He wrapped his arms around Kane's torso mid-air and let his weight carry them forward until they crashed onto the centre of the mattress.

Without a word being spoken between them, the chase morphed seamlessly into a wrestle for supremacy.

Everet grappled for Kane's wrists. Light, contagious laughter filled the air as Kane managed to squirm around and trap his hands beneath his own stomach so they were hidden from Everet.

Everet straddled the backs of Kane's thighs and reached around him. Their bodies lined up perfectly. His crotch rubbed against Kane's arse again and again as he tried to worm his hands beneath Kane's torso.

Success! Everet finally caught hold of one wrist, then the other. Sitting back on his calves, Everet pulled Kane up off the mattress to kneel in front of him, as if they were spooning.

Breathless, half from their tussle and half from laughter, Kane cheerfully collapsed back against him.

"Screw me." It was a demand, not an invitation.

All at once, neither of them was laughing.

"I thought I was supposed to be the bossy one," Everet growled in Kane's ear.

"You want to be boss of this bed? Prove you can take the title from me."

In less than two seconds, Everet had rolled Kane onto his back and straddled him again. Shock filled Kane's eyes for a second, then he was back in form. He parted his lips, no doubt to utter something bratty.

Every cell in Everet's body reacted to Kane and his challenges. His desire to take control of another man had never been so strong. His need to make sure the guy in his care was well-treated had never felt so desperate. Everet clamped his hand over Kane's mouth, testing the way forward.

"There's only one word you're allowed to say from now on," Everet informed him.

Kane nipped at Everet's hand, catching the sensitive spot where the skin at the base of his thumb curved up toward his index finger. Everet ignored the stab of pain.

"No."

Kane's eyes narrowed, obviously furious at hearing the word directed at him in any circumstances.

"That's the only word you're allowed to say," Everet went on. "You want this to stop, say no." Everet frowned as he considered his own statement. "No, scratch that last bit. *Whatever* you say, that's what's going to happen." Everet smiled. "No more smart remarks, no more coy flirty little bits of nonsense. Either you want this, or you don't. If you don't, just say something, anything at all. But if you do want it, then you have to stay completely silent. Not one word."

Kane stared up at him, his eyes as calculating as ever. Everet turned the situation around inside his head, studying it from every angle, but he saw no way in which Kane could manipulate the order.

He held Kane's gaze as he went on, determined that Kane should see how serious he was about this. "You can speak up at any time. I won't be angry. You won't be punished." Everet kept his hand over Kane's mouth, making sure Kane had time to think about what he'd said, and if he wanted to speak up or not.

"You understand your options?" Everet checked, one last time. Every fibre and sinew in him prayed Kane wouldn't back off now, but he somehow kept his expression neutral. "Nod if you do."

Kane nodded, taking the opportunity to dig his teeth a little deeper into Everet's hand. He might as well have saved himself the bother. Everet was so focused on the importance of the moment he barely even felt the bite.

Lifting his hand away from Kane's mouth, Everet straightened up. "Give me your answer."

Kane didn't say a word. Not one single blessed syllable left his mouth.

A wave of relief rushed through Everet. He knew how hard it was for Kane to remain silent at any time. If he was making the effort to keep quiet now, it was because he *really* wanted this.

A few more seconds of silence, and Kane poked out his tongue. There was a smudge of blood on it — Everet's blood.

Everet glanced down at his hand. The little bugger had bitten down hard enough to break the skin; he looked wonderfully proud of that achievement.

"Careful, Kane, you're not the only man in the bed with teeth."

Everet still sat over Kane's legs, but the top half of the Kane's body was free. When Kane moved to sit up, Everet didn't try to stop him.

Watching him warily, Everet allowed Kane to retain that little bit of freedom, simply because he was curious to see what Kane would do with it. Catching hold of Everet's wrist, Kane guided his hand up to his mouth.

He very gently kissed and licked at the wound, as if he was doing his damnedest to clean it up and make it better.

It might have looked like an apology, but when Kane glanced up at Everet's eyes, his gaze was all seduction. No one should have been able to make licking an open wound look erotic, but somehow Kane managed it.

Everet took his hand away. Pulling himself off Kane, he got off the bed completely. Kane opened his mouth, no doubt a complaint already rushing to his lips.

"Remember the rules," Everet warned.

Kane stopped short, unable to say a single word without bringing the game to a halt. Folding his arms across his chest, he settled for lifting one eyebrow in silent challenge.

"Take off your clothes," Everet ordered.

Kane held Everet's gaze for a moment. Then, a smile curved his lips. He pulled his shirt over his head and threw it aside.

Everet made a mental note to make tossing clothes on the floor against the rules in future. He wasn't about to play the maid and pick them up.

Kane reached for his fly. Everet had seen Kane naked a hundred times before, but it felt different this time. This time they were both thinking about sex. Everet sent up a silent prayer that they were both doing all this for the right reasons, but it was too late for him to back off now. The only one with a safe word was Kane.

*

Kane took off his jeans and tossed them off the bed.

Everet looked so bloody serious about it all. But, if Everet actually thought there was any way in hell that them having sex wasn't going to completely alter everything between them, he was far more naive than any man his age had a right to be.

Naked now, Kane knelt in the centre of the bed. If he was going to pretend that Everet was in charge, there was little he could do except wait for the next order. That wasn't as difficult to do as Kane had thought it would be. He even managed to keep his hands by his sides and not play with his erection. Not talking—now *that* was a challenge.

Kane bit down on his bottom lip as he fought to keep words back. There were no particular words that he wanted to say, but that was irrelevant. The urge to speak, to be heard, to prove he was worth hearing, was almost overwhelming.

Everet finally stopped doing his statue impression. He pulled his own shirt over his head and set it on the chair in the corner of the room. Other items of clothing followed. Kane watched every movement, taking in each line of muscle revealed to him.

The raven wasn't pretty; he was too strong to suit a word like that—too male. There was so much raw power in him, it almost took Kane's breath away, and he had a truly gorgeous cock.

It really was a case of no payment necessary in Everet's case. The guy was so—

What the hell? Kane shook his head at himself. Other men might think with their cocks, but he didn't think with his. There bloody well had better be a pay-out on the cards! Otherwise, he was—

"Second thoughts?"

Kane opened his mouth, but quickly shut it in favour of silently frowning at Everet.

"You're allowed to speak to answer a direction questions."

"I'm not having second thoughts," Kane said. "I'm ready to go, aren't I?" He waved a hand at his flourishing erection.

"You shook your head."

"No, I didn't."

Everet said nothing. He just stood there, stern and disapproving, with his arms folded across his bare chest.

"And even if I did, it doesn't mean you have to stop everything," Kane bit out.

"Yes, it does," Everet said. "I have no interest in an unwilling partner, remember?"

He said it so patiently, as if it wasn't already the millionth time he'd said it, as if he'd say it another billion times if he thought he needed to.

Kane glared at him, remaining perfectly still while his brain went into overdrive.

Everet meant what he said. And he wasn't going to be easy to fool. Nest security. Nest cop. Being lied to all the time would have given him a really good bull-shit detector.

There was only one way to proceed with a man like that.

Kane looked deeply inside himself, searching for that part of himself that wanted to believe that the version of reality Everet spoke of actually existed for a magpie.

It was far easier to find that part of his psyche than it had been the last time Kane had turned to his tactic of last resort. Barely a split second passed before that side of Kane stepped forward, more than ready and willing to take over.

It would be good to be able to enjoy having sex without focusing on any end game that didn't involve an orgasm. Yes. Being aware of his own pleasure rather than constantly focusing on the need to please someone else so they'd give him what he wanted…

It was strangely freeing and undeniably scary.

Kane let it all flood to the front of his mind, safe in the knowledge that the regular part of him was still there in the background, ready to resume control once it was in his best interests to do so.

He looked up and met Everet's eyes. Everet's frown deepened. Kane didn't even blink.

Everet moved forward until he stood with his bare legs pressed against the edge of the mattress. Kane remained perfectly motionless as Everet dipped his head and brought their lips together for the first time.

The kiss was simple and strangely sweet. For the first time he could remember, Kane didn't keep his eyes open in order to monitor the other person's reactions. He let his eyelids drop closed so he could focus solely on the way Everet's mouth felt against his.

Everet's lips were far softer than he expected. There was nothing insistent or demanding about the way he kissed. It was all very un-raven like.

Kane parted his lips, curious if that would get Everet started in earnest. No such luck. Everet completely failed to jump at the chance to claim Kane's mouth. Instead, Everet slid his hand into Kane's hair and encouraged him to tilt his head back.

Kane let Everet do that. Yes, that was right. He *let* Everet do it. Kane was the one in control, whatever Everet might think. Kane was the one who could stop it all with a word. And, for once in his life, it really felt like he was kissing someone who would stop if he said no.

Everet wouldn't simply grin and keep going, enjoying himself all the more because the man trapped beneath him was in the middle of a panic attack. Ravens were an honourable flock — more fool them.

Kane shuffled his knees on the bed, impatient for a real kiss. Everet ran his tongue gently across Kane's bottom lip. Frustration bubbled up inside Kane, demanding action, demanding movement.

Lifting his hands from his sides, Kane slid them into Everet's hair. Tugging hard at the thick, black strands, he pulled Everet's head down, demanding that Everet deepen the kiss *now* rather than whenever the hell the mood struck him.

Everet made a grumbling, pissed off noise in the back of his throat as he swayed forward. He almost lost his balance and sent them both tumbling onto the bed, but he recovered at the last moment.

As far as Kane was concerned, a lover proving he was that strong, that stable, was issuing an irresistible invitation to use him as a climbing frame. Kane let Everet take his weight as he fought for control of the kiss.

He nipped at Everet's bottom lip, demanding to be allowed to explore his mouth. Everet took no notice. So bloody controlled!

Kane tugged at Everet's hair so hard he knew it had to hurt. With each movement he made, his bare cock rubbed against Everet's torso. Everet's hard shaft rubbed against his body in return.

Everet made that pissed off sound in the back of his throat again. A tingle of expectation raced all down Kane's spine. He moaned his approval as he pressed himself ever more firmly against Everet's body.

One moment Kane hung from Everet's conveniently broad shoulders. The next, he lay flat on his back. His eyes snapped open. He stared up at Everet in shock. Everet still wasn't smiling, but at least he didn't look like a man inclined to think with any body part above his waist. That was a definite improvement.

Even better, Everet looked like a man who was ready to screw. As if to confirm that possibility, Everet grabbed a tube of lube from the drawer in his nightstand.

Kane immediately twisted around to put himself on his hands and knees.

"No, stay on your back. I want to be able to see your face."

Kane gave a mental shrug and rolled over again. Everet coated his fingers with lube so quickly, Kane barely had a chance to pull his knees back toward his chest before Everet had his fingers against Kane's hole, smearing the lube around the tight ring of muscle.

As Everet knelt on the bed alongside Kane, he loomed taller than he had any right to appear. Without any warning, he turned his attention from Kane's hole to his face.

"You remember what you need to do if you want me to stop?" Everet asked.

It was a bloody stupid question. Kane glared at him in annoyance. Everet's fingers stilled, pressing against his arse, but not yet inside him.

He was waiting for an answer? Seriously?

Kane squirmed, trying to push himself onto Everet's fingers. It was no use. Everet was as stubborn as a sodding rock.

Finally, purely because it was in the interests of gaining his own pleasure, Kane nodded. Yes, he knew what he needed to do to make Everet stop. He just wished he knew what to do in order to get the stubborn bastard to hurry the hell up.

As if someone had flicked a switch inside Everet the moment Kane nodded, Everet started to move his fingers, working them deep inside him, stretching him, preparing him to take Everet's cock.

The whole time, Everet kept looking away from what he was doing, and staring at Kane's face. It was completely unnatural. All the interesting stuff was going on elsewhere, damn it!

"Just because you're not allowed to speak, that doesn't mean you can't let me know what you like." Everet crooked his fingers, obviously looking for Kane's prostate.

On the second try, he found it. Kane gasped. That wasn't obedience, though. It was an uncontrollable instinct. He couldn't have kept it back if it would have saved his life.

Everet smiled slightly. He crooked his fingers again. A wave of pleasure rolled through Kane's body. It wasn't like the bliss that came from quicksilver, but it still felt good and his body was quick to latch onto it as a possible replacement, however ineffective it might ultimately end up being.

Kane moaned, arching his back and pushing himself down on Everet's fingers. It was easily the most wonderful sensation he could remember feeling. If Everet wanted to be soppy and try to make it good for the guy he topped, Kane wasn't going to complain.

Five minutes later, Kane changed his mind. He bloody well would complain. He didn't want Everet's fingers. They weren't enough. He wanted Everet's cock. Now!

Dizzy with a combination of pleasure and frustration, Kane reached out and wrapped his hand around Everet's shaft.

Everet let out a surprised grunt. His cock slid against Kane's palm, slicked with a liberal supply of pre-cum but Everet grabbed Kane's wrist with his free hand before Kane had a chance to deliver more than a few strokes.

Kane looked up. A moment later, Everet lifted his gaze too. Their eyes met. Seconds stretched out until they felt like hours.

Finally, Kane felt a subtle pressure against his wrist. Everet nudged Kane's hand, encouraging him to stroke his cock again. At the same time, Everet crooked the fingers he still had lodged in Kane's arse. The tips of his fingers pressed against Kane's prostate. When Everet rubbed his thumb against the sensitive strip of skin between Kane's hole and his ball sac, it felt like he was surrounded by so much pleasure he was going to find it impossible to remain conscious.

Kane arched his back as another wave of bliss rolled through his body. He pressed his head back against the mattress. Scrabbling at the blankets alongside him with his free hand, he grabbed fistfuls of them in an effort to anchor himself to reality. His mind swirled with pleasure. He gasped for breath, unable to stop himself moaning with both pleasure and frustration.

Everet kept complete control of Kane's hand movements and used his grip on Kane's wrist to make his hand move faster and faster around his cock.

Kane's own cock remained untouched. He didn't have the coordination to reach for it. Hell, he wouldn't even have been able to keep jacking Everet if Everet hadn't been so willing to help him along.

Kane closed his eyes very tightly as bliss took flight inside him. Quickly gaining height, it soared through the sky high above anything he'd ever be able to control. Kane clenched his teeth, but there was no way he could hold back now; no possibility of calling that kind of ecstasy back to the perch. Kicking out at the mattress, Kane lifted his arse up off the bed as he came.

Cum spilled across his stomach and chest. His hole clenched around Everet's fingers. Ecstasy stabbed him again and again—pleasure so sharp it felt more like pain.

Kane's breath lodged in his chest. He jerked against the sheets, unsure if he wanted to squirm further into ecstasy or escape from it. It had been so long since he'd come, and now his body seemed determined to punish him for that.

Panic rushed through him as his lungs screamed for oxygen. It seemed possible that he might never be able to breathe again. Then, as quickly as it had claimed him, the moment of pure sensation slipped away. He collapsed back on the bed as he finally managed to pull a breath into his lungs.

He lay there for what could have been hours, slowly letting all the parts of his scattered mind come back to him one by one. He lay completely still.

Kane frowned.

Still.

Motionless.

That was a problem. Part of him should be moving, that was important, wasn't it?

His hand. Damn. Kane pried opened his eyes and looked down at his right hand. It still encircled Everet's shaft. It was also splattered with Everet's cum. Everet had come, and Kane hadn't even noticed!

Lifting his gaze, Kane looked Everet straight in the eye.

Everet appeared completely emotionless. He should have looked impressed. Men were supposed to be impressed after they screwed Kane—that was a fact that he was very certain of.

No, that didn't quite fit. Everet should actually look embarrassed about coming too early. They hadn't even got to the screwing and being impressed stage, and Everet was as finished as any man could ever be. As Kane continued to stare into Everet's eyes, Everet retrieved his fingers from within Kane's body.

Kane straightened his legs. Everet lay down alongside him on the bed, apparently perfectly at ease with the whole world.

Kane frowned more deeply. "Bit quick off the mark, weren't you?"

"No," Everet said, very simply.

"So you never intended to screw me?" Kane didn't even try to make it sound like he believed him for a second.

"Oh, I imagined it," Everet admitted. "I even let myself pretend that I'd do that tonight. But no, I couldn't let that happen."

Kane rolled away from Everet and sat on the edge of the mattress, his feet on the floor by the side of the bed.

"Messing around was one thing. Actually screwing you would have risked screwing us up in too many ways," Everet said.

Kane clenched his fists around the edge of the mattress as he tried to pull his thoughts into order. He looked down at his body. Cum stains streaked his torso. His hand was covered in the stuff. Kane absentmindedly wiped his palm on the sheet as he worked out his next move.

It didn't take Kane long to come up with a plan. He pulled himself to his feet. As he stepped forward he fully expected Everet to leap off the bed and catch hold of him, but Everet didn't move a muscle. A stupid part of Kane was actually disappointed.

Everet didn't make any move to leave the bed and pursue him. He didn't even speak until Kane's hand was on the door handle.

"You can go into the bathroom and clean up, that's fine. But you're not to leave the apartment without my permission."

Kane looked over his shoulder. *And who's going to stop me?*

It was only his complete certainty that Everet's inevitable answer would be *"me"* that stopped Kane from asking the question. The annoying thing was, Everet would probably follow through, too.

Kane slammed the bedroom door behind him. He slammed the bathroom door too. In the small, spartan space, he stared in the mirror above the sink.

He tried to remember the last time a guy hadn't screwed him at the first opportunity. It was useless. He couldn't recall it ever happening before. It was simply unheard of.

Kane frowned at his reflection. All his injuries had healed. Granted, he still looked a fraction tired around his eyes, but if he wasn't an out and out ten, Kane reckoned that he could at least manage a nine and a half on most men's scales.

But, for some reason, Everet hadn't wanted to...

No. Everet had wanted to—Everet had wanted him. Kane was sure of that. Everet had wanted him, but he'd held himself back.

Kane stared at his reflection as his frown deepened. He blinked rapidly and forced the expression from his face. Running his fingers over the lines where the frown had been, he checked carefully for wrinkles. No, he was still safe from that. There were no crow's feet at the edges of his eyes.

Kane turned away from his reflection, suddenly uncertain that what he saw there could get him what he wanted. He shook his head in an effort to clear such a preposterous idea from his mind, but he wasn't entirely successful.

Once he'd cleaned himself up, Kane wandered out into the living room. Everet sat on the sofa. He'd pulled his jeans on, but he hadn't bothered with anything else. His feet were bare, so was his chest. If he'd wanted to look as hot as possible, he'd succeeded. Kane stopped halfway across the room when their eyes met.

"Tomorrow, before you start work, we'll need to put some ground rules in place."

Kane folded his arms across his chest in a pretty good impression of Everet's habitual pose and said nothing.

Everet leaned forward in his seat and rested his elbows on his knees. "By then, you'll need to decide if you want what we do together to be strictly about getting your behaviour up to a standard the nest considers acceptable, or if you also want there to be a completely separate arrangement between us that could run alongside that. The second option would include sex. The first wouldn't."

Unable to think of a witty, or even a sarcastic response, Kane raised an eyebrow.

"It's your decision, and whatever it is, I'll respect it." Everet nodded toward the bedroom door. "Go get some sleep."

"What about you?" Kane said, before he could think better of it.

"The room is yours for the night," Everet said. "A bit of distance will probably do us both good." With that, he moved a cushion to one end of the sofa and lay down.

He was far too tall for the undersized piece of furniture. He had to rest his feet on the far arm of the sofa to even pretend to fit.

Kane shrugged and went into the bedroom. There was no reason why he should care if Everet got a good night's sleep or not. So, why did part of him hesitate as he closed the door, wondering if he should offer to take the sofa?

Chapter Seven

Everet tilted his head to one side, then the other, as he rubbed the back of his neck. He was really going to have to get a full night's worth of sleep at some point. Preferably one that involved lying stretched out in a nice comfortable bed. Otherwise, he was going to end up with a permanent crick in his neck.

"Sleeping on the sofa wasn't as much fun as you'd thought it would be?"

Everet spun around.

Apparently, he'd been wrong to assume he'd have to drag Kane out of bed to face his second day at work. Kane stood in the bedroom doorway; he was completely naked.

"I slept fine, thank you," Everet lied.

Kane's lips twisted into a disbelieving smile.

Everet squared his stance and folded his arms across his chest in an effort not to fidget nervously under Kane's gaze. "Have you made your decision?"

"Yes." Kane said, nothing more.

Everet clenched his teeth, determined to outstare the magpie. Kane made him wait for what felt like hours before he finally spoke again.

"Yes, I think a little arrangement on the side would be a very pleasant way to pass the time."

Everet didn't give himself time to look relieved. He strode across to the bedroom door. Kane had left it ajar in his wake. Now, Everet pushed it open the rest of the way, and drew a line across the threshold with the toe of his boot.

Kane raised an eyebrow. "Are we playing charades? I hope it's a movie. I've never been one for reading—unless you include the kind of magazines that have pictures of hot men and sticky pages, of course."

"This is the boundary line," Everet said.

All the time he'd spent silently rehearsing the words inside his head during the night paid dividends. Each syllable came out smooth and confident. There was no way Kane could guess just how fast Everet's heart raced, or how unsure he was about whether this was the right thing to do.

"Oh?" Kane prompted.

"On this side of the line, in the bedroom, we're lovers and equals. Perhaps one more dominant than the other and more inclined to give orders, but still—lovers and equals. You can say no at any time." Everet stepped back into the living room. "On this side of the line, my only concern is making you a productive and trustworthy member of the nest. I don't care how hot you are. I don't care if you think I'm being too tough on you. I expect complete obedience. You have no right to disobey any order you're capable of following."

Kane frowned, apparently not the least impressed, but Everet didn't miss a beat.

"Nothing we do in the bedroom will affect anything that happens out here. It won't change what work you're expected to do, or anything else. That sort of manipulation isn't going to be an option."

"You've got it all sorted out very neatly, haven't you?" Kane asked, perching nonchalantly on the arm of the sofa and displaying his naked body at a singularly attractive angle.

"I wouldn't be a good master if I didn't think things through in advance," Everet said.

Kane nodded slowly. It was impossible to tell what he thought of the arrangement, but if his previous behaviour was anything to go by, it seemed reasonable to assume he'd try to sabotage his plans in every conceivable way.

Everet took a deep breath. "Do you have any questions?"

"What happens if you want to screw me somewhere other than in the bedroom? What if you want to bend me over the back of the sofa? Or if you feel like pushing me up against the tiles in the shower? Or, what if—?"

"None of those things are an option for the foreseeable future," Everet cut in before Kane had a chance to paint any more erotic little sketches for him.

Kane grinned, and Everet knew that Kane had already spotted the way his jeans tented over his erection. Everet held back a sigh. He wondered if Kane knew he hadn't even needed to try to turn him on, being in the same room as Kane was enough to have him painfully hard.

"It's time for you to get dressed, and go to work," Everet announced, as impassively as possible.

Kane laughed as he walked past him and disappeared into the bedroom. Everet didn't really blame him.

* * * * *

"You'll have to let him out of your sight sooner or later."

Everet didn't look heavenward. He didn't sigh. But only because he was aware that Raynard deserved his complete respect—as an individual, as well as a higher ranking avian. That didn't change just because Raynard's tone of voice made it clear he intended to deliver a sermon in Everet's direction.

Everet didn't turn to face Raynard, but he managed to convince his vocal cords to produce words that sounded polite and calmly unconcerned about the upcoming lecture. "Good afternoon, sir."

Everet sensed Raynard step forward to stand alongside him, but he didn't look away from Kane. The magpie's dusting still wasn't enthusiastic, but at least he seemed to have realised that he wasn't going to be able to get out of doing a good job. Everet no longer needed to nag and prompt him through each individual task.

"You've watched him all day, every day, haven't you?" Raynard observed.

"He belongs to me, sir."

"That doesn't change the fact you must be as bored as hell."

Everet spared Raynard a brief glance. "No one said it would be an interesting job all the time, sir."

Raynard smiled slightly, but soon reverted to his usual, serious expression. "When was the last time you stretched your wings?"

Everet watched Kane crouch down and dust the side moulding on an elaborate mahogany cabinet.

"I'm still waiting for an answer," Raynard mentioned, calmly. "I have nothing to do until Ori finishes in his meeting. I won't walk away from this conversation just because you've decide to adopt some of your submissive's brattier tendencies."

Everet pushed down his annoyance. He probably deserved that. "I haven't stretched my wings since I brought him to the nest," he admitted.

"That's a mistake. You should shift."

"There hasn't been a suitable opportunity, sir. When he's more settled, I'll —"

"Now."

Everet turned and looked up at Raynard's profile. "He's not ready to be left on his own, sir." There was no avoiding that admission.

Raynard turned, and they stood face to face, directly squaring off against each other. "I agree."

Everet hesitated, completely prepared to do battle, but not at all sure how to deal with a peace offering.

"But that doesn't change the fact you are going to go and stretch your wings. Now."

Everet opened his mouth.

Raynard raised a hand, commanding his silence. "I'll watch him until you get back."

There were a great many things Everet could have said, but none of them felt suitable.

No! was the first response that tried to rush to his lips, but Raynard was a hawk. A raven didn't say no to a hawk on a whim.

You? Jumped up as a second option. He bit that back too.

"Sir, with all due respect, Kane is..." Everet finally began. "Kane is quite different to the kind of submissive you're used to, sir."

"You mean he's the complete opposite of Ori."

Everet thought it best to remain silent at that point.

Amusement danced in Raynard's eyes. "I told you before that a man's first submissive isn't always his last. I do have a little more experience than you give me credit for."

"I mean no disrespect, sir."

Raynard waved the apology away with a careless gesture. "None of this changes the fact that you've been given an order—one I expect you to obey. Go and stretch your wings. You have one hour, starting now."

Everet glanced toward Kane.

"You may go and tell him who he will be answerable to in your absence," Raynard allowed.

Everet held back a sigh and walked down the corridor to where Kane was half-heartedly going about his duties. He must have sensed Everet's approach because he suddenly became far more industrious.

"Mr. Raynard will be watching over you for the next hour."

Kane straightened up. "What? Why?"

"Because, I need to step away for a little while, and you're not ready to be left unsupervised just yet."

Kane's eyes narrowed. "Where are you going?" he

demanded.

"Everet, now!" Raynard ordered.

"We'll speak about it later," Everet said to Kane, as quickly as he could. He turned on his heel and strode along the corridor.

Every step was like fingernails on a chalkboard.

Leaving Kane was unnatural. It was only pure bloody mindedness that kept him going. That, and the knowledge that he'd hardly be setting a good example for Kane if he failed to obey what was, on the surface at least, a very reasonable command from a man fully entitled to give him orders.

Parts of him were obviously very much in favour of following Raynard's instructions, because he didn't need to think about where he was going. Instinct quickly carried him up to one of the highest floors of the nest.

At the top of the flight of stairs leading to the mid-level avians' changing rooms, he pushed open a door. A couple of other men were standing by lockers lining the left-hand wall, but Everet's attention was inexorably drawn to the windows on the right-hand side of the space.

Each square aperture offered a glimpse of sky that called out to him, tempting him closer. The door behind him swung open again, only just missing his shoulder. With one last glace toward the pale blue sky, Everet made his way to a spare locker and pulled his T-shirt over his head.

Within seconds, he'd stripped down to his bare skin. Hanging his clothes in the locker, he put his boots on the shelf below them, and tucked his watch inside one of them.

Everet took a deep breath.

One hour. Kane would be fine without him for one hour. Maybe just as importantly, Everet needed to remember he'd be fine without Kane for one hour, too. Closing the locker, Everet turned to the window directly opposite him.

Fresh air caressed his skin as he opened it. A shiver ran down his back, but that had less to do with temperature and more to do with his body's increasing desire to shift. He closed his eyes and placed his hand on the small wooden perch positioned just inside the window.

Part of his mind still wanted to hold on to its human shape, but as Everet sensed another man change into his avian form just a few windows down from him, the need to shift overwhelmed everything else.

He was helpless to resist the pull toward the avian half of his psyche. With a flap of wings and a toss of the head, he found himself already half transformed into his raven form. It had been far too long since his last shift. The transformation coursed through him in a rush of physical and mental changes.

It was more luck than judgment that allowed him to lift his legs and wrap his claws around the perch in time. He unfurled his wings to their full span in an effort to maintain his balance. The squawk he'd let out hadn't been very dignified. Everet ruffled his feathers as he looked both ways along the long, narrow room, almost daring anyone to have noticed his silliness.

The space looked different through a raven's eyes. The colours were more muted, the distances shortened. Everet turned his attention to the window. The sky was oh, so much more inviting seen through these eyes.

This time, when the wind blew against his face, it teased and tempted him, calling to him like a lover. Everet was sure that no one who was entirely human could understand that feeling. Even an avian who'd yet to complete his first shift couldn't fully comprehend what it would be like to see the whole world there, and know that it was his for the taking.

Kane would be safe with Raynard for a little while. Everet partially extended his wings for balance and hopped onto the windowsill. One more leap, and he was out there, hanging high in the empty air, with nothing between himself and the ground but his muscles and his wits.

Flapping his wings, he climbed high above both the nest and the city at large. This was the way humans and their society should be viewed—from up here on the wing, where they were unable to hurt anyone. Kane should never have been let loose in their company.

Everet worked his way higher, anger pushing him faster. No. This wasn't the time for that kind of fury. Kane was safe now. The only men Everet needed to worry about were other avians, and he understood them. Turning in the air, he spotted a few other members of the nest out getting some fresh air into their lungs—or at least air as fresh as they could find, considering the sprawling city below them.

Two finches were flying together. From the other side of the nest, a falcon left the highest changing room, which was reserved for the birds of prey, and took to the air. Everet's attention darted from one patch of sky to the other, carefully checking on the progress of each species, ready to make sure everyone remembered that, under no circumstances should any member of the nest be considered an appetiser, no matter how their entirely bird-brained brethren of the same species may act toward each other.

The finches flittered away in the opposite direction of the falcon. For a little while, Everet found himself completely alone and able to simply enjoy how the sun felt on his back and the way the wind played beneath his outstretched wings.

Feeling that sensation of freedom, after so long spent in an unnatural position in that wooden chair alongside a sickbed, sent Everet's heart beating faster than even its avian form was used to. He flew higher, forcing his body to work harder and harder as he let out an angry caw at the entire world.

Freedom.

If he had any sense, it probably should have been what he craved more than anything else. So why was it that getting back to the nest was the only thing he could think about?

* * * * *

Kane watched the other men from the cleaning flock wander off in various directions. Their shift was over. They were free to go and do whatever it was that passed for fun among really boring people.

Unfortunately, Kane was well aware that he couldn't walk away and do as he pleased. The hawk was no less bloody minded than Everet was when it came to keeping a watch on someone. He'd done nothing but stare at Kane for over half an hour. No conversation. No small talk. Not even a smile.

Raynard was obviously enjoying playing hard to get. Kane mentally rolled his eyes, but he'd always known that his little holiday with Everet wouldn't be able to last forever. Sooner or later, he'd known he would have to get back to reality—and a job that paid more than dusting.

"So," Kane said, turning to face Raynard. "What are you going to do with me now?"

Rather than accept the obvious invitation to step forward and close the gap between them, Raynard frowned as if Kane had insulted him rather than propositioned him.

"You belong to Everet, that hasn't changed just because he's gone to stretch his wings." Each word was colder and more clipped than the last.

Kane shrugged. If Everet had wanted to keep him to himself, he should have thought about that before wandering off. Leaving him, however temporarily, was a move that Everet was going to regret—Kane was going to see to that.

"And I already have a submissive. You'd do well to learn to respect both facts."

If Raynard wouldn't come closer, he'd just have to go to him. Kane pinned his most seductive smile to his lips and moved slowly, letting Raynard get a good look at him as he approached. "I won't tell them, if you don't."

He was less than a step away when Raynard reached

114

out and grabbed hold of his arm. Success!

Without warning, Raynard set off at a fast march. Kane had no choice but to scurry along at his side in an effort to keep up. He doubted Raynard would let go of his arm if he fell. The bastard would probably just drag him along the corridor Kane and the other cleaners had spent the best part of the day polishing.

"Where are we going?" Kane demanded, as soon as he caught his breath.

"Down to one of the public areas. We'll wait for your master there."

Kane laughed. "Don't you trust yourself to be alone with me?"

Raynard made a disbelieving sound in the back of his throat. "I think you'll find a man who has a swan for a lover will have no use for a magpie."

Flames of pure humiliation coursed through Kane. Unwilling to blush, there was only one way he could let out the heat burning through his veins. Anger.

"Let me go!" Stepping back, Kane fought against Raynard's hold on him with all his strength. He didn't care if they were now halfway down a flight of stairs—that just meant Raynard would be more likely to give in more easily, rather than risk a fall.

If Raynard had had any sense, he'd have let go immediately. But Raynard was obviously an idiot as well as a bastard. His hold on Kane wasn't tight enough to be painful, there was no chance of it leaving a mark, but it was still infuriatingly unshakable.

"Stop squirming, before you have us both tumbling down the stairs," Raynard snapped.

"You're not my master. I don't have to obey you!" Kane pushed against Raynard with his other hand. "Where's Everet? I want Everet. Now!"

Raynard ignored the question. He set off down the remainder of the stairs, and nothing Kane could do seemed to make the damnedest bit of difference to their progress.

Raynard was so much bigger and stronger than him, Kane couldn't even tug him off balance. They reached the bottom of the long flight of stairs without Kane gaining a single inch of ground against him.

Raynard stopped and pulled Kane around to face him. "That's enough. Your master left you in my care. That should be all you need to know in order to conduct yourself appropriately."

Kane pushed against Raynard's chest, not sure if he wanted to get away from him or just hit him because he was so pissed off at the world.

Raynard pulled Kane closer, automatically tightening his hold on him as they entered into another battle of wills.

Kane sensed the anger building in Raynard. That was good. Anger wasn't all that different from passion. Raynard already held him so close they were almost in an embrace. Their lips could easily be brought together if Raynard dipped his head. That would teach Everet not to leave him alone, and—

"Raynard?"

Raynard pulled back, jerking his face away from Kane as if he'd been slapped. He glared at someone standing just out of Kane's line of sight. Suddenly, Raynard shoved Kane away from him. Caught off guard, Kane flailed at the empty air, only just keeping his balance.

He glared at Raynard, but Raynard's attention was elsewhere. Kane followed the hawk's line of sight. A group of old men, probably some of those elders that Everet was always on about, congregated a few yards farther down the corridor. The swan was there too—standing close to them, but still appearing slightly removed from the group.

"Raynard?" the same voice repeated. It was the grumpy git from Kane's first day there—the eagle, Hamilton.

Hamilton turned his attention to Kane. "Where is your master?"

Kane waved a hand toward Raynard. "Ask him. No one told me a damn thing. Everet just said I had to do whatever this guy wanted. As if it's *my* fault he's not getting what he wants from his own submissive."

Kane didn't need to look in Raynard's direction to sense the pure fury emanating from him. Good.

"Ori," Raynard said, with clearly forced calm.

The white haired boy hurried past Kane to stand in front of Raynard, as eager to obey him as a puppy who'd just learnt a new trick.

"You have too much sense to believe anyone who says something like that," Raynard said. It was a statement, not a question.

"Yes, sir," Ori said. "You told me earlier that you would be watching over Kane while Everet stretched his wings." His tone was as mild as ever.

Kane mentally cursed. How hard could it be to drive a wedge between two guys? Come to that, what kind of bird of prey refused string-free sex from an expert?

"If Everet can't handle—" Hamilton began.

"Everet's managing fine. He didn't ask for my help. I ordered him to take a break from watching the brat," Raynard cut in.

Kane looked up at Raynard. Everet hadn't wanted to rush off? Everet had wanted to stay with him?

Hamilton and Raynard were still glaring at each other, and no one seemed brave enough to disturb them. The sudden sound of footsteps pelting down the hallway to their left seemed very loud in the silence.

Everet appeared around the corner. He seemed to blur for a moment, as he went from a full out sprint to being determined to look as if he'd never achieved anything above a moderate pace on his way across the nest.

He strode down the short length of corridor that still separated him from the group. Every man's eyes were on him. For some stupid reason, Kane found himself not just looking at, but truly feasting his eyes on him.

Everet wasn't the best looking guy on the planet. On a purely points-based scale, Kane knew that Raynard would have easily outscored him. Yet, somehow, it was impossible for Kane to look away from Everet.

There was a new ease and confidence in Everet's movements now. He was even hotter than he'd been before he went to stretch his wings. Raynard didn't play in the same league as him when it came to a pure, raw *I want him to screw me* score. Even reminding himself how much richer Raynard was didn't help Kane there.

"Sire, sirs, is there a problem?" Everet asked. He glanced at Kane for a moment, but soon transferred his attention back to the other men in the hallway.

"No problem at all," Raynard said. He pushed Kane's shoulder, shoving him toward Everet. "He's all yours."

"Thank you, sir," Everet said to Raynard, as if he'd just been handed a bloody parcel.

Kane stepped backward. The moment he moved, Everet's attention snapped toward him. Success rushed through Kane. Yes, that was the way things should be. Everet should be focused on him and no one else. "Raynard and I had a wonderful time," he said.

"*Mr.* Raynard," Everet corrected, not even blinking at the suggestion Kane had been screwing around behind his back. It was as if he found it impossible to believe that Raynard would want to screw him. Another wave of embarrassment coursed through Kane as he tried to work out when the entire world had decided it didn't even consider him to be worth a quickie in a conveniently discreet alcove?

Everet turned back to the others. "I'm sorry if he was any trouble, sir." He paused for a beat. "If there's nothing else?"

"No," Raynard said, with an idle wave of the hand. "You may both go."

"Thank you, sir." Everet reached out and caught hold

118

of Kane's arm. When Everet set off down the corridor, he went even faster than Raynard had a few minutes earlier. The main difference was that Kane didn't mind Everet's grip on him. In a strange way, it actually felt good.

Everet didn't slow down until they were back in his apartment. He closed the door behind them before he released his grip on Kane's wrist.

Not entirely sure he was ready to forgive Everet for leaving him with Raynard, Kane pulled sharply away from him.

"Tell me exactly what happened," Everet ordered.

"Why?"

Everet fell perfectly still, staring at some apparently random point on the wall. Silence descended. Several seconds passed before Everet looked toward Kane and met his gaze. "Because I am your master, and I can't look after you properly if I don't know what's going on."

"Maybe you should have thought about that before you buggered off and left me with that trumped up bastard!"

Everet's expression changed. The skin between his brows furrowed as if he were thinking deeply about something. "I'm sorry if I scared you by leaving so suddenly. I wasn't thinking as clearly as I should have been. Now that I've stretched my wings, things will be better."

Kane gawped at Everet as if he'd just beamed down from a spaceship filled with little green men. Everet's reaction was so at odds with anything he expected, it took Kane a full minute to take in what he'd just said, what kind of accusation he'd actually levelled at him. "I wasn't scared!"

Everet sat down on the sofa and indicated the chair opposite him.

Kane planted his feet.

"Sit down, Kane," Everet said, very calmly. "That's an order which you are quite capable of obeying. I am your master; I expect you to do as you're told."

"And if I don't?" Kane demanded.

"Then I will pick you up and put you in the chair. If I need to tie you to it in order to make you stay there while we have this conversation, I will. It's time certain things were made far clearer. Obedience is not optional. You're going to end up in the chair one way or another."

He was serious. Kane saw that in his eyes. As tempting as it was to disobey, just to force Everet to make good on his threat, Kane knew when it was better to play a slightly longer game. He didn't rush — there was no need to let Everet think he was going to be jumping at anyone's command — but Kane walked across to the seat and sat down.

"That's good," Everet told him. "And, as I said, I'm thinking a lot more clearly now. I can see that I made mistakes before —"

"Like making out with me?" Kane demanded, very ready to hear the insult and retaliate by any means necessary.

Everet seemed to think about that very carefully. "Like making out with you before things were more clearly settled between us outside the bedroom," he specified. "I don't regret what we did, just that we didn't talk more first. We're not doing things in the right order."

Kane frowned. Leaning back in his seat, he pulled his feet up to rest on the cushion in front of him and glared at Everet over the top of his knees. If Everet thought that they could go back to a time before they'd fooled around, he was going to have another thought coming very quickly.

"You need to try to understand that, as your master, I have your best interests at heart. The orders I give you outside the bedroom are all ultimately for your own benefit."

Kane huffed his disbelief.

"I know you don't see that yet, but in time, you will," Everet promised.

Kane didn't bother to argue. He knew that tone of voice from back before he left his original nest. Everet had flown high in the sky and seen the whole world stretched out beneath him. All the people had looked like little toys he could push around on a whim. It would take a little while for reality to reassert itself and for him to remember that Kane wasn't the type to take that kind of treatment quietly; that Kane was someone who would always shove back.

"Now, I want you to answer my original question. When you were with Raynard, what happened?"

Kane shrugged, but deep down he knew that it wouldn't get him anywhere with Everet. He sighed. The path of least resistance was obvious. "He's a grumpy sod. I flirted. He frowned. That's about it, really."

Everet nodded to show he had heard. "Will Raynard say the same when I speak to him?"

"You're going to check up on me behind my back?" Kane demanded.

"No." Everet smiled slightly. "I'm not going to do anything behind your back. I'm telling you to your face that I'm going to ask Raynard the same question."

Kane rolled his eyes. "Yeah," he muttered. "He'll say the same."

"Good." Everet straightened in his seat. His tone changed, as if he was done with that subject and was more than ready to set it aside. "Do you have any questions for me?"

"Yeah." A god-like feeling of authority wasn't often the only side effect an avian experienced after stretching his wings.

"Go ahead, you can ask me anything." Everet encouraged him, with a nod and a slight smile.

Kane raised one eyebrow and smiled back. "Wanna screw?"

Chapter Eight

Everet didn't laugh, but it was a close call.

He probably should have expected that to be the question in the forefront of Kane's mind. It was obviously his default state; if in doubt, turn to sex.

"Every avian wants to get laid after being on the wing," Kane said. "You can't be that different."

"I want to," Everet agreed.

Kane's gaze turned suspicious. "Does that mean you're going to, or are you going to get all talkative again?"

Everet allowed a smile to touch his lips, but his calm façade was maintained through sheer force of will. Behind his unruffled exterior, his mind raced faster and faster. He knew what he wanted. But what was the right thing? What would a good master do? What would —

No, it was no good wondering what Raynard would do. Ori and Kane were so unlike each other it would be useless. Raynard wouldn't have made a good master for Kane.

Hamilton? He didn't give a damn about anyone other than the ranking birds of prey. It was impossible to consider him to be a good potential master for anyone.

There was no suitable example for Everet to follow; no one whose advice he could take. Flying through unchartered territory, all he had to guide him were his own instincts. But this soon after his shift, while the raven side of him fluttered so close to the surface, it was easy to believe that his avian instincts would guide him toward the right solution.

Everet stood up. He extended his hand toward Kane.

For several seconds, Kane just stared at him as if he were an idiot. He still looked sceptical when he finally reached up and put his hand in Everet's grip.

Leading Kane to the bedroom door, Everet stopped just short of entering it. "Do you remember what we discussed earlier?"

"Yeah, yeah, inside the bedroom we're screwing, outside we're all serious. I've got it, okay?" Kane stepped over the threshold. "I'm not an idiot, or a child—stop treating me like I'm both."

Suddenly, his grip on Everet's hand was as strong as Everet's hold on him had ever been. Kane's expression damn near dared him to try to retreat.

Everet didn't say a word as he joined Kane in the bedroom. Closing the door, he sealed them inside, away from the rest of the world.

Kane stood just a few feet inside the room. He made no attempt to run away this time. He even held his ground when Everet stepped forward. Cupping Kane's cheek with one hand, Everet kissed him, firmly but gently.

With the adrenaline from his recent flight still swooping and twirling through his veins, even that chaste bit of contact was enough to make Everet moan with desire. With his other hand, he pressed against the small of Kane's back, ordering him forward until their bodies were jammed tightly together. Everet gasped as their erections rubbed against each other through the fabric of their trousers.

Kane moaned in return, balancing on his tiptoes in an effort to bring his lips to a more accessible height, and his crotch in line with Everet's. He responded so perfectly to every prompt, his tongue duelling with Everet's and exploring his mouth in return. Sliding one hand around to the front of Kane's body, Everet rubbed his palm against Kane's fly, stroking his cock through the material.

Kane moaned into Everet's mouth and thrust

determinedly against his hand. Kane was very pleased to see him, Everet had no doubt about that. But there was something else, too – something in Kane's pocket.

Everet frowned. Pulling back, he broke the kiss and peered down between them.

"You look like you've never seen a hard on before," Kane grumbled.

Everet made no reply. He slipped his fingers into Kane's pocket and pulled out whatever it was that created that second bulge.

"Hey, that's mine!" Kane made a grab for it.

Everet automatically lifted the thing out of Kane's reach.

A wallet. Everet's heart lurched.

It wasn't Kane's. Kane hadn't arrived with it. Everet hadn't given it to him. That left only two options, neither of which were in the least bit palatable. He wasn't sure which option was worse – that someone had given Kane a wallet in an effort to tempt him away from Everet, or that Kane had acquired it by some other means.

Everet undid the catch and opened the wallet.

Frederick Raynard.

Everet damn near felt the blood drain out of his face as he saw the name printed on the driver's license.

"Give it back," Kane demanded, snatching at the wallet.

"You picked his pocket," Everet said, lifting Raynard's wallet out of Kane's reach. There was no accusation in his tone, no anger, it was a simple statement of fact.

"It's—"

"It's not yours, Kane," Everet said, as Kane made another grab for it. "You stole it."

Catching hold of Kane's shoulders, Everet forced Kane to face him and look him in the eye. Finally looking away from the wallet, Kane stared up at him. Anger and confusion filled his expression, as if he really didn't get what all the fuss was about.

He didn't get it. In that moment, Everet realised that was the real problem—Kane truly didn't understand that what he'd done was wrong—that picking someone's pocket was something that the very vast majority of avians would consider to be wrong. Maybe Kane knew that he'd broken a rule, but he really didn't understand how important that rule was.

"Have you taken anything else from anyone since you arrived here?" Everet demanded. "From a man, or from the nest?"

Kane's expression turned mutinous. He pressed his lips firmly together and remained silent.

A bitter taste filled the back of Everet's mouth. "If you give me everything you've taken right now, then you won't be in trouble with me," he promised. "But I need to have everything you've taken. Now."

"I haven't taken—"

"Kane," Everet snapped. "We both know you're lying. If I have to search every part of the nest you've so much as walked through, I will. I'll find whatever it is."

Kane held out for almost thirty seconds before his gaze flicked toward the bottom of the chest of drawers set against the far wall. Everet was quicker than Kane. He reached the drawers first. Wrenching open the bottom one, he shoved all his clothes aside until he spotted a little hoard of items pushed into the back corner.

He grabbed them before Kane had a chance.

Kane scratched and tugged at Everet's arm, but Everet ignored all of Kane's attempts to snatch the stolen items from him. His lack of reaction only seemed to infuriate Kane even more. Kane swore, he demanded, he threatened everything under the sun—even coming up with several things that it had never occurred to Everet to do to someone in his entire life. He was reasonably sure most of them were physically impossible.

Keeping a firm grip on all the stolen items, Everet turned away from the chest of drawers.

As suddenly as someone might flip a switch, Kane's entire demeanour changed. He smiled. His expression turned coy. When he placed a hand on Everet's arm, his attitude was all flirtation.

And this was the moment that would make it or break it for them. Everet had no doubt about that. It was all so clear inside his head now. If he'd ever prove that he was a good master, that Kane could always have complete trust in his word, he'd do it now.

Brushing past Kane, Everet went to the bedroom door, wrenched it open and strode into the living room. He dropped everything Kane had stolen onto the coffee table. Turning around, he was back in the bedroom before Kane had even stepped outside it.

"What do I need to do to get them back?" Kane asked.

Everet pushed his hand through his hair and made a concerted effort not just to appear calm, but to actually *be* calm. Two deep breaths and he knew he was as near to achieving that goal as he'd ever be.

"Everything you stole will be returned to its rightful owner. Nothing you can do will change that."

"What?"

"Nothing that happens in this room affects how you'll be treated out there, and nothing you do out there affects us in here, remember?" Everet asked, very levelly.

Kane seemed to study him for a long time. Everet remained perfectly still and let Kane look his fill. He wouldn't see any hidden agenda. There wasn't one to see.

"So, you're not going to punish me?" Kane asked, carefully.

"No." Everet tilted up his chin, determined to keep his word on that, no matter what else happened.

Kane stepped forward until they were almost touching. "You're not even going to be angry with me?"

They were close enough together that Everet had to dip his head to keep looking into Kane's eyes. "No, I'm not." There was little point when Kane didn't even seem to know right from wrong yet.

"You're still going to screw me?" Kane asked, placing one hand in the middle of Everet's chest and stroking his way down to his abs.

"There's no reason why we shouldn't do whatever we want in here."

Kane smiled and looked up at Everet through his lashes. "I still want you to screw me."

Everet's body certainly didn't care what was going on in the real world. As he gazed down at Kane, Everet couldn't help but see him not as a thief, but as someone who was desperately in need of a lover who could show him what it was like to be with a man for no reason other than the pleasure they hoped to find in each other's bodies.

Everet didn't hesitate. He brought their lips together in a kiss just as confident as the first they'd shared that evening.

I really can leave all your bad behaviour out there.

Everet slid his arms around Kane once more, praying that Kane understood the silent message.

Kane kissed him back. He slid his hands up Everet's body and into his hair. His movements weren't as self-assured as Everet's, but that could only feel like a good thing right then. Being with a man for any reason other than payment was new for him. It would take him time to find his feet.

"I want to screw you right into the mattress," Everet whispered as he trailed his lips back to Kane's ear. "That sound good to you?"

Kane nodded.

"Tell me," Everet ordered.

"I want your cock buried in my arse," Kane bit out, frustration coating every word. "How many times do you need to be told?"

Everet grinned. Pushing everything else out of his

mind, he concentrated entirely upon the fact that they were two guys who really wanted to come.

A nudge against Kane's shoulders had him toppling backward onto the bed. Everet watched him fall. Kane bounced as he landed. His eyes opened very wide with surprise, but he didn't complain.

Everet didn't need to issue an order for Kane to undress this time. They were both too close to the edge. They both began to tear their clothes off at the same time and they both rushed and tugged at each item of clothing, not caring if they teared seams or popped buttons in their haste.

The moment they were both naked, Everet jumped onto the bed with Kane. His hands slid against gloriously bare skin. There was so much to touch, and neither of them seemed to be able to do anything other than frantically grope and hump each other.

It didn't take long for Everet's body to give up on waiting for his brain to issue sensible orders. Before he knew it, physical instinct had taken over, and he was lying over Kane, pressing him down against the blankets.

Kane wriggled and spread his legs spread further apart. Everet's cock slid against Kane's exposed hole. Kane scrabbled at his back, pulling him forward, clumsily demanding that their bodies come together.

Lube.

Even with the raven side of him so close to the fore, some part of Everet knew that looking after his lover meant remembering that lube was important. He forced himself to pull away and grab a tube from his nightstand drawer. As he slicked his fingers, Kane swore and grumbled at the delay.

Everet pushed two fingers inside Kane, trying to prepare him as quickly as he could.

"I want your cock."

Everet made himself ignore the demand. He kept his complete attention on the way his digits worked inside Kane's hole.

128

Suddenly, Kane put his hands on either side of Everet's face and turned his head — demanding that Everet look him in the eye. "I want your cock, not your fingers."

He sounded serious, but Everet could see in Kane's eyes that he was afraid, too.

As soon as he saw Kane's fear, Everet automatically began to pull away. But, as he held Kane's gaze, Everet hesitated and stopped short with his fingertips resting against Kane's slicked hole. The longer their eyes remained locked, the more certain he was that Kane's only fear involved him stopping at fingers again and never actually screwing him.

"Cock," Kane repeated, wiping away the last of Everet's doubts.

Everet reached up, and, with the fingers of one of his hands still smeared with lube, caught hold of Kane's wrists. He tugged Kane's hands away from his face, but he didn't stop there. He kept moving until he had Kane's arms pinned firmly against the mattress.

Looming over him, Everet let his cock rub against Kane's well-lubed hole. It was a tease, nothing more. Kane moaned with frustration and squirmed beneath him, but there was little he could do in his current position. Everet was the only one with either freedom or leverage. He dipped his head. Kane helped bridge the gap too. He leaned up into the kiss.

"Cock," Everet whispered against his lips.

He pushed forward, sheathing himself slowly inside Kane's body. Kane let out a breathless little groan filled with pleasure and relief. The sound vibrated against Everet's lips and tingled through his body.

Kane's muscles tensed and relaxed around the top portion of Everrt's cock, as if Kane was determined to squeeze every possible bit of bliss from their joining. A lifetime seemed to pass before Everet finally had his erection buried to the hilt in Kane's hole. He fell still, savouring both the physical sensations and the wave of success that rolled through his mind.

Kane barely waited for a millisecond before he squirmed impatiently beneath him, trying to get him to move.

Everet stared down at him. Kane had his eyes closed very tightly. Everet tensed his muscles, unwilling to move until that changed.

Eventually, Kane blinked open his eyes. He glared up at Everet.

"That's right," Everet said, before Kane could say anything. "I want you to look at me."

On the last word, he began to move his hips. He ground down against Kane, not real thrusting, just making sure Kane could feel every inch of him.

Kane whimpered his approval and adjusted his position so his legs wrapped around Everet's body, pulling him closer still. Above Everet's grip on his wrists, Kane's hands clenched into fists.

"I've got you."

Kane frowned. He shook his head. "I don't need —"

"Whether you need it or not," Everet cut in, his voice just slightly breathless. "That's the way things are. You're mine. I've got you." He tightened his hold on Kane's wrists as proof. He wouldn't let anyone hurt Kane now.

Kane looked away and squirmed again.

This time, Everet didn't make Kane wait. Bracing his feet against the bed, he pulled away, then thrust deep into Kane's arse.

Their groans of pleasure hit the air at exactly the same time. Kane was so tight around Everet, and it was so soon after Everet's flight, and he'd wanted Kane for so long. Everet scrabbled for control of his own body as he pushed into Kane over and over again.

The need to make Kane happy pounded through Everet's mind, just as determinedly as his need to come. Every inch of his skin tingled with increased sensitivity, but the frantic signals sent up from his cock overpowered everything else.

The generous coating of slick lube, the heat of Kane's body around his shaft, the strength of Kane's muscles as he worked them around Everet's cock, it was almost too much. If he hadn't been so determined to make Kane come first, Everet would have been able to reach his orgasm a dozen times or more. But, no, that wasn't an option.

Kane had to come first—in all meanings of the term. If Everet had ever doubted that before, he couldn't avoid the knowledge anymore. Every single part of his mind and body knew it was true. Kane was his, and Kane had to come first.

*

Please, please, please.

Kane didn't say a word out loud. He just kept repeating the plea over and over inside his head. He needed to come so badly, he could barely think.

When he'd lived with the humans, he'd only ever wanted to beg because he knew the guy screwing him would probably give him a better tip if he put on a good show. This time, the words stayed inside Kane's head. He didn't plead for anyone's benefit but his own.

Writhing on the mattress, Kane did his damnedest to meet Everet's thrusts and tighten his internal muscles around Everet's cock, but that wasn't for Everet's pleasure either. Kane was incapable of thinking of anyone other than himself.

Forget manipulation. Forget payment. Kane wanted to come. That realisation scared him more than any kind of kinkiness could have. Pain was one thing, but power was different.

If Kane couldn't focus on Everet and making sure Everet really enjoyed screwing him now, then he'd be far less likely to be able to use their sex life to make Everet do whatever he wanted later. If he didn't pull himself together soon, he'd have no way of ensuring Everet would treat him right after they zipped up.

Kane gasped. Whatever thoughts he'd managed to hold on to until that point slipped away into darkness and oblivion. Everet thrust into him again, pushing against Kane's prostate, sending sparks of bright, shiny bliss shooting through him.

Everet still had Kane's hands pinned to the mattress; Kane couldn't reach for his own cock to jack himself off. But, the tip of his erection rubbed against Everet's stomach every time he thrust forward, and suddenly that was enough.

Jerking within Everet's hold on him, Kane came. His cum spilled across his stomach and smeared between their bodies on Everet's next thrust.

Everet's grip on Kane's wrists tightened.

The only thing Kane could do then was fly high on whatever air currents his pleasure offered to him, and hope it wouldn't eventually drop him some place he didn't want to be.

Everet let out a yell. The sound was muted and seemed to come from very far away, but Kane still knew what it meant. Everet had come, too.

All was right with the world. Kane had been good enough. The man who'd just screwed him would be pleased with him.

Very slowly, the ecstasy drained away, leaving them both panting for breath on the mattress. As the minutes passed, Kane sensed Everet begin to recover.

Everet pulled away, separating their bodies, but he didn't release his hold on Kane's wrists. Even when he rearranged them in the bed so they lay facing each other, Everet maintained his grip. He brought Kane's wrists together and let him rest them comfortably on the small amount of empty mattress between them, but he still didn't let go.

Kane tried to breathe more evenly, but his heart rate showed no sign of slowing. Panic bubbled inside him. He closed his eyes very tightly as he fought against it.

"I've got you," Everet said again.

I don't need to know that. I can look after myself. Kane

pressed his lips firmly together. If he said those words right then, he had the terrible suspicion that they would sound like a lie.

Everet tightened his grip on Kane's wrists.

Kane didn't want that to make him feel better, but it did. So did the gentle kiss Everet placed against his lips.

"Open your eyes."

Against all his instincts, Kane obeyed. He glared at Everet, determined not to let any honest emotion show.

Everet smiled and relaxed comfortably with his head on one of the pillows. That was it. He just lay there, pleased as heavily spiked punch and twice as intoxicating.

At least he seemed to have forgotten all about the stuff he'd found in the back of the drawer. That was good. Kane closed his eyes and pretended to rest just as easily as Everet until Everet finally released his wrists and sat up.

Wriggling toward the opposite side of the bed, Kane immediately headed for the door.

"No."

Kane found himself stopping short as the order hit the air. There was no reason for him to do that. Everet couldn't physically stop him from the other side of the room, yet for some reason the door remained a yard away, and Kane didn't take another step.

Everet got up and walked past Kane. He opened the door and stepped out into the living room. Before Kane realised what he intended to do, Everet had picked up all the pretty little things Kane had acquired, placed them in a drawer, and locked it.

"Get dressed, come out here, and we'll deal with this."

"Deal with it how?" Kane said, suspiciously.

"Get dressed," Everet repeated. He stepped into the bedroom, but only for long enough to grab a clean set of clothes from his wardrobe. He was soon back in the living room.

Kane looked from Everet to the rumpled bed. It was as

if nothing that had happened there existed in Everet's mind. That was…that was just wrong.

"I told you before that nothing we do in the bedroom will affect the standard of behaviour I expect you to achieve in the nest at large," Everet said, pulling a black long-sleeve T-shirt over his head.

He'd actually meant that? Kane cursed Everet in a dozen different ways, but he didn't open his mouth to share his opinions.

"Get dressed, Kane," Everet said once more.

Pulling his clothes on gave Kane time to think. Unfortunately, it didn't give him any clue how to handle a raven on a mission. All too soon, he sat on the sofa facing Everet, still without any firm idea of how he could get out of this without having to accept some sort of punishment.

"Do you remember the rules I've given you?" Everet asked.

Kane studied him warily. "Don't leave the apartment without your permission. Don't try to use sex to manipulate you."

"That's good," Everet said.

It was like watching a volcano and waiting for it to explode. Every muscle in Kane's body tensed as he waited for Everet's anger to be unleashed. Unfortunately, it was only then that he realised that being perched on the edge of a rocky outcrop looking down into the bubbling magma probably wasn't the safest place from which to observe proceedings. If Everet flipped out, there was no way Kane would be able to get past him and out of the apartment.

"I'm adding a new rule," Everet went on, still outwardly calm.

"Okay," Kane said, since some sort of contribution seemed expected of him at that point.

"You're not to take anything that doesn't belong to you. There are things I've given you since you came to the nest — those things are yours. No one is allowed to take them from you. If you come to me and tell me you need or want something, I'll listen and we can discuss whether or not your request is reasonable. But I want your word that you won't take anything from anyone else at the nest unless you have both my and his permission to take it."

Kane just stared at Everet, wondering which one of them had finally lost touch with reality.

"It's wrong to take something that doesn't belong to you," Everet continued, his expression as serious as ever. "Just like it would be wrong for someone else to take something that belonged to you. Can you understand that?"

"I'm not a child," Kane snapped.

"I didn't say you are," Everet said, still as mild as ever. He hadn't moved anything but his lips the whole time he spoke. His gaze hadn't left Kane's face. It was freaky.

Kane shifted his position on the sofa, pushing his hands through his hair and wiping his fingers across his lips.

"Can you give me your word you'll remember that rule and follow it from now on?" Everet asked.

Saying no obviously wouldn't get Kane anywhere. That only left one answer he could give. "Yes."

"If you break your word, you'll be punished. Understand?"

"Yeah." Kane shifted in his seat again. "Are we done now?"

Everet leaned back in his seat and took a deep breath. "With this part, yes."

Kane frowned, all his suspicions roused once more. He straightened the edge of his T-shirt, as if that would help him face whatever was about to come. "This part?"

"We need to return the things you took."

Kane shook his head and crossed his arms. There was no way in hell he was going to do anything of the sort. "No. They're mine now."

"Things become yours if someone gives them to you of their own free will, or if you buy them—but not if you just take them." Everet walked across to the locked drawer and took out the little bundle of items Kane had acquired since he'd arrived at the nest.

Kane rushed across. Everet moved the stash out of his range before he could grab a single thing, leaving Kane standing at his side empty handed.

"We'll see Raynard first." Everet glanced at his watch. "He should be with Ori and Hamilton in the elders' meeting room now." He set off toward the door.

"I don't want to go."

Everet glanced over his shoulder. Whatever he saw on Kane's face, it made him turn around and look at him properly. "Nothing bad will happen to you, Kane. You won't be punished."

Kane stayed right where he was.

"This isn't optional," Everet said.

"They'll be mad," Kane pointed out as fear peaked inside him, invading all those parts of his mind where pleasure had reigned a few minutes earlier and claiming them for its own. Not far behind that came anger. If Everet wasn't stupid enough to make him go and admit to picking up the things, then no one would be angry with him, and there would be no need for him to be afraid. It was Everet's fault.

"Yes," Everet agreed. "They'll be mad, but I'll be there with you."

"But you can protect me?" Kane demanded, sceptically, as he moved back toward the far side of the room.

"Yes." He said it with complete confidence. He held Kane's gaze without a blink. "Have I ever given you any reason to think I'd lie to you?"

"You're really promising I'm not going to be punished?" Kane asked, doubtfully.

"I promise." Either Everet really believed that, or he was the best liar on the planet—better even than Kane could claim to be himself.

With a heartfelt sigh, Kane gave in. He followed Everet

through the corridors and hallways, but he saw no reason why he should have to act as if he was happy about Everet's stupid decisions.

Long before Kane was ready for it, he found himself outside the door to the elders' meeting room. Everet spoke quietly to the man guarding the space from unwanted intruders — which Kane was pretty sure meant anyone below the rank of a bird of prey.

Pretentious bastards.

He scuffed his heels on the carpet as he waited for Everet to finish babbling with the guard. The lover of a bird of prey wouldn't have to wait around like this. Kane glared at the mark his shoes had left in the carpet's pile. He'd have to upgrade to a better master soon — preferably before he became the guy cleaning the carpets rather than leaving marks on them. He's find a rich, indulgent man — one who wouldn't care about a few acquired bits and pieces.

As for Everet...

An uncomfortable feeling knotted Kane's stomach. If he found a new master, he'd have to find a way to keep seeing Everet, too — for sex, if nothing else. Maybe Everet could be his bit on the side...

Kane smiled down at the carpet. If the other guys could have the best of both worlds, why couldn't he? Everet would keep screwing him, but he'd lose the right to order Kane around whenever he was doing anything other than sneaking a quickie behind the sugar-daddy's back. Throw in a bit of quicksilver, and the picture would be truly perfect.

Hell, he might even share the quicksilver with Everet...

"Kane."

He jerked his attention away from the carpet. Everet stood next to the open door, beckoning him forward. There was no way to keep pretending this wasn't happening. In some horrible version of autopilot where he couldn't help but obey Everet, Kane walked into the meeting room at Everet's side.

The same elders who'd been present when Kane first arrived at the nest sat facing them.

Everet stopped in front of the table. Not sure what else to do, Kane stood next to him.

"Is there a problem?" Hamilton demanded, impatiently.

Everet stepped forward and put Raynard's wallet on the table in front of the hawk. "Kane took it from your pocket while you were watching over him. I don't think anything has been taken from it, but I'd appreciate it if you'd check so I can be sure, sir."

The room fell silent as Raynard rifled through his wallet.

It was all there. Kane knew that. He hadn't even had a chance to look through the thing before Everet took it off him. Whether or not Raynard would admit he hadn't taken a penny was a different matter. He was just the type of avian who'd love to drop someone he considered to be a "lower rank" into the shit.

"Everything's there." Kane barely had time to be surprised that Raynard hadn't taken the chance to make life worse for him before Raynard continued. "Was mine the first pocket he's picked since he arrived?"

"It doesn't matter if it's the first or the hundredth," Hamilton snapped. "He is evidently unable to conduct himself in an acceptable manor. Everet is just as clearly unable to control him. Everet, you will find out if there is a cage free in—"

"With all due respect, sir," Everet cut in.

The silence that followed was deep and frigid.

Eagles weren't used to being interrupted, arrogant sods. Kane glared at him, pissed off on Everet's behalf.

"What?" Hamilton's tone rattled like a glass full to the brim with ice.

"You put him under my protection, sir," Everet said. "I'm his master. He belongs to me. Until one of us backs out of our arrangement, I'm the only person who has a right to punish him."

"Have you?" Raynard asked.

"No, sir, I haven't, and I don't intend to. I've spoken to Kane. He understands what is expected of him in future," Everet said, ever so calmly.

Kane turned his head and downright gawped at Everet. He was actually going to try to keep his promise? He really thought he could do that? Kane mentally shook his head. It was blatantly pointless. There was no way in hell a bird of prey would allow a mere raven to speak to them like that.

Bloody hell. Everet should know that, and —

"Completely unacceptable," Hamilton burst out, confirming every suspicion Kane had. "I will not have a magpie running amok in my nest. The precedent of not punishing a thief is — "

"I'll be taking the punishment on his behalf, sir."

Kane's eyes opened even wider as he stared up at Everet.

Everet didn't turn toward him, or even glance in his direction. It was as if he'd forgotten Kane was in the room. Everyone else seemed to have done the same. Everyone's attention was on Everet. Kane might as well have been invisible.

"I believe the punishment you currently hand out to thieves is a period of time spent in the cages," Raynard said.

"Yes, sir. But, with your permission, the more traditional punishment is twenty lashes," Everet said. "I'll take that punishment."

The elders exchanged looks and muttered to one another in voices too low to be audible on Kane's side of the table. The only ones who didn't offer up any opinions were Ori and Raynard.

"Do you have anything to say, Ori?" Raynard prompted, after all the other elders seemed to have had their say. He made no attempt to speak quietly enough to stop

Kane and Everet hearing him.

Ori frowned.

Kane held his breath.

Ori turned to Everet. "You're sure this is what you want?" he asked.

Everet didn't waver for a second. "Yes, sire. Very sure."

Ori took a deep breath. "I don't think we should interfere with a master's care for his submissive unless it's essential. Unless there's a particular reason why Everet can't take that punishment, we should do as he asks."

Raynard nodded, a curt little motion. "Seconded."

Hamilton huffed, but finally waved a hand as if to indicate that they might as well get on with it, if they really were intent on such an action. "But keep him on a shorter rein in future," he snapped, as a parting shot.

"Understood, sir," Everet said with a polite nod.

"Leave the other things he stole here," Raynard said. "I'll see that they're returned to their rightful owners and places."

Everet set them all on the table.

The sparkle of highly polished silver called to Kane. It was only a teaspoon, but it took all his fear of the punishment being transferred to him to keep him from trying to pocket it again. The pen he'd taken from the owl's desk lay next to it. The little gilded box that had once decorated a hall table was there too.

"Go back to your apartment," Raynard ordered. "I'll arrange for the punishment to take place this evening. I'll send someone to fetch you when necessary."

"Yes, sir."

Everet turned toward the door. Kane followed closely at his side. All in all, the meeting had gone a hundred times better than he could have ever expected. After all, *he* wasn't the one due to get whipped.

So why the hell did Kane feel as if someone had punched him in the stomach?

Chapter Nine

Everet took a deep breath and mentally counted to ten. Perhaps that made it a little easier for him to keep his emotions to himself, but it didn't magic away the bizarreness of the situation.

He wasn't used to feeling so many men's eyes wandering over his body while he removed his shirt. He didn't want to get used to it either. There was a time and a place for public nudity; it was when the men undressed in the locker rooms so they could shift into their avian forms unencumbered by yards of fabric unnecessary to a man who wore feathers. No one stared then.

Still, he told himself, this had to be better than being put in a cage. The very thought of that sent a shudder down his spine. At least this way, he'd be free and able to keep an eye on Kane. That was the important thing.

Everet didn't look up. It seemed like every man in the nest had turned up to watch him take off his shirt. Everet had never seen so many avians in the nest's play area at one time, let alone clustered around the same station.

The whipping post stood in the middle of a carefully delineated area. Folding his shirt neatly, Everet set it on the table to the left-hand side of the area.

Kane stood alongside the table, nibbling at his bottom lip. He was the only man in the room whose attention wasn't on Everet. Kane hadn't met his eyes once since they'd left the elders' meeting room. He hadn't said a word either. Now he looked everywhere except at Everet.

Unable to afford to give Kane any extra time to mentally process everything that was going on, he touched Kane's cheek and made him look up.

Kane glared into Everet's eyes, as if daring him to change his mind about accepting the punishment in his place.

"You can trust my word," Everet said. "No one will raise a hand to punish you while you belong to me. Not me, not anyone else."

Kane said nothing. His expression wavered, but he didn't seem to know what emotions the situation called for. Distrust and anger seemed to be easy for him; anything else still remained just outside his grasp.

"Whenever you're ready, Everet," Raynard said, from behind him.

Everet smiled down at Kane for a moment, pushing all his other concerns aside in favour of reassuring his charge as best he could. "Everything will be fine. It won't take long. Just wait here for me. Understand?"

Kane nodded. His cheek rubbed against Everet's palm.

It was hard to turn toward the whipping post, but not because Everet was afraid of the whip. Turning away from Kane when he was confused and hurting went against every instinct Everet possessed.

Raynard stood at one corner of the area around the whipping post. Hamilton and Ori flanked him. Whispered words passed between them as Everet approached. Stopping a few steps away from them, just out of eavesdropping range, he patiently waited to be invited closer.

Ori noticed him first. He placed his hand lightly on Raynard's arm to get his attention and nodded toward Everet.

"You're ready?" Raynard asked.

"Yes, sir."

Raynard stepped away from the others. Everet remained motionless as Raynard approached him. He felt strangely calm now that the moment had arrived.

"Have you ever been whipped?" Raynard asked.

"No, sir, not seriously." Not since he'd indulged his curiosity as a very young man, before he'd even reached his avian maturity.

Raynard didn't need to tell him that this would be a serious whipping. They both knew they couldn't permit it to be anything else. The law of the nest was the law of the nest, and if Everet had any intention of remaining one of the men who enforced it, he couldn't be seen to either disobey it, or to suffer less when he admitted his guilt.

"Ori and Hamilton both think you should accept some time in the cage in lieu of this form of punishment," Raynard said, idly running the tails of the whip through his fingers as he spoke.

Everet met Raynard's eye. "You don't, sir."

"I'd choose whichever punishment allowed me to best care for the man under my protection. I won't try to convince you to do otherwise—not even if our resident swan thinks I should."

Everet smiled slightly, but his attention quickly returned to the whip.

"If you ask me to stop, I will," Raynard said. "But if you can take the twenty in one block, it will be easier for you and over more quickly."

Everet nodded.

"As soon as you reach the whipping post, find whatever mental place you need to go to as quickly as you can and stay there. Don't worry about Kane. Ori will keep an eye on him during the punishment. He'll let me know if the little brat moves an inch."

Everet had never been more relieved to hear anything in his life. Kane would be fine. Even when his master was distracted, Kane would be looked after. "Thank you, sir."

"Any questions?" Raynard asked.

"No, sir."

"Go ahead and get yourself in position. There'll be no

bondage."

Everet met Raynard's eyes once more. Raynard understood what it was like for an avian who naturally craved dominance to have to put himself in a position of weakness. Perhaps being in love with a swan wasn't the same as taking a whipping, but, yes, Everet had no doubt that Raynard understood how he felt.

He'd never been more grateful that Raynard had stepped forward and volunteered to administer the punishment on behalf of the nest, rather than leave it to one of the security flock.

"Thank you, sir." Everet hoped Raynard knew how sincerely he meant that.

He turned away from Raynard. Keeping his chin up and his shoulders back, he approached the whipping post. He had nothing to be ashamed of, and he'd be damned before he'd act like he had any reason to blush in front of men who'd turned up to see a punishment-whipping as if it were a novel form of entertainment.

He knew there were more than a few avians who weren't thrilled that he seemed to be a favourite of two high-ranking elders. He had no doubt they'd love witnessing what had to look like a spectacular tumble from grace. But he didn't have time to worry about pride, or vanity.

He reached the whipping post. Reaching up, he caught hold of the metal ring set at the top of the thick wooden support.

He didn't need to keep his head up and watch over Kane while the punishment took place. All his concerns there had been allayed. Everet allowed himself to rest his forehead against the wood and close his eyes. No one would know if his mask slipped as the whip fell against his back.

The whole room fell silent. Even the gossips must have stopped babbling. After all, what would they have to talk about tomorrow if they missed some important detail tonight?

Everet's muscles tensed as he waited for the first lash to

fall against his skin. Raynard didn't make him stand there and suffer as expectation built up. Only a few seconds passed before the leather snapped against his skin. A line of fire roared across his shoulders, from one side of his body to the other.

Everet gasped. It was nothing like he'd expected. The only experience he'd had to go on had been part of an experiment he'd conducted with a few other ravens a lifetime ago, so that they would, in theory at least, know how it felt— just in case they were ever called upon to whip a man as punishment. In that moment, Everet realised that the experiment had failed. None of its conclusions were in any way valid.

That sensation and this were as far apart as a single match being struck against the sole of a shoe, and the result of that match being applied to a forest full of dry kindling.

Clenching his teeth, Everet kept his curses to himself.

There was a point behind this, and it was a point that was worth making whatever the cost.

Find whatever mental place you need to go to as quickly as you can, and stay there. Raynard had given him good advice. But there was no pleasant beach scene for Everet to call to mind. He couldn't imagine that he flew high above the nest, unconcerned with anything that happened beneath him.

There was only one thing Everet was able to think about. Kane. He needed to focus on Kane and on how to be a better master for him. He needed to focus upon his duties to his submissive.

The whip struck Everet's back again. This time there was no gasp. Everet didn't have any breath left in his lungs for that.

He pulled air into his body the moment the whip left him, but that was just survival instinct. His mind was now entirely focused upon what Kane needed him to do differently in future.

Another blow fell.

Everet needed to make sure he took time to stretch his wings, so he could make the right decisions for Kane.

Raynard had established a rhythm. Pain spiked inside Everet at easily predictable intervals.

He needed to make sure he explained exactly what he expected from Kane, so that the rules were simple and clear.

Again and again, the whip fell. Everet made no attempt to count the lashes. That was Raynard's job, not his. Everet's job was to take all this pain and use it to make his resolution to be a better master stronger than ever.

He didn't try to fight the pain. He welcomed it, hailing anything that enabled him to be a better dominant as a gift he should cherish.

His mind welcomed the whip. His body didn't. His body hated it and everything it represented. His back burned. Everet pressed his forehead hard against the whipping pole. His grip on the metal loop tightened until his fingers cramped around it.

A little part of Everet had always wondered if he might like pain the way some of his previous lovers had; if it were to be properly applied by a man who knew what he was doing.

Now, Everet knew for sure, and he didn't find it the least bit erotic. His cock remained soft. It was only steel cold determination that kept him standing there. It was only his need to become a better master, a better man for Kane, which stopped him spinning away and launching himself at Raynard to try and wrestle the whip from him.

Kane.

The image of the magpie rose up in Everet's mind. *Kane as he had first seen him, huddled in a pathetic little ball in the back room of a human club.*

As another lash of pain exploded inside him, the image changed. *Kane standing in the middle of the living room, his arms folded, his expression mutinous.*

Every new fall of Raynard's whip brought another picture of Kane to Everet. Kane was his, and Everet had never been more determined to do right by him.

*

Kane closed his eyes tighter as yet another crack of the whip filled the air. The twenty lashes seemed to go on forever, echoing around inside his head until he was sure the leather must have connected with Everet's back a hundred times. He desperately wanted to lift his hands and cover his ears, but he couldn't. He was frozen in place. He couldn't even turn and run away.

It probably wouldn't have helped. Even if he'd been able to sprint out of the room, out of the nest, out of this whole screwed up world, the sight of the whip landing on Everet's back for the first time had burned itself into his retinas. He'd never be able to un-see it. And he'd never be able to un-hear the sickening sound of flesh trapped beneath the lash.

The breath caught in Kane's throat. He'd received plenty of beatings, but they were different. They had been filled with anger and fuelled with alcohol. It had been about some guy catching hold of him as quickly as he could and raining down blows until his arm got tired or he needed another drink.

Anyone standing around when Kane had fallen foul of a punter's temper had either cheered or joined in with sadistic enthusiasm. Kane had thought those nights had been bad, but this…

The room was filled with avians who seemed to have turned up just to watch Everet get whipped. And now, they just stood there, impartial observers. The crack of the whip was the only sound. The cold clinical nature of the punishment somehow made it far worse. The nest wasn't lashing out at Everet in drunken fury. It wasn't acting before it thought things through.

Without needing to open his eyes, Kane knew that Raynard wasn't getting off on hurting Everet. He was just going through the motions; doing a job that he might consider distasteful, but which nevertheless needed to be done.

And Everet...

Kane managed to make a few muscles escape the icy stillness that filled his veins. His hand curled into a fist at his side. His teeth cut into his bottom lip. He whimpered, but another crack of the whip made it impossible for him to open his eyes. He couldn't watch Everet get whipped because of him, he just couldn't...

In that moment, no piece of sparkly treasure was worth it.

A small, selfish part of Kane knew that just because he wasn't the one getting whipped, that didn't mean the punishment wouldn't hurt him in the long run. Everet could easily decide that he was too much trouble, and he wanted to trade him in for a submissive who didn't have his skill at pick-pocketing. What if Everet gave up on him? What if Everet didn't want to screw him anymore? What would happen to him then?

But that wasn't the only reason why Everet should never get hurt. Hurting Everet was just wrong—it was as simple as that. Everet was...Kane didn't know what he was, but he was someone who shouldn't get hurt—not by anyone, not ever.

The silence following that blow was longer. Kane tasted blood as his nerves built up, and his teeth cut through the thin, sensitive skin on his bottom lip.

"It's over now," Ori whispered, from somewhere to Kane's right. "You can go to your master."

That was a lie. Kane couldn't do that. He couldn't do anything. Fear still paralyzed him.

"Kane?" Ori said again.

Through super-avian strength of will, Kane managed to pry open his eyes. They'd been so tightly closed, they'd started to water. Ori now stood directly in front of him. He appeared concerned. He was also blurry.

Kane swiped at his eyes. They'd watered a lot.

Ori extended a hand to Kane, offering him a handkerchief. He was so bloody nice. He was probably just the kind of sub Everet wanted.

"I'm not crying," Kane snapped, in no mood to help Ori show him up in front of Everet.

Striding past the swan, Kane marched across the whipping square. He was halfway to Everet before he realised that he was about to come face to face with the very sight he'd closed his eyes against.

His steps faltered. All the air rushed out of his lungs. Everet stood next to the whipping post, his hand resting on the thick wooden pole as if to steady himself. His head was bowed, as if all his strength had deserted him.

Raynard stood alongside Everet, speaking to him in a low voice. Ori must have walked around the other side of the post because he appeared at Raynard's side and offered the hawk a small pot of something. Raynard handed it to Everet with more softly spoken words.

Then, Raynard looked up and caught sight of Kane.

"Come here, Kane."

Kane reluctantly shuffled forward.

Everet looked over his shoulder. His face was white. His back wasn't. There was no blood. Raynard hadn't broken the skin, but thick red marks crossed his skin in long straight lines.

Kane managed to take another step forward. Everet's expression was impossible to read, until it suddenly morphed into one of acute concern. He partially released his hold on the post and held one hand out to Kane. "It's okay. Everything's fine. It's over now."

"You're very fortunate," Raynard snapped, almost at the same time.

Kane turned his attention toward the hawk, mostly because it was easier than thinking of something to say to Everet.

"Not many masters would have taken that punishment in your place. I suggest you show your appreciation by altering your behaviour—rapidly."

"With all due respect, sir," Everet said. "Kane and I have already spoken about this. What's done is done." His voice wasn't entirely steady. Inside, Kane wept to hear it, but he kept his expression blank.

Raynard humphed with obvious disapproval. "He's your submissive. You have to do as you see fit, I suppose." He looked at Ori for a moment. When he spoke next, his tone was far more mellow. "Do you need help back to your room?"

Everet shook his head. "I'll be fine, thank you, sir."

Raynard and Ori turned and walked away; the swan casting concerned looks over his shoulder as they went. Kane glanced around the room. Most of the men who'd filled the space were leaving.

It seemed as if only a few short seconds had passed before they stood alone in the centre of the huge playroom. That was when Kane made the mistake of turning his attention back to Everet. All at once, Kane's thoughts scattered. He was incapable of doing anything but stare in horror at Everet's back.

"It looks worse than it is," Everet said, lifting his head and purposefully straightening his stance.

Kane's gaze snapped up to Everet's face. "I thought you said I could trust you to tell me the truth."

Against all of Kane's expectations, his words caused Everet to smile.

Something inside him sang with joy as he saw the raven's lips twitch and curve with approval. He'd made Everet smile. He could make him happy. That was it—that was the perfect way for him to make up for making Everet get whipped.

"Do you want a blowjob?"

Everet laughed. For a moment, he sounded even happier, but the noise quickly morphed into a hiss of pain.

"Not right now, thanks," he murmured.

Kane frowned. "You have to. It will make you feel better."

Everet's expression changed. He stared at Kane for several seconds, his scrutiny so intense Kane had to struggle not to squirm.

"You remember what I told you about trying to trade sex for things?" Everet turned away from the post and put his hand on Kane's shoulder.

It wasn't obvious if he still wanted to touch Kane the way a man touched a lover, or if he just needed something to stabilise him. No matter how desperate Kane was to step back and run away from the entire situation, he found himself unable to deprive Everet of anything that might help him stay on his feet.

"I wasn't trading; I was just offering," he muttered, pushing his hands into his pockets.

"Because you think I'm angry with you, and you think sucking me off will fix that?" Everet shook his head. "No."

"Maybe I just thought that getting off would make you feel better," Kane snapped.

Everet smiled again, but he also shook his head. "At the risk of making myself sound far more vanilla than I could ever actually be, sex is for the bedroom, not the whipping station."

"Okay." That wasn't a deal breaker. "We'll go back to the bedroom." Kane turned around. The sooner they got back to the bedroom, the better.

Everet's grip on his shoulder tightened.

Damn. That was right. He couldn't run away and expect Everet to chase him right now.

Kane frowned down at the floor, unsure what was the best way to handle the situation. "If you want to lean on my shoulder on the way up to the room, I don't mind," he hazarded.

Everet nodded his acceptance. "Thanks. Just fetch my T-shirt first, please."

Kane hurried across to the table, snatched up the garment and returned to Everet. He gave it to him, but Everet made no attempt to put it on. He just held it in one hand, and put his other hand on Kane's shoulder.

Leading the way back to their apartment, Kane instinctively found himself monitoring Everet's pain levels via the weight the raven placed on his shoulder. By the time they were in the living room, Everet needed a hell of a lot more support than he had when they first left the whipping post. His steps had shortened, his grip on Kane had tightened, but his back remained straight, his chin up.

It was only when they got inside the apartment that Everet's energy seemed to completely desert him. He slumped down onto the sofa, but he made no attempt to lean back against the cushions. He sat right on the edge of the seat, his elbows resting on his knees and his head bowed.

Kane didn't need to remain at his side any more. He walked away, only to stop halfway across the living room.

Damn! Belonging to Everet had made him so weak, so stupid. He'd come dangerously close to missing the perfect trick. The raven had kept him so busy, Kane had almost forgotten what his main priority should have been the whole time.

Carefully schooling his features into a neutral expression, Kane retraced his steps and sat alongside Everet on the sofa. "I should call the doctor to check you out."

"There's no need," Everet said, his head still bowed. "Raynard knew what he was doing. I don't need a doctor to tell me that my back will heal well enough without any help. Time is all it needs."

"It can't hurt to check," Kane pushed.

Everet looked up. His hair had lost its slicked back style. Several black locks fell forward into his face. He stared past them at Kane, a slight smile on his lips. "You don't need to worry about me."

"But I do!" Kane protested. "I should get the doctor. If

nothing else, he'll be able to give you something for the pain and—"

Everet's expression changed from one extreme to the other in less than half a second. His brow creased as his eyes narrowed. Any hint of a smile left his face. "No."

"I just meant…" Kane began quickly.

"There will be no drugs in this house."

The inside of Kane's elbow screamed in protest. Damn it, he needed it. The moment he'd remembered the easiest way to make his heart sing and his pain disappear, it had become vital he get his hands on a hit.

He wouldn't have to feel guilty if he had quicksilver rushing through his veins. None of this would be important if he could get a high. Everet wouldn't matter to him if he could just have a little sparkle injected into him. His hands curled into fists, as if he really could reach out, grab hold of the idea and hold onto it no matter what Everet said.

He stood up, but he had no idea where he intended to go. Pacing across to the fireplace, he turned and made his way back to Everet, only to repeat the process all over again.

The apartment door called to him. He could escape now. Everet was in no condition to catch up with him. He would be in far too much pain to—

Kane shook his head. No. That was wrong. Most men worked that way. But Everet wasn't most men. He worked according to his own rules. Everet would run after him no matter how much it hurt.

Hell, he'd probably try to chase him down if he had two broken legs, and a broken wing to boot. He'd catch him, too—even if he had to claw his way forward by his fingertips. He was stubborn like that. And Kane had already hurt Everet enough. Forcing him to give chase now would be wrong.

Kane shook his head again. He pushed his hands through his hair, trying to straighten out his thoughts from the outside. He was all muddled. Belonging to Everet was so different than belonging to any other man he'd ever known, it had completely messed up his brain.

He'd known lots of men who'd completely scrambled their minds on drink and drugs, but he hadn't realised it was possible to do that simply by over-indulging in the presence of another person.

"I'll help you into the bedroom," Kane decided. It was all simpler in there.

"I told you before," Everet said, his voice taking on a slight edge even though he was obviously still trying to sound all nice and patient. "Sex isn't a bargaining chip. You don't have any ground to make up with me. I'm not mad at you."

Kane glared down at him. "What if it's not about any of that? What if I'm just horny?"

"So you liked watching me get whipped?" Everet asked.

"Yeah, it was hot. All I could think about the whole time was how much I wanted to jump you. It's only your stupid sex is for the bedroom rule that made me wait until we got back here."

Everet raised an eyebrow as if he didn't think that particular lie was even worthy of comment.

Kane sighed and looked down at his fly. His cock had never been softer. He wasn't going to fool anyone. "Maybe I just want everything to be as simple as two guys in bed together," he said. "As simple as pleasing the man I live with and making him feel better when he's in pain."

Everet blinked. His eyes revealed his shock, even while his other features remained impassive. Kane kept his own expression blank, but no one could have been more surprised than he was by the words that had just left his mouth.

Now they were out there, he realised, to his great surprise, that they were true. One part of him wanted a high, but another part of him just wanted to help Everet. And right then, that helpful bit of him was the stronger of the two. If he had an angel on one shoulder and a devil on the other, the angel had just taken off his halo and beaten the devil over the

154

head with it until the poor little bugger gave up any attempt to whisper anything at all in Kane's ear.

Kane didn't understand it. He wasn't even sure he wanted it. But he knew in that moment, without any shadow of a doubt, that was the way things were.

*

Everet watched confusion flicker in Kane's eyes. The magpie was a good actor, but he wasn't *that* good. He looked so lost, so scared, as he tried to work out what was going on in his own head.

The desire to wrap Kane in his arms and hold him for the rest of his life overpowered every sensible thought in Everet's head. He pulled himself to his feet. The flames that had burnt across his back raged all the more fiercely as molecules of oxygen brushed across his skin and fed the blaze. Everet forced himself to ignore that. He stepped forward.

Kane remained perfectly still as Everet took his hand.

"The bedroom," he said. "Just because we can make each other feel good."

Kane nodded.

It was impossible to tell who led the way. Everet knew his balance was still shot. His grip on Kane's hand was only partially intended to reassure Kane. Everet wasn't sure he'd have made it to the bedroom door without Kane's support.

Inside the room, Everet headed straight for the bed and sat down heavily on the edge of it.

"What do you want to feel better first," Kane asked. "Your back or your cock?"

Everet managed to lift his head and peer up at him. Kane held the little pot of ointment Raynard had given him in one hand. His other hand was empty. Apparently, Kane didn't need any props in order to make someone's cock as happy as hell.

"My back," Everet said, ignoring the fact that, in spite

155

of everything else, his cock had started to harden.

Kane nodded. The mattress tilted slightly beneath Everet as Kane climbed onto the bed behind him. Even the tiny movements Everet made as he automatically balanced himself sent new bolts of heat searing through the muscles in his back.

Everet gripped the edge of the mattress and gritted his teeth, riding it all out as best he could. He heard plastic move against glass as Kane took the top off the pot. The ointment had a strong metallic smell. Anything that smelled that bad had to do someone some good.

"I just rub it into the whip marks, right?" Kane asked.

"That's right." Everet closed his eyes, determined not to react however much the application hurt. Kane wanted to help. Everet couldn't let any negative reaction to such a positive sign of progress creep past his defences.

Everet wasn't sure what he'd expected as he waited for the first touch. Clumsiness? Carelessness? For Kane to quickly lose interest in the task and leave it half done? He quickly realised that all those guesses would have been wrong.

Kane's touch was gentler than anything Everet had ever felt. It slid over the injured skin so tenderly, it was barely possible to feel his fingers moving against him.

The lotion quickly cooled on Everet's skin allowing Everet to track Kane's progress across his back and down toward the lowest whip marks. They'd been placed as low as they could go without the risk of doing Everet serious damage. Raynard really had done his best to space out the lashes and stop them crossing over each other. Everet made a mental note that he should thank Raynard for that.

Everet felt his breaths become less laboured as his skin stopped protesting against each lungful of air he took. He opened his eyes and stared down at his boots.

"Did I miss anywhere?" Kane asked.

"No." Everet turned just far enough to be able to look over his shoulder and meet Kane's eyes. The skin across his back only protested mildly at the movement.

Kane looked so sad. Everet's stomach clenched. A ferocious need to make his submissive happy wiped every other thought from his head. Twisting a little farther, Everet brushed their lips together. "You did a fantastic job. Thank you."

He tried to catch Kane's gaze, but Kane quickly looked away, as if afraid of what Everet might see in his eyes.

"Are you ready for your blowjob now?" Kane asked.

Everet had been ready to see Kane's lips wrapped around his cock since the first moment he'd recovered his health. He'd wanted Kane on his knees in front of him for so long, he wouldn't have been able to remember a time before that, even if he'd been inclined to try.

"Yes," he said, softly, as if it was a secret that only Kane would ever hear. "Very ready."

Lifting one hand, he trailed his fingertip across Kane's lips. They instantly parted as Kane offered his mouth to Everet's finger.

Everet swallowed rapidly in an effort to gain some patience, but he couldn't bring himself to delay the forthcoming blowjob by messing around with his fingers. He dropped his hand back to his side.

Kane chuckled, but for once he didn't seem to be interested in playing the brat. Everet had never been more relieved in his life. He remained perfectly still on the edge of the bed as Kane moved around him.

He seemed about to drop to his knees, when he stopped short.

Everet held his breath.

Grabbing a pillow off the top of the bed, Kane dropped it on the floor at Everet's feet before lowering himself gracefully down onto it.

Everet remembered how to breathe. Gradually releasing his grip on the edge of the mattress, he reached for his fly.

His whip marks didn't object too badly to that kind of movement, but Kane put his hand over Everet's fingers, stopping him before he had a chance to pull down the zipper. As their eyes met, they both froze in place.

Chapter Ten

"Let me?" Kane asked.

Everet didn't seem inclined to grant his request. The silence stretched out, so thin and taut that it could have been used as a trampoline.

"I'm not trying to take control," Kane said, when the hush became too much for him. "I just—" *I just want to do this for you.* Kane mentally cursed himself, but the words wouldn't rise to his lips. There was no real way for him to explain the desperate need that burned deep down in the pit of his stomach anyway.

He had to do this, for Everet, for himself, for…he didn't really know, he just had to.

Everet took his hand from beneath Kane's. He stroked Kane's cheek very gently, then lowered his hand to the edge of the mattress. Everet didn't say it was a bad idea; he didn't say anything at all.

Kane grinned as if he'd been given an expensive gift; something made from a precious metal that would sparkle and shine whenever it caught the light. He reached for Everet's fly and carefully drew it down. He still didn't have enough room. There was too much fabric in the way. He tugged at Everet's jeans, but he couldn't get them down while Everet sat on the bed. Kane looked up.

Everet didn't make him ask. Resting a hand on Kane's shoulders, he stood up. No wince, no intake of breath. Kane mentally added a tub of whatever that cream was onto his "must get—now!" list.

Kane quickly pulled the denim all the way down to Everet's ankles, so he didn't have to stand for any longer than was absolutely necessary.

Everet sat down again. He was already more than a little hard. Kane smiled as he wrapped his fingers around the long, thick shaft. God, but he was gorgeous; and Kane had seen enough cocks, had gone down on enough cocks, to know what he was talking about.

He stroked Everet firmly, coaxing him to grow harder under his watchful eye. The foreskin slid back, exposing the glans as he worked, tempting Kane and making him abandon all thought of taking it slow and trying to make the game last.

He wanted to dive on Everet and deep throat him, but he fought back the impulse. Dipping his head, he just wrapped his lips around the tip. Stilling his hand, he circled the head with his tongue before sucking to create a snug little vacuum. Everet gasped.

Kane looked up through his lashes.

For the first time since Everet had finally allowed them to start playing together, Kane wasn't so distracted by his own need to come to pay proper attention to his lover and ensure that Everet had a bloody wonderful time.

If he pleased Everet, then…

Kane hesitated—not physically—his tongue continued to play around Everet's cock with the ease and confidence that came from long hours of practice and an almost endless list of former partners. No, Kane's hesitation was all mental.

If he pleased Everet, then…

Part of him wanted to finish the thought with the possibility that Everet might let him get high, or that Everet might give him something bright and shiny to keep all for himself. Neither idea formed the right shape inside his head. Everet wouldn't change a damn thing just because Kane proved he gave really good head.

Kane frowned slightly, staring down at the base of Everet's cock as he dipped his head and took a little more of Everet's erection into his mouth.

If he pleased Everet, then…then Everet would be pleased with him?

Kane whimpered and bobbed his head lower again as he realised that he'd been wrong—not about if he should give Everet head, he still knew it was the perfect way to cheer up any man. But he'd been wrong about something else very pertinent to that moment.

Damn it! Kane knew he was just as distracted by his own needs and desires as he'd ever been. The only difference now was that he was concerned with how happy he'd be if Everet was pleased with him rather than how good his own orgasm might feel when he eventually got to come.

It was no use. Magpies obviously weren't cut out to think and

160

fool around at the same time. Another dip of his head. Kane pushed all the complicated, confusing things aside and concentrated on facts that he didn't require a single brain cell to understand. Everet's cock was delicious.

Yes, that was a straightforward fact that he could focus on.

Kane let his eyes drop closed as he stroked the satiny soft skin. The taste wasn't the only wonderful thing about sucking Everet off. The sensation of his mouth being filled again and again sent a shiver rushing down Kane's spine and straight to his balls.

The texture of Everet's shaft as it rubbed against his lips, the scent of Everet's pleasure, and the flavour of Everet's pre-cum as it leaked onto his tongue—everything combined inside Kane, making his cock harden and his head spin with pleasure.

A touch to the back of Kane's head jerked him out of his daydream. He opened his eyes and looked up. Everet stroked his fingers through Kane's hair again, his touch firm, but still strangely gentle.

Kane stilled, waiting for Everet to take up a tight grip around the longest strands of hair he could find, so he could take control of the blow job. Kane waited for Everet to force his head down until his shaft pushed into the topmost section of his throat and choked him. He waited for Everet to thrust his hips forward and start using his mouth in earnest.

"That's good, Kane. So good."

That was it. Everet stroked Kane's hair again before settling his hand near the nape of his neck. Then he smiled. Apparently, he had nothing else to say. He was once more content to let Kane get on with it.

Kane swallowed in confusion.

"Feels great," Everet murmured.

Frowning, Kane dropped his gaze down to Everet's cock. While he still held the tip between his lips, it was impossible to see most of the shaft, but that wasn't the point. It didn't matter what he stared at, as long as it gave him an excuse to avoid Everet's gaze.

He tried to dip his head but, all at once, it was impossible. Everet's thumb pressed firmly against Kane's forehead, just where his frown creased his skin.

Kane stubbornly kept his gaze down, staring at the dark, wiry hairs that grew around the base of Everet's cock, as if they were the most interesting things he'd ever seen in his life.

"If you want to stop, you can," Everet said.

Kane jerked his gaze up.

Everet sounded so understanding, as if he really wouldn't mind if Kane quit in the middle of it. Kane was more than ready to pull away and remind Everet that only a fool insulted someone who had their teeth that close to his cock. Except, when their eyes met, it was obvious that he would mind if Kane stopped—he'd mind *a lot*. He was just being an idiot—or being a nice guy, same thing really.

Kane made a distinctly unimpressed noise in the back of his throat. It would serve Everet right if he did stop after he scared him that way, making him think that he did such a bad job of sucking him off that he couldn't care less if Kane even bothered to finish what he'd started. Reaching up with his free hand, Kane took hold of Everet's wrist and pointedly moved his hand away from his forehead.

Everet didn't protest. He allowed Kane to resume bobbing his head at whatever pace he liked. Good. That suited Kane just fine.

It had been a long time since he'd been able to simply concentrate on the pleasure of going down on another man rather than how best to manipulate the situation. He was going to enjoy the end result too; nothing was going to stop him.

Curling his tongue and caressing the underside of Everet's shaft each time he lifted his head, Kane began to take Everet all the way to the base on every descent. No more teasing. It was time to bring out his A-game and show Everet just what he'd been missing out on during all those years before they'd met. He was going to make sure that Everet knew he'd never be able to find another lover that could make him come as hard as Kane could.

He was going to make himself indispensable to Everet's future happiness. He whimpered at the thought. As if reading the idea right out of his head, Everet moaned his approval, too. He stroked Kane's hair again. His hips jerked; the tiny movement of a guy who'd been driven too close to the edge and was no longer able to stay still, no matter how fantastic his self-control usually was.

"That's right," Everet ground out, his voice deep and rich with lust.

Yes. Everything was right in Kane's world. He settled a hand high up on Everet's leg, but he didn't attempt to control Everet's movements. He just wanted the pleasure of feeling more of Everet's skin.

Everet's thigh muscles bunched and twitched beneath Kane's palm. Kane whimpered, loving both the strength he felt in Everet and the control he was practicing. No other man had ever shown an inclination to control his strength around Kane.

Magpies were for using hard and rough. Gentleness was for other people. Self-restraint was for lovers who weren't going to be paid by the number of orgasms they induced.

Everet slid his hand down onto Kane's shoulder and gasped. His head dropped back. It was a clear warning for what was about to happen. Kane had plenty of time to move away. Instead, he stilled and held his tongue in front of the very tip of Everet's cock. Everet's semen landed directly on Kane's taste buds.

The raven didn't make a single sound as he came. He didn't even appear to breathe. Head back and staring up toward the ceiling, he just spilled his cum over Kane's tongue in long, creamy ropes.

Kane had to swallow as fast as he could to keep up. Then, as suddenly as it had struck Everet, his orgasm ended. The only things left in the world to prove that Everet had ever reached his orgasm were the taste in Kane's mouth and the tight grip Everet had on his shoulder.

Even when he'd first stepped away from the whipping post, Everet hadn't needed Kane to steady him this much. He was really dizzy with pleasure. Yes, Kane liked that idea. He smiled to himself as he sucked almost tenderly around Everet's softening shaft.

A far less attractive thought involved the fact that, at some point, Kane would have to pull away and separate them. He didn't like that prospect at all. He'd have much preferred to stay right where he was for the rest of the night, maybe even for the rest of his life.

Everet was his, and Kane had no more interest in giving up the raven than he would have had in giving up the most sparkly jewel in the world.

"Come up here."

Kane reluctantly obeyed. He moved to sit on the edge of the bed alongside Everet but he didn't look in Everet's direction. It was far easier to stare at the floor between his feet instead.

"You want me to help you get comfortable?" Kane eventually blurted out, trying not to feel pathetic for wanting any excuse to break the silence, even one involving menial labour.

"Yeah, thanks," Everet said.

Kane clumsily helped Everet out of the tangle of denim around his ankles and tossed the balled up jeans down near the base of the bed. Picking up the pillow he'd knelt on, Kane pitched that toward the top of the bed.

The bed…

There was no way in hell Everet would get a wink of sleep on the sofa. Kane looked once more at the beautiful, big bed he'd slept in so comfortably the previous night. He glanced at the whip marks on Everet's back while Everet moved the pot of ointment onto the nightstand. If Everet had taken the whipping for him, then…

"I'll take the sofa tonight," Kane said, as levelly as he could.

Still perched on the edge of the bed, Everet looked up at Kane, a slight frown furrowing the skin between his brows. "Take off your clothes."

Kane pursed his lips. Everet obviously thought that he was going to take the opportunity to escape from the flat. Well, if he thought that being stark bollock naked would keep him there, he was about to have another thought coming pretty bloody fast. Nothing could keep Kane there now. Nudity would only help him find another master more quickly!

Making no attempt to hide his anger, Kane tore off his clothes and threw them on the floor next to Everet's. The seam on his shirt ripped. Kane didn't care. He didn't care about anything or anyone. That was the way it had always been, and that was the way it would stay.

"Come here."

Kane stomped forward. Maybe he'd only remained in the room this long because he fully planned to give Everet a piece of his mind before he strode out of there, but he could just as easily do that up close.

When he stopped directly in front of Everet, the raven settled his hands on either side of Kane's hips. Kane was ready for the forthcoming lecture, and was determined not to listen to a word of it. What he wasn't so ready for was the way Everet dipped his head and took the tip of his cock into his mouth.

Kane grabbed hold of Everet's shoulders. It had been so long since anyone had cared if he came too; it hadn't even occurred to him that Everet would want to get him off, let alone on today of all days.

It was impossible for Kane to hold back a startled little cry.

Once that first sound was out, others followed hot on its heels. Kane clawed at the tops of Everet's arms as he fought for some sort of self-control.

Everet deftly caught hold of Kane's wrists. A moment later, he had them both pinned behind the small of Kane's back.

Squirming was out of the question. It might make Everet stop, and that wasn't something that could be allowed to happen. Kane stared down at Everet as he dipped his head and took him all the way to the base in one smooth motion.

Long strands of dark hair obscured Kane's view of Everet's eyes, but they didn't stop him from seeing how beautiful Everet's lips looked while they were thinned out around his shaft.

Everet caressed along the underside of Kane's cock as he pulled back. Then, just in case Kane hadn't been able to believe his eyes the first time he saw Everet's lips slide down his cock, Everet repeated the action several more times, letting Kane take in every wonderful detail. A few extra flicks of his tongue against the sensitive spot just where the head joined the length of his shaft and Kane came into Everet's mouth.

Sparklers lit up behind his eyelids. His knees shook. His hands clenched into fists behind his back as if there was some way he could hold on to ecstasy and make it last a little longer.

Despite his every effort, it slipped through his fingers, intangible and oh-so fleeting. The bliss that had extended all the way to his fingertips faded all too quickly, leaving a strange emptiness in its wake.

Kane groaned. There was no way he could stay on his feet a moment longer. He slumped forward until his knees rested against the mattress between Everet's legs. Everet's grip on his wrists didn't falter as Kane collapsed against him.

"That's right," Everet whispered, as Kane bowed his head down to rest it upon Everet's shoulder.

While Kane was still mussy-headed with afterglow, Everet rearranged them on the bed. Kane couldn't bring himself to protest being nudged and prodded right then. No suitably sarcastic thoughts rose up inside him. The idea of sharing a bed with Everet was curiously appealing—and not only because it gave him a good excuse to avoid making do with the sofa.

Within a few short minutes, Kane was spooned in front of Everet; all wrapped up under the blankets, with the heat of Everet's body pressed against him at every point. Everet's chest moved against Kane's back each time either of them took a breath. His knees fitted neatly against the back of Kane's knees. Even Everet's feet followed the line of Kane's feet. Their toes rested against each other.

Kane smiled against the pillow. It would be easy to get used to this safe, cosy feeling. Sleep claimed him the moment he closed his eyes. He didn't move again until he suddenly felt Everet pull away from him.

Kane had no idea how much time had passed. He could have been asleep for moments or hours, but he still knew that Everet shouldn't be leaving him.

"Where are you going?" he demanded, pushing himself up onto one elbow and glaring at the shadowy outline moving toward the edge of the bed.

"Bathroom," came the sleepy reply.

"Oh." Kane supposed he couldn't complain too much about that.

He lay down and waited impatiently for his raven-shaped hot water bottle to return. The bed was cold without Everet to keep it warm.

Kane hadn't noticed before, but the bed was far too large for one man to sleep in on his own. He pulled the blankets up around his neck and grumbled under his breath. Everet had been gone for ages.

Kane turned over. Even while grumpy about being temporarily left in the bed on his own, he couldn't help but smile at the fact Everet had invited him to share the bed with him. He'd never want to leave the soft comfortable confines of the bed now that...

Kane's smile died an agonizingly slow death. A frown spread across his forehead at much the same pace.

The bastard!

A bitter taste filled Kane's mouth. All of a sudden it was obvious that the only reason Everet had let him sleep there was because it was the easiest way to make sure he didn't sneak off in the middle of the night.

No wonder Everet had wrapped himself around Kane and held him so tight. He was playing the bloody guard dog again.

The door swung open. Everet stepped back into the bedroom. In the half-light, Kane saw that the raven's hair was disordered. His movements lacked their usual fluidity. The magic cream had obviously worn off. The pain from the whipping showed in every move Everet made.

Kane refused to feel any sympathy or responsibility for that. Everet had chosen to take the punishment. It wasn't Kane's fault he was in agony. Everything was Everet's fault. He deserved to hurt.

Everet slipped between the sheets and immediately moved across the mattress to trap Kane in there with him.

It took everything Kane had learned when he'd whored himself out to force his body to relax and accept an embrace he no longer had any interest in receiving. He lay meekly within Everet's arms, even as his anger burned all the more viciously inside him.

He listened carefully to the rhythm of Everet's breaths. By the time fifteen minutes had ticked past, he was sure Everet was fast asleep. Moving slowly, doing his best to make it seem like he just wanted to be considerate and to not wake up his lover unnecessarily, he began to extract himself from Everet's hold.

He didn't even make it to the edge of the bed.

One moment Everet was sound asleep. The next, his hand encircled Kane wrist.

"I'm just going to the bathroom," Kane said. Damn, but whoring made a man a good actor. Not one iota of his fury infected his tone.

Everet let go of his wrist. "Go ahead."

Kane left the bed and moved toward the door. Two paces later, he glanced back. Everet already appeared to have fallen asleep. He blatantly didn't give a damn.

He was just like all the other guys who'd screwed Kane in the past. The fact Everet's back wasn't covered by the sheets, because even thin cotton was probably too painful against his whipped skin, was irrelevant. Kane still hated him.

Picking up his clothes from the bottom of the bed en route, Kane moved into the living room. He was dressed within seconds. Ignoring the bathroom door, Kane headed straight to the apartment's exit.

He tried the handle. It turned easily. Everet hadn't even cared enough to lock him in. Kane closed his eyes for a moment, wondering why he had ever thought Everet might be different.

Shaking his head at his own stupidity, Kane opened the door. It wouldn't take him long to find someone with a little bit of quicksilver. At least he knew where he was with that. Quicksilver never let a man down.

*

Everet launched himself out of bed. The response was purely instinctive. His brain was still asleep when he raced out of the bedroom. He was barely any more awake when he sprinted through the open front door of his apartment and out into the corridor.

Eyes open wide, adrenaline pumping, unaware of anything except a few very basic facts about the world, he threw himself down the corridor after the figure that was running away from him.

Predatory predispositions were everything in that moment. Everet couldn't have stopped to think if he'd wanted to, and he didn't want to. He wanted Kane. The magpie filled his whole world.

Everet's legs were longer. Kane might have recovered his health, but his fitness still lagged way behind Everet's. Kane was less than ten yards ahead of him by the time he reached the top of the stairs leading down towards the main part of the nest.

As Everet stepped onto the first tread, Kane had just made it down to the first landing. An expanse of carpet covered a flat area that led to a ninety-degree turn and the next flight of stairs.

Everet leapt.

Clearing all twelve stairs in one swoop, he landed just behind Kane. His momentum carried him forward. Crashing into Kane's back, he took Kane's smaller figure down with him and they tumbled together.

The carpet did little to cushion the fall. They landed heavily and both of them had the breath knocked out of their lungs. Everet caught hold of Kane before he could roll away toward the next flight of stairs. He fought for a better grip on the squirming figure, but Kane seemed to have more limbs than any man had a right to.

"Get off me! Help! Someone help! He's trying to kill me!"

Everet finally got a firm hold on him. Making use of fistfuls of Kane's clothes to keep him under control, he finally managed to wedge Kane beneath the weight of his body.

He pressed his hand over Kane's mouth. He didn't know what the hell was going on, or what had prompted Kane to completely lose his mind, but Everet was pretty sure an audience wouldn't help either of them sort it all out.

Kane bit down hard. Everet cursed. Blood seeped from the

deep bite marks on his index finger, but he didn't try to pull his hand away. A little bit of pain wasn't important.

Everet's body had already started to remind him that he'd have far more pain to deal with once he allowed his mind a moment to process it. He didn't care about that either. He'd deal with that when he had time.

His first concern was far more immediate.

"Kane. Kane!"

Everet grappled for a hold on Kane's hair with his other hand. Finally, he managed to make Kane turn his head toward him. He held him still, trying to force Kane to meet his gaze.

"I'm not going to let you go. Stop struggling. You're just going to tire yourself out."

Either Kane saw sense or, more likely, he was already exhausted. Whatever the cause, he fell still beneath Everet. He stopped trying to scream against Everet's blood-stained hand.

Everet waited a few heartbeats, then carefully removed his fingers.

"You booby trapped the door!" Kane accused.

"Yes," Everet agreed.

Kane stared up at him in shock. He opened and closed his mouth a few times before he finally settled on something to say. "Why?"

"Because I didn't want you to sneak out while I was asleep."

Apparently, that kind of logic didn't appeal to Kane. He started to wriggle again. "Let me go."

"No. You're mine."

The pronouncement made Kane freeze. This time, he looked at Everet voluntarily. Their faces were so close together, Kane was more than a little blurry, but Everet could still see that something about what he'd just said appealed to Kane.

"You're mine," he repeated. "Did you start doubting that?"

Kane said nothing, but the answer was obvious.

Everet dropped his head until his forehead rested against Kane's temple. "There's no need to be scared," he said. "You're mine. I won't let you wander off."

Kane took a deep breath and let it out very slowly. "Why did you let me sleep with you in your bed?" As calm as he'd somehow managed to make his voice, confusion still infiltrated every syllable. Each word was carefully spaced out. The answer to the question was important.

"Because I wanted you there," Everet whispered, keeping the words just between them, a wonderful little secret they could keep entirely to themselves. "That's the only reason anything happens in that room, isn't it? I wanted us to sleep curled up close, because I knew it would feel good—for both of us."

Another deep breath shifted Kane's torso beneath him. "It wasn't just to stop me from running away?" Suspicion filled each word.

Everet let out a chuckle. "Sweetheart, my early warning system was the only thing I needed for that. It let me know you were trying to leave in plenty of time to catch you, didn't it?" Everet lifted his head so he could look down at Kane and see him more clearly.

The little magpie nodded his agreement.

"Did you like sleeping in my bed with me?" Everet asked.

Kane offered him another even smaller nod.

"Do you want to go back to bed?"

Kane hesitated.

"You're still allowed," Everet said, the moment he guessed the reason. "Nothing that happens in that room can be taken away as punishment, remember?"

Kane graced him with one more mini-nod.

Everet smiled encouragingly as he painfully pulled himself to his feet and helped Kane to stand alongside him.

Kane was dressed. Everet was stark bollock naked. When he managed to tear his attention away from Kane for a moment, Everet noticed that there were several men leaning against the railings that looked down over the staircase.

"Show's over," Everet said, his tone of voice very different to the one he'd used with Kane. "I suggest you all go back to your beds." Hand in hand with his magpie, he walked up the stairs and past the group.

"No one would have blamed you if you were trying to kill him."

Everet turned on his heel and faced the group. It was impossible to tell which one of them had spoken. "I'll put any avian who hurts the man under my protection into a bird cage," he told them all. "And I'll see to it that he grows old down there."

He might not have looked like the head of the nest's new internal security department, but he bloody well was. Any avian who forgot it would have to deal with him—naked and whipped, or otherwise.

He spun away from them and led Kane back to the apartment. The siren that went off if anyone opened the door after he'd sealed it for the night had obviously been a very good precaution.

When Everet closed the door behind them this time, he pressed the button on the discreet little device fitted high up on the doorframe, reactivating it so Kane could see that he still cared if he left or not.

"Come on," Everet said. "We've still got a few hours before we have to get up. Back to bed."

The moment Everet sat on the edge of the bed, his body presented him with the bill for all that energetic chasing around. It was to be paid immediately, and in throbbing discomfort. He bit down on his tongue as the first wave of it ripped through his body. A thousand needles stabbed into his back, burying themselves deep in his flesh along every line where the whip had left its marks.

Everet closed his eyes, sick to his stomach. It took several minutes before he was able to risk opening his eyes again. Moving very cautiously, he looked over his shoulder.

Kane sat on the other side of the bed, uncertainty radiating from his every pore. "I could put more ointment on your back, if you like."

Despite it all, Everet managed to smile. "Yes, that would be good. Thank you." Anything to do with Kane's first ever attempt to offer someone anything other than sex to make up for something he'd done wrong was fantastic in Everet's book; even if it involved letting someone touch his back when every logical bit of his mind protested at the top of its voice.

Logic couldn't compete with either his instincts or his desire to be a good master to a man he cared for more deeply by the day.

Chapter Eleven

"Just out of curiosity, how pissed off with me are you?"

Everet blinked and tried to focus on the world around him. His brain was still more than half-asleep. The signals it sent out were sluggish after a night of pain and yet more disturbed sleep.

Kane had picked the worst possible day to decide to be a morning person. Everet peered up at him. Kane was wide-awake, sitting upright and cross-legged on his side of the bed. He'd pushed the blankets back and was completely naked.

Being able to focus well enough to admire the view became an even bigger priority. Everet's cock stiffened rapidly. His brain was stumbling into action at a far more leisurely pace, but it managed to point out that Kane had asked him a question, and that he'd yet to answer it.

"I don't remember saying I'm pissed off with you at all," Everet said. His voice sounded thick with sleep. He yawned. He thought about stretching, but checked that idea before it even made it out of the gate. While he lay very still on the bed, his back was only moderately sore, but he was sure any kind of movement would make that change very quickly. "What time is it?"

Kane's eyes narrowed. "You didn't have to *say* you were pissed off. I'm not an idiot. I can put one and one together."

Everet bit back a sigh. "The time, Kane."

He huffed, but he looked at the alarm clock on the bedside table. "Ten past six."

Everet relaxed slightly. He still had plenty of time to get Kane to work on time. "Thank you. And, to return to the original subject—you might not be an idiot, but you are wrong about this. I'm not mad at you."

"I ran away," Kane said.

"I remember." Everet doubted he'd ever forget that heart-stopping moment when the alarm went off, and he realised Kane was no longer at his side.

"I broke the rule about leaving the apartment," Kane pushed.

"Yes, you did."

"Well?" Kane demanded.

Everet took as deep a breath as he dared. The skin on his back complained, but it didn't burst into flames, so he'd apparently calculated an acceptable lung capacity correctly. "We do need to talk about that," he admitted.

However, he was damn sure that wouldn't happen while he lay face down on the bed. Some conversations required easy eye-contact and he had no doubt that this would prove to be one of those exchanges.

"Have you been in the shower yet?"

"What does that have to do with anything?"

"You can have the bathroom first," Everet said, ignoring the anger in Kane's voice. "Go on. We'll talk in the living room once we're both dressed."

Kane huffed again, but he also did as he was told without further argument. It was a welcome blessing. Everet listened to doors open and close. Straining his hearing, he heard the shower start up, quickly followed by Kane splashing about in there.

Everet risked a slightly deeper breath and winced as the skin across his back pulled against the whip marks.

It was like the biggest sticking plaster ever invented, and there was only one way to deal with removing it. Kill or cure. Everet jerked himself into a sitting position, pulling the sticking plaster off in one harsh movement.

His head spun. His stomach heaved. He braced himself with his hands on the mattress in front of him and waited for the worst to pass. How anyone could find a whipping erotic was beyond him, but how anyone could put up with the after-effects just to get off—that was an even bigger mystery.

He shook his head slightly. It took every scrap of courage he could muster to make himself shuffle across to the edge of the bed, alter his position, and drop his feet onto the floor.

"You can do this," he muttered, as he forced himself to stand.

Standing wasn't easy while dizziness ruled his world, but he managed to stay on his feet. Each new movement made him wish he could claw the skin off his back. He thanked any god who listened that Kane wasn't there to see him take his first tottering steps that morning.

A shower was out of the question. The idea of water falling on his back made a cold sweat break out across his skin. Everet moved shakily to the wardrobe and grabbed a pair of jeans.

He wasn't sure if the worst of the pain dissipated once he'd made his first major movements of the day, or if he just got accustomed to it. It was quite possible that the sheer bloody mindedness, that most people considered the hallmark of a raven's psyche, had kicked in.

Clothes. Unfortunately, they weren't optional.

Black jeans, black boots, black T-shirt. Everet nodded to himself when he finally stood fully clothed near the base of the bed. He was ready to face the whole world, or at least ready to square off against a magpie in a bratty mood. It could easily feel like the same thing.

Kane didn't knock before he walked into the bedroom. His arrival should have looked confident, maybe even cocky, but Everet wasn't fooled. Kane was even more anxious than he had been before. He couldn't have proclaimed his fear of retaliation more plainly if he'd cowered in the corner with his arms raised to fend off the beating from hell.

He'd obviously been whipped often enough to know how a man felt the following morning. Lying would be pointless.

"Get dressed and join me in the living room." Everet walked out, making sure he held his head high and kept his spine straight, no matter how uncomfortably his T-shirt rubbed against his back.

Sitting down on the sofa, Everet leaned forward and rested his elbows on his knees to spare his back any contact with the sofa cushions. Kane didn't linger in the bedroom. Everet only just had time to work out what his first question should be before Kane appeared in the doorway.

"Sit down." He nodded to the chair opposite him.

Kane obeyed with uncharacteristic obedience. "Tell me how you felt just before you left the apartment," Everet ordered.

"Why?"

Because I told you to. Everet bit back the words. That wasn't the way to deal with Kane—that didn't change just because Everet was in pain. "Because if we can work out what made you do the wrong thing last time, we'll have a better chance of making sure you do the right thing the next time you feel the same way," he said carefully.

174

Kane shifted uncomfortably in his seat. A second later, he was on his feet. "We should go. I don't want to be late for work."

Everet caught hold of Kane's wrist when Kane would have walked past him, heading for the door. "Tell me how you feel right now," he ordered.

"Angry," Kane spat.

"Good."

Kane hesitated. He tried to snatch his hand out of Everet's grip on him but failed. Everet wouldn't have let him go for anything.

"You want me to be mad at you?" Kane demanded. "Well, in that case, well done."

"I want you to be honest with me," Everet corrected. "Did you feel the same way last night?"

Kane shrugged.

"You'll have to do better than that."

Kane huffed. "Yeah, okay. I was pissed off then as well."

"And afraid," Everet added.

Kane tried to pull his wrist out of Everet's hand again. Everet remained perched on the edge of the sofa, keeping his back as motionless as possible while still maintaining his hold on Kane.

It wasn't that difficult to keep his grip, especially when Kane had yet to put any real effort into shaking it off.

"You were afraid that you liked sharing my bed more than I liked having you there," Everet said.

Kane stared at a blank patch of wall alongside the window and made no reply.

"I love having you sleep next to me. I like keeping you close. You never need to doubt that, or to doubt that I want you to belong to me. There isn't a mistake you can make that could change that."

Everet had no idea he intended to say all that before the words hit the air. Perhaps the adrenaline from his injuries had altered his ability to control his tongue. Still, every syllable was true. He couldn't deny any of it.

Kane still didn't look toward him.

"Next time you feel angry or afraid, I want you to tell me rather than try to leave the room. Do you think you can do that?"

Kane shrugged.

"You can shout or stamp your feet. You can lunge at me and try to claw my eyes out if that's what you need to do. But, whatever happens, I want you to stay close to me and let me know how you feel."

Another shrug.

This time, Everet returned Kane's silence. He sat there, as still as any statue in the fancy human museums, and simply waited. Kane remained on his feet in front of him, pulling ever so slightly against Everet's hold on him, constantly testing to see if Everet still wanted to keep him there.

It might have been a minute or an hour. Time didn't matter as they mentally stared each other down, waiting to see who would give in first.

Finally, the pressure against Everet's hand eased. Kane stopped leaning away from him. More time slipped by.

"I'll try," Kane muttered.

Everet smiled and squeezed Kane's wrist, in what he hoped felt like a reassuring way, then released him. "Good." Everet stood up. "Let's get you to work."

"Are you staying with the cleaning team today?" Kane asked. *Are you staying with me? Please?*

"Yes." What other answer could he give to that kind of silent plea?

Kane seemed to relax slightly. He wanted his master close to him.

Everet didn't tempt fate by grinning like an idiot, but his lips twitched into a small smile. It was probably a tiny shuffle forward, even as baby steps went, but it still felt good to think that some sort of progress had been made. As Everet led Kane to his duties and took up his post watching over him, his T-shirt rubbed against his whipped back like wire wool dipped in saltwater.

He squared his shoulders and pushed aside the pain. It had definitely been worth it.

* * * * *

"Everet, may I speak to you for a moment, please?"

Kane looked up from his dusting just in time to see Ori beckon Everet across to the other side of the hallway. It was a blatant attempt to put several yards between Kane and his master.

"Of course, sire." Everet smiled slightly as he joined Ori.

Kane straightened up, all thought of dust-free surfaces forgotten. Narrowing his eyes, he glared at the back of the swan's neck. He had no right to speak to Everet in private—let alone practically throw himself at him.

Anger twisted and swarmed within Kane, green-eyed and furious. Ori had a master. There could be no possible need for Ori to wander around pestering other people's masters—men who were supposed to be watching over their own submissives.

Kane turned away from the table he'd been dusting and made no attempt to be subtle as he observed every detail of the softly spoken conversation.

Ori stood far closer to Everet than he needed to. From the way Everet had to bow his head to put his ear nearer Ori's lips, Kane could tell that Ori was speaking really quietly. Kane had used that trick himself, dropping his voice to a seductive whisper to get a prospective sugar-daddy leaning in close. He knew how to spot a slut making a play for a guy.

As for Everet—he should have had more sense than to fall for it. Where were all his copper's instincts now?

Kane tossed his duster on the floor and folded his arms across his chest. The conversation continued for several minutes, and neither Everet nor Ori so much as glanced in Kane's direction. Well aware that his existence had been forgotten, it took all of Kane's self-control to remain on his side of the hallway.

Finally, Ori stepped back. Then, of all the bloody cheek, he tilted his head slightly, smiled, and looked up at Everet through his lashes. It was the final straw. No one in his right mind would have allowed another submissive to flirt with his master that way without taking immediate action.

Kane strode across the freshly vacuumed hall carpet and stepped straight past Ori. He heard something that might have been Everet starting to ask what he wanted, but Kane didn't have time for silly questions.

Kane slid his hands around Everet's neck and up into his hair. Pulling Everet's head down, he brought their mouths together.

For a second, Everet seemed too startled to kiss him back. Kane made the most of it, thrusting his tongue past Everet's lips to explore his with impunity. For once, Kane was the one in control of every detail.

Everet made a frustrated noise in the back of his throat, but he didn't push Kane away. He slid his arms around Kane's body and pulled him closer. Kane was all in favour of full body contact, but when Everet demanded that he instantly hand over all control of the kiss, Kane was in no mood to let that happen without a fight.

He nipped at Everet's bottom lip and squirmed against his body. Their crotches rubbed together as he wriggled—he made sure of that. They'd barely had enough time to lose their breath before they were both hard and ready to do far more than kiss.

Kane mentally grinned, but he didn't waste time celebrating before the end of the game. It wouldn't be long before Everet's brain caught up with his body. Kane had to make the most of every second before that happened.

Unable to risk touching the whipped skin on Everet's back, Kane kept his hands on the back of Everet's head. He yanked at thick black strands of hair, using his grip as leverage in an effort to bridge the gap between their heights a little more perfectly.

Suddenly, Everet stopped trying to embrace him. He caught hold of Kane's wrists and jerked him bodily away, breaking the kiss and putting clear air between them all the way down to the floor.

"What the hell's got into you?" Everet demanded.

Kane glared up at him. Could he really be that clueless?

"I think this might be my cue to head to my next meeting," Ori murmured.

Everet twisted around to look at Ori. His eyes opened wide with shock. He'd obviously completely forgotten Ori was there.

Kane grinned. Success!

"Yes, sir. Thank you, sire," Everet said, but it was obvious to anyone listening that his mind was elsewhere—that the only man he had on his mind was a magpie rather than some stupid swan.

Ori walked away. Kane strained his avian senses, listening to his footsteps until they faded out of hearing. Everet didn't glance after him once. Perfect.

Job done, Kane tried to take a step back. Everet stopped him short, refusing to let go of his wrists. "Where are you going?"

"Back to work," Kane said, with a nod to the discarded duster.

Everet frowned. "Do you think I'll give you the afternoon off so we can get laid?"

"Sweetheart," Kane said. "If a little bit of frustration was going to make that happen, you'd have given in days ago. Why would I think today would be different?"

"Then what was this all about?" Everet demanded.

Kane shrugged. "Can't I just want to kiss you?"

"The truth, Kane."

"You said I could do whatever I wanted when I was pissed off with you, providing I didn't run away," Kane reminded him.

The expression in Everet's eyes changed. He still didn't get it, but he seemed more inclined to smile than to frown. "Are you still in a bad mood?" he asked.

"Nope."

Everet nodded, as if making a decision. "Good. You did the right thing. Well done. You're free to get back to work."

Kane smiled. When Everet released him, he picked up his duster and resumed his duties. He was aware of Everet's eyes moving over his body every time he bent down to reach a bit of low carving. Everet was just as turned on as Kane was, just as desperate to come as he was.

Everet didn't take his eyes off Kane during the rest of the day, and Kane didn't stop smiling, either. The world was once more just as it should be—with Everet's attention completely focused on him.

And, just to make the universe an even better place, Kane was able to spend the rest of the afternoon sure that Everet would jump him the moment they got back to Everet's apartment and closed the bedroom door behind them.

Talk about having something nice to look forward to.

* * * * *

"You're going to be doing something different today."

Kane froze, his T-shirt halfway over his head. His skin was warm and slightly damp from his morning shower, but he still broke out into a cold sweat.

A punishment.

It had taken just four days for Everet's back to heal. He no longer appeared to be in any kind of pain—not even when he thought he was unobserved. Deep down, Kane had known the punishment was on its way. He was ready for it.

Everet was fully fit. Last night he'd been more than capable of pinning Kane to the bed and screwing him hard and rough, just the way Kane loved. And now, he obviously felt healthy enough to exact his revenge on Kane for trying to run away, too.

Kane dropped his T-shirt to his side. "Should I bother putting this on?"

"What do you mean?"

Kane turned toward where Everet stood in the doorway between the bedroom and the living room, already dressed and ready for the day. "The punishment for leaving the apartment without your permission that night," Kane muttered. "You're going to whip me, right?"

Everet shook his head. "There's not going to be a punishment. If you still have questions about that, we'll have another chat this evening about why you're not going to be punished." He stayed in the doorway, his arms folded, his stance squared. "First, you have a day's worth of work to do."

Oh, joy, Kane thought. Now he'd be able to spend the whole day in anticipation of yet another awkward conversation where he had no idea what to say, no idea how to explain how scared he felt when he thought about a future which didn't involve Everet and him being together.

Bloody wonderful. Kane pulled on his T-shirt, his movements jerky and impatient.

Everet led the way out of the apartment. Kane followed along behind him, his feet dragging along the carpet. Damn, but dusting was enough to bore anyone to tears. It was only Everet's supervision that made it bearable and—

Suddenly, Kane looked up. They were heading in the wrong direction.

"Where are we going? You said I had to go to work?"

You're going to be doing something different today.

Everet's earlier words floated to the front of Kane's mind. Kane had been too focused on the prospect of a punishment to question that statement properly, now he realised how big an error that was.

"You're still going to work. You'll just be doing a different job today."

All of Kane's senses were immediately on high alert. He stopped halfway along a corridor he'd never seen before. "A worse job?"

Everet shook his head as he retraced a few steps, caught hold of Kane's hand, and led him forward once more. "Not a worse job, just a different one."

The sound of clattering dishes dropped some not very subtle hints about their destination.

Hell, no! "I can't cook, so there's no point—"

"Hush," Everet chided. They turned down another corridor. The rattling of dishes grew quieter until it completely faded from hearing. "Do we need to go over the newest rule you've agreed to follow?"

"No nicking stuff," Kane muttered, purely to avoid the longer version of the conversation.

Everet smiled. "Well done."

They turned another corner, and the big dumb albatross came into view, standing outside a heavy looking wooden door.

"What's he doing here?" Kane asked, glaring up at Ambrose.

Everet might think the guy was all sweetness and light, but Kane had no doubt the oaf would jump at the chance of fooling around with Everet if he was given half a chance. Kane pursed his lips. The sooner he found the opportunity to get the albatross alone and make it clear that Everet was going to be his *master* and no one else's, the better.

"It's standard protocol to have a member of security down here at all times," Everet explained, still leading Kane forward.

"Why?"

"You'll see."

Ambrose nodded a greeting to Everet with a great deal more friendliness than was required. Everet returned the gesture, and rapped on the door. Someone called for them to enter. The door swung open. It was only luck that stopped Kane coming in his pants right there and then.

A gentle tug on Kane's hand pulled him into what was easily the most beautiful room he'd ever set eyes on. As Everet closed the door behind them, Kane turned, taking in every glorious detail surrounding him. He'd never imagined a place like this could exist, let alone that he would find it in the building where he lived.

"I thought you might like it here."

Kane managed to glance toward Everet for a moment, but his eyes were soon drawn back to the beauty of their location. Every wall was covered in shelved cabinets, and every shelf was weighed down with more glitter and sparkle than Kane could wrap his mind around.

There was more silver in there than he'd known existed in the entire world.

"It's beautiful…"

"Yes, it is." That wasn't Everet's voice.

Kane's attention snapped toward a small figure sitting at a table on the far side of the room.

"Good morning, sire," Everet said from Kane's left.

Ori stood up and made his way across the room. "Good morning." His attention settled on Kane. "It takes a great deal of work to make sure all of the nest's silver remains in the best possible condition."

Kane glanced toward Everet. "This is the new job you were talking about?"

Everet nodded. His expression remained serious, but Kane saw a light in his eyes that hadn't been there when he'd looked at Ambrose, or even when he'd looked at Ori.

"Kane?" Ori prompted.

When Kane turned back to him, Ori lifted his hands. He held a polishing cloth in each hand and one extended in offering toward Kane. "Would you like to help me polish some of the nest's silver?"

Kane wasn't sure why, but he turned to Everet to see what Everet thought of the idea before he made his own decision. He waited for Everet's verdict, even though he had to clench his hand into a fist at his side to stop himself from grabbing the cloth before the offer was withdrawn.

Everet nodded his approval. "That's a good idea. I need to get on with some work of my own, but I'll be back to collect you later."

"You're going?" Kane blurted out.

"Yes. But, you'll be fine. Ambrose will be right outside the door if you need anything, and Ori will show you what to do."

Kane frowned, torn between his desire to have Everet within sight, and to remain surrounded by sparkle.

Everet stepped forward and pressed a kiss on Kane's cheek.

No one had ever done that before. Kane's fingers twitched, but he managed not to make a complete idiot of himself by lifting his hand and touching the chaste bit of skin Everet had chosen to kiss. He was so distracted by a kiss that had nothing to do with sex, Everet was gone before he could think of anything to say.

"He's a good man," Ori said from behind Kane.

"Too good for someone like me, you mean," Kane translated

as he turned to square off against the swan.

Ori dropped his gaze. Against all of Kane's expectations, Ori retreated to his table. "I've only just made a start on this set of spoons," he said.

Row upon row of silver lines stretched out across the table. Kane gravitated toward them. Before he knew it, he had one of the spoons in his hand.

"Please, take a seat," Ori invited, sitting down on the opposite side of the table.

Kane lowered himself onto the chair, but he couldn't take his eyes off the silver.

"I'm not sure how much you know about silver, but it needs to be polished regularly to stop it from tarnishing," Ori said, his words soft and gentle, his tone exactly the same as that he'd used toward Everet. "If it's left for too long, the surface starts to go dull and it loses all its shine. Eventually, it goes completely black. Would you like me to show you how we keep it sparkling?"

"Yes." Kane's grip on the spoon in his hand tightened.

"That's the one I just finished," Ori said, with a nod toward the spoon Kane held. "Maybe you'd like to keep it in front of you for comparison, so you'll know when the first one you do is finished?"

Ori wasn't going to try to take it off him. That was the only thing Kane really cared about right then. The spoon, with all its gleam and shine was his. Kane nodded.

Setting it down carefully in front of him, he managed to release his grip on the handle. He picked up another spoon. It was nigh on impossible to believe that it could ever look like *his* spoon.

Ori set to work on another part of the cutlery set. Carefully copying Ori's actions, Kane worked on his task in silence. Very slowly, he saw something like a glisten begin to emerge from beneath the polish and the cloth.

Pure silver glittered and shone under the bright overhead lights. Kane gazed down at it in wonder.

"It's almost like magic, isn't it?"

Kane jerked up his head. He'd almost forgotten Ori was there.

"That's one of the things I like about this job," Ori added.

"This is your job?" Kane asked.

Ori took a deep breath. Unless Kane was mistaken, it took a lot of effort on Ori's part not to let that breath out as a sigh. "No. Not really. I'm not supposed to want to do things like this." As he spoke, his hands kept working without a single hesitation. "I'm supposed to be all delicate and pretty—useless for anything other than offering the occasional opinion."

Kane turned his eyes back to his own work, unable to resist trying to make the spoon shine as brightly as possible, but he didn't stop listening.

"My master says that my role in the nest is to counteract the birds of prey's more aggressive nature with instincts that are all about tolerance. I am slowly getting better at that, I think. But this…"

Kane glanced up.

"This is still the kind of work I like best."

Kane nodded. Part of him felt like he understood. "It's a good job, getting the sparkle out of things." He frowned, knowing he sounded like an idiot.

Ori didn't laugh. "The avian who used to look after the silver left the nest a few weeks ago—he's living in a breeding colony now. Nobody's found a suitable replacement yet," Ori said.

For a moment, Kane actually believed that the nest might actually consider him as that replacement. He shook his head. He wasn't suitable for anything. "They'd never leave a magpie alone in a place like this," he muttered.

"Why not?"

Sudden anger fired up inside Kane. His grip on a half-polished knife turned white-knuckled. He wanted nothing more than to lash out at the whole world, to stab the universe deep in the heart and watch it bleed. It wasn't fair.

"Because you all know I'm a thief," Kane ground out, each word more bitter on his tongue.

"People can change."

Kane closed his eyes. "Magpies can't." He'd known it all his life, even if he sometimes managed to push the knowledge to the back of his mind when he was with Everet.

Thieves, whores, and disgraces to the avian nation. Magpies couldn't change. The best anyone could hope for was that they'd behave reasonably well under very close supervision. Hamilton was a bastard, but he was a bastard who was right about magpies.

"Maybe they can change if they have a master who believes in them—a master like Everet."

The sheer unexpectedness of the statement made Kane look up and meet Ori's eyes. For the first time, they held each other's gaze for several seconds.

"I wouldn't be who I am without my master," Ori said. His brow furrowed as he obviously thought carefully about each word he said. "I think, over time, belonging to a man, or owning a man, changes someone. Part of the master rubs off on his submissive. A little of the submissive is passed back to the master. I know I'm far more confident than I was when I first met Raynard. There's no reason why Everet's self-control couldn't rub off on you. He has quite a bit to spare."

Kane looked down at the knife. It took a man with a hell of a lot of confidence to sit opposite him not to be worried about getting stabbed right then. Even most birds of prey would have faltered.

Kane looked up. Ori didn't pull away in fear. He didn't even blink.

"Everet is very controlled," Kane allowed.

"Yes." Ori said. He paused for a moment, as if debating whether or not he should say something. "There's another reason why none of the elders would need to worry about you wanting to take anything from here."

Kane waited, hoping like hell there wasn't a punchline on its way. He wasn't sure he'd survive it, if there was.

"Because, in a way, you'd know everything in the room would already be yours," Ori said. "You'd know that it was all your responsibility and that you'd be coming back here to work with it every day. And you'd know that it would be safer here than it could be anywhere else in the nest."

For a few minutes, both of them remained completely silent and absorbed in their work.

"Do you think you'd need to take anything out of the strong room if you knew it would be there for you to look after whenever you came back to it?" Ori eventually asked.

Kane stroked his fingers over the glistening metal. A swan was part of the group who ran the nest because he didn't think like a bird of prey.

An eagle would send a thief to prison.

A swan… Kane looked up at Ori. A swan tried to make sure he had exactly what he wanted because then there'd be no need for him to steal anything in the future.

"You really think you could get me the job?" Kane asked.

Ori smiled slightly. "I can get you a trial period in the job. If you do well, there'd be no reason why anyone could object to you taking up the position permanently."

Kane nodded very slowly. Everything around him, even the ideas in his head, they were all so new and interesting. Even better than that, they were all shiny.

Chapter Twelve

Everet raised one hand and knocked on the door leading into the nest's strong room. His heart raced so fast he was sure that the guard standing alongside the door had to be able to hear every beat.

It wasn't a good idea to look like an idiot in front of a man he'd probably need to give orders to in the future. Everet couldn't allow himself the luxury of hesitating when Ori called out permission for him to enter the room.

As he stepped inside, Everet's eyes went straight to the workbench. Kane sat hunched over something. He had a polishing cloth in his hand and was apparently so hard at work he hadn't even registered Everet's arrival.

"Good afternoon, sire," Everet said to Ori, even though his attention remained completely focused on Kane.

The words had barely left his mouth when Kane's manner did a complete one-eighty. He leapt out of his chair and raced across to Everet.

It was only his first day. Everet couldn't expect too much from him. It would have been cruel to think that one day in—

"Look!"

Kane caught hold of Everet's hand and dragged him across the room. Everet was so shocked it didn't occur to him to try to hold his ground. At his work station, Kane indicated several rows of sparkling silverware. They were laid out on a length of purple velvet with a neatness that bordered on reverence.

"Look!" Kane ordered again.

"You polished all of this today?" Everet asked.

"Yes. Isn't it beautiful?" Kane whispered. He moved even closer to Everet's side, his left hand crossing his body to grip Everet's nearest elbow. It was hard to know if the posture was a request for reassurance or if Kane just wanted to snuggle into his side after a day of being apart. Either way, Everet was entirely in favour of it.

He turned to Kane. The cutlery was nice enough, but Kane, high on success and with pleasure softening his features, was gorgeous.

"Everet!" Kane protested, tugging at both his hand and arm. "You have to look at them, not at me!"

Everet smiled down at him. "You did wonderfully," he said. "You must have worked non-stop since I left."

Kane nodded, grinning with triumph. There was a smudge of silver polish on his cheek. Everet lifted his free hand and wiped it away with his thumb.

Dipping his head, he brushed their lips together. He'd intended it to be a chaste little bit of praise, but the moment their mouths touched, it became something very different.

Kane's shorter frame moulded itself against Everet's body, like ivy growing up and around an oak tree, covering every branch and completely engulfing a creature far larger than itself.

All at once, Kane was pure sex, pure submission. He wrapped his arms around Everet, threaded his fingers into Everet's hair, and tugged him down into the kiss.

Somehow, Kane managed to demand more from Everet and make it feel like he'd offered to submit and follow his lead at the same time. It was a bloody good trick and one Everet instantly fell in love with.

Relief at finding out that Kane had taken to the new job like the infamous duck took to water, mixed in with the lust Everet always felt whenever he was in the same room as Kane, and soon it was impossible to untangle them.

Sliding his arms around Kane's smaller frame, Everet braced himself for the stab of pain he expected to burn across the skin on his back. Nothing. He was finally free to do whatever he liked without the after-effects of the whipping holding him back.

He grabbed Kane's arse and pulled him even closer, rubbing their crotches together. Deepening the kiss, Everet took complete control of Kane's mouth. Of course, Kane didn't just let that happen, he made Everet fight for it. But the way he thrust even more firmly against Everet's body, his cock hard and his whimpers needy, let Everet know that Kane was desperate to lose that particular fight and—

A polite little cough cut through the air like a very well-polished silver knife through butter that had melted under the sexual heat that filled the room. Everet jerked his head up.

Ori smiled shyly across at them from the other side of the room. "You're very welcome to have the room to yourselves," he offered. "I wouldn't have interrupted at all, except you're between me and the door."

Everet automatically looked over his shoulder. As they'd rubbed against each other, they had indeed moved toward the door.

"I'm sorry, sire," Everet began.

"I'm not," Kane said, still grinning.

Everet couldn't bring himself to chide Kane for being cheeky, especially when it sounded more like friendly banter than petulance toward a man he'd previously shown an unaccountable dislike of.

"I'll leave you to, um…" Ori blushed as he hedged past them. "I hope you'll join me here again tomorrow, Kane."

The door was heavy and, no matter how gently it was closed, the mechanism still thudded loudly into place.

For several seconds after Ori left, neither Kane nor Everet moved a muscle; neither of them uttered a single word.

"I did really well today," Kane eventually said.

Everet stared down into Kane's eyes, loving the peace and happiness he saw there. "Yes, you did."

"I know I can't be rewarded for that," Kane said. "But does that mean you're not allowed to celebrate with me."

Even as he smiled, Everet studied Kane a little more warily. "What are you plotting?" There was more than a touch of warning in his voice.

"I'm thinking: you and me, right here, right now, coming harder than either of us ever have in our lives." Kane whispered each part of his plan into Everet's ear. Heat ran down Everet's spine as Kane brushed his lips against the lobe.

Lifting his head, Everet used their height difference to take his ear out of range. "I said no sex outside the bedroom," he reminded Kane.

"You also said *for now*. I remember."

Everet swallowed and did his best to keep his brain above his belt.

"I know you're not screwing me because I was a good little silver-polisher all day," Kane said. "You'll just be getting us off because we're both really, *really,* happy right now."

Everet glanced around the room. He'd seen Kane's expression when they'd arrived there that morning. He knew how much he liked the sparkle and glitter that surrounded them.

Maybe there wasn't any reason why they couldn't have sex there... Maybe it was the perfect time to make the line between their sex life and Kane's training, a mental rather than a physical barrier... Everet sighed, maybe he just really wanted to screw Kane and any excuse that let him do that was fine with him.

Was he thinking like a good master or a horny man? He had no idea, but he also knew that, while he'd been busy thinking it all through, the decision had been made in a far more instinctive part of his brain.

"Stay exactly where you are." Everet stepped back as he gave the order.

Kane glared at him with obvious disapproval, but he also obeyed.

Striding across to the door, Everet jerked it open. The guard in the corridor leapt to his feet and shoved the book he'd been reading behind his back.

Everet glowered at him, but he didn't say anything. They'd talk about keeping his attention on his job another time. "No one is to enter this room until we leave. No one. Understand?"

"Yes, sir." The guy straightened his back as if springing to attention. It did nothing to make up for his earlier lapse in concentration.

Everet slammed the door and turned to face Kane.

"Strip."

"Because you want to make sure I'm not hiding any of the cutlery in my pockets?" Kane asked.

"If I wanted to know that, I'd frisk you," Everet corrected, folding his arms across his chest and leaning back against the door. "I want you naked because I want to see every single inch of you. Now."

Kane pulled his T-shirt over his head and dropped it on the floor at his side. Their eyes met across the room. Kane paused for a moment.

Everet didn't move. He didn't even take a deep breath.

Smiling to himself, Kane kicked off his trainers.

Socks. Jeans. Boxers. One by one, he tossed each item aside. Finally, he stood in the centre of the room stark bollock naked.

It was only then that Everet allowed himself to step forward. He walked around Kane very slowly. Kane remained as motionless as Everet had a few moments before. He didn't turn to watch Everet. He didn't say anything bratty. The atmosphere in the room was very different to that which usually fell over their bedroom when they were about to play.

Even if he was in control in their bed, the atmosphere was light and friendly. In this room, it all felt far more serious, much more important. It wasn't just about making sex about something other than money now, it was about wrapping it up in the tight bindings of dominance and submission. Down here, sex wore a collar and walked at heel on a lead made from heavy silver chains.

Kane's breaths became uneven, and Everet hadn't even laid a hand on him yet.

"I told you I want to see every inch of you." When Kane would have spoken up, Everet put a fingertip against his lips. "That's because, as soon as we make our time here about sex, I own every inch of you."

Kane's eyes sparkled with interest. For once, he didn't bite Everet's finger the moment it came within a yard of his mouth.

Everet's lips twisted into a smile as he dropped his hand to his side and began to walk around Kane once more. "You love all this glitter, don't you?"

"Yes."

Everet picked up one of the knives Kane had polished. The handle was moulded into some complicated pattern that had probably been the latest fashion a few hundred years ago. Every nook and cranny of it gleamed.

Kane's back was toward Everet. He had no warning before Everet brought the knife to rest upon his bare shoulder.

"What?" Kane twisted his neck and peered around at it.

"It looks good against your skin," Everet mused, as if entirely to himself.

Kane's jaw dropped as he managed to catch a glimpse of it. A tiny whimper escaped from the back of his throat.

The knife wasn't sharp enough to hurt anyone. Everet was able to trail the blade across Kane's skin without worrying that it might do him any sort of harm.

"Feel good?" he asked.

"It would feel even better if you'd do it around the front and I could watch you properly."

Everet was sure Kane was right, but that wasn't the point. "I can see fine from here," Everet said. "You don't need to see; you just need to feel."

Kane huffed.

"Close your eyes," Everet ordered.

"Why?"

"Because I told you to. I warned you that I like to boss my lovers around. It's time you got used to obeying me properly when we play."

Everet walked around to face Kane. Kane raised an eyebrow at him, but he made no attempt to cover his erection and hide how turned on he was by Everet's orders.

One last moment of mutiny, and Kane finally closed his eyes. Everet rewarded him by touching the handle of the knife gently against each eyelid. Kane's breath caught in his throat. He licked his lips. Nerves, Everet wondered? No, excitement—that was it.

"Can you feel it glittering against you?" Everet whispered. "It feels good, doesn't it? Smooth and clean, and so shiny…"

He let the silver brush against Kane's lower lip. "Taste it."

Kane opened his mouth in acceptance and Everet offered the blade to him very slowly, slipping it past his lips until it touched against his tongue. The look on Kane's face was little short of pure ecstasy.

Under no pressure to maintain a sombre expression while Kane was blind to everything that happened around him, Everet grinned.

When he took the silver away, Kane frowned. He kept his mouth open for several seconds, obviously hoping to feel the silver slip inside him one more time.

"Tell me what it tastes like," Everet ordered.

Kane licked his lips. "Good."

"You can do better than that."

Rather than open his eyes and argue, Kane closed his eyes even tighter and frowned in concentration.

"Shiny," he whispered, his tone more uncertain than Everet had ever known it.

"Good," Everet said. "What else?" He moved to stand directly behind Kane. With his free hand, he reached around Kane's torso and guided him to lean back against him.

Kane didn't try to fight whatever Everet wanted to do with his body. He was far too caught up in what Everet was doing with his mind.

"Silvery," Kane offered.

"Yes," Everet said, encouragingly. Keeping one hand on Kane's abs to hold him in place, he brought his other arm around Kane as well, and guided the knife to rest against Kane's collarbone.

A shiver ran down Kane's spine, so fierce, Everet felt it echo through his own body.

"Cold?" Everet asked.

Kane huffed. "You bloody well know that temperature has nothing to do with it."

"True," Everet allowed, as he slowly traced the blunt point of the knife around one of Kane's nipples. The little bud immediately peaked and hardened for him. "It's all to do with how good the silver feels against you, isn't it?"

*

Kane tried to take a deep breath, but he couldn't seem to force enough air into his lungs. His head spun, but he knew damn well that it had nothing to do with a lack of oxygen, temperature, or any of that bull. It had everything to do with an overload of silveryness.

His mind swirled with sparkling clouds. "It's almost like being high."

"It is?"

Kane hadn't realised he'd uttered the confession out loud until Everet replied. It was too late to take it back now, pointless to curse himself for an idiot. Kane simply nodded. "The silver, it's..." He shook his head. There were no words to describe the way the element seemed to seep through his skin every time Everet traced it over his body.

As Kane stood there, naked and mute, Everet moved the knife down. He had to slide it around to the side of his stomach to pass his other hand. Then, suddenly, it was on Kane's thigh.

It was right next to his cock.

Kane gasped and thrust forward his hips.

Silver against his cock. His mind came dangerously close to disintegrating at the prospect.

"Tell me what you want," Everet commanded.

The knife. Sex. You. Silver. Everything. So many things sprang to the front of Kane's mind, but if he could only have one thing then there was really no choice for him to make. Only one of those things was truly essential to his future happiness.

"You."

Everet hesitated, as if Kane's answer had caught him completely off guard.

"I want you," Kane repeated, with complete conviction. "I want your cock buried in my arse, your body pinning me down and your lips against mine. I want you wrapped around me, filling me, grabbing me, everything. You said you own me. I want you to prove it." By the end of his speech, Kane's words tumbled out so fast he had no control over them and barely any breath left to say them.

Everet made no immediate reply. Kane tensed, pleading with any deity who might be inclined to take pity on him.

Still without saying a word, Everet very slowly began to slide the silver knife blade up and down Kane's shaft.

Kane dropped his head back until it rested on Everet's shoulder. He parted his lips and gasped up toward the ceiling, but he didn't open his eyes—not while he lacked permission to do that.

Everet's touch was so controlled, so determined. Then, without any warning, it changed into something so different, it was almost impossible for Kane to believe he still shared the room with the same man.

Everet pushed Kane forward. There was no way Kane could stop himself opening his eyes as self-preservation kicked in. He reached out to break his fall. His hands slid against the spoons and knives laid out across the table. Silver caressed his palms. As he lost the last of his balance, his whole torso came to rest on the rows of freshly polished silver.

Even before his brain had processed what had just happened, Kane reached out to touch and caress his hoard. Everet caught hold of Kane's wrist and twisted it up behind his back, stopping him short, forcing him down against the silver. His cheek pressed down on the bowl of a spoon. A blunt knife pushed along the line of his neck.

So much silver. So much sparkle. So much perfection...

Everet soon had two well-lubed fingers working inside Kane, preparing him for his cock. Kane couldn't work out what felt better—what happened inside him, or what pressed against his skin.

It was too much for any man to be able to take in silence. Kane didn't even try to control the words that left his lips anymore. He had no idea if he praised Everet or cursed him. He might have told Everet he loved him or hated him. Silver, quicksilver, submission, sex. Everything blurred together in Kane's mind.

It was only when Everet thrust deep inside him, lodging his shaft in Kane's arse to the hilt in one harsh movement, that events crystallized into one solid reference point that Kane could focus upon.

He cried out as he bucked against the table and silver stroked the whole underside of his body. Even the head of his cock rubbed against a highly polished surface.

Kane squirmed, relishing every bit of it. Everet strengthened his grip around the wrist he had pinned to Kane's back, sending another wave of bliss through him.

Closing his eyes, Kane watched flashes of silver and gold explode in the darkness. He couldn't do much except flex his muscles around Everet's cock and try to make sure Everet enjoyed the ride, too.

All too soon, Kane felt the ice crack beneath him. He crashed down into the arctic water beneath the winter freeze. There was no air, just pleasure so sharp and brittle it felt more like pain. Water splashed above his head. He had no idea if he was waving or drowning, if he wanted to be rescued or not.

He cried out, but heard nothing past the ringing in his ears. Finally, he managed to drag a full breath into his lungs. He gasped and spluttered, his whole body shaking as he pulled himself back to the surface and came face to face with the real world.

Everet tugged at Kane's wrist, forcing him to stand long before he was physically capable of attempting such a mammoth undertaking. Kane immediately stumbled.

Both Everet's arms slid around him, but they didn't hold him up, they merely made his descent toward the bare wooden floor of the silver room a little more controlled.

Everet went down with him. Wrapping his arms more firmly around Kane, he held him close to his chest and cradled him there. Everet made a noise in the back of his throat, which he probably intended to be reassuring. It sounded more like the kind of sound a sabre-toothed tiger might make if it tried to purr like a tabby kitten.

Kane closed his eyes. He didn't need so much fuss made over him, but he couldn't deny that it was very nice to have a strong warm body to rest against while he came down from his high.

He smiled. He'd always known that Everet would let him get high sooner or later. It involved silver, and there had even been a certain sort of quickness involved, on Kane's part at least. He was reasonably sure Everet hadn't lasted that long either.

"Don't look too pleased with yourself," Everet whispered in his ear.

Kane raised an eyebrow. "You came too." He had no doubt about that. Everet's softened shaft pressed against his skin, sticky with the residue of both lube and Everet's cum.

"Yeah, I did," Everet agreed. "I wasn't talking about that."

Kane sluggishly lifted his head. "Then what?"

"I mean, before we leave the room, someone is going to have to wash the cum off all the silverware you just came all over."

Kane glanced up toward the table. Damn. He had, hadn't he? He shrugged. "Was worth it."

Everet pressed a kiss to the top of Kane's head. "Yeah. It was." He chuckled then. "How about you wash and I help you dry?"

* * * * *

"Good evening, sire." It took all of Everet's self-control to look straight at Ori and not immediately turn his attention to Kane.

"Hello." Ori smiled. "Did you have a good day?"

"Yes, thank you, sire."

Everet didn't need to ask the same question in return. He knew what a poor liar Ori was. If Kane had done anything wrong during the day, it would have shown plainly on the swan's face.

The tiny bit of tension that had lingered in Everet's spine dissipated. This made it twelve days in a row that Kane had proved to be an exemplary worker—a true credit to his master and his nest.

Everet took a deep breath. He'd done his duty and made conversation with a man who thoroughly deserved his respect—not to mention his thanks for the silver-room suggestion. And, now, Everet would have his reward for remembering to be polite to Ori. He allowed himself to turn toward Kane.

Hard work suited the magpie. Nothing else had ever made his eyes shine so brightly—not just with pleasure, but with pride as well.

"Did you have a good day?" Everet asked.

Kane nodded rapidly. He strode across to fetch Everet from his place by the door, just as he had every other day.

Everet dutifully followed his somewhat polish-stained lover across the room and happily praised the progress Kane and Ori had made on cleaning and polishing a huge silver punch bowl. The thing was monstrous. Filled to the brim, it would have held enough to get every avian in the nest thoroughly sloshed.

"You did really well," Everet said. He pressed a kiss against Kane's lips, but this time he managed not to let Kane lead him too far astray. He kept the kiss chaste and quickly turned his attention back to Ori before he forgot the swan was even in the room.

"I'd better be on my way," Ori said, halfway to the door already. "Raynard is expecting me upstairs." It had never been more obvious that he knew exactly what they did in the silver room once he left. His hand was halfway to the handle when an unexpected knock sounded on the other side of the door.

Everet turned his attention to the door, suddenly on his alert as both a member of the security flock and a master.

Ori frowned slightly and opened the door. "Yes?"

"A visiting party has arrived from another nest. Mr. Hamilton requests that you come to the main reception room to greet them as soon as it is convenient, sire."

Ori indicated his willingness to do that, but the messenger didn't step back to make way for him to leave the way Everet expected him to.

"Mr. Hamilton also orders Everet and Kane to attend him in the main reception room, immediately."

Ori glanced over his shoulder. Everet wished he could have told him what was going on, if only because that meant he'd have known for himself. All he could do was shrug.

Ori turned back to the messenger. "You may tell Mr. Hamilton we are all on our way. Thank you."

"Yes, sire."

"I don't want to go to some boring meeting," Kane began.

"It's possible that we could come back down here after the meeting," Everet said.

He didn't actually add the words *unless you throw a temper tantrum* to the end of his sentence, but Kane still seemed to hear them, loud and clear. He sighed, but uttered no further complaint as they made their way up through the nest. They eventually reached one of the big reception rooms used to entertain high-ranking avians from nests both near and farther afield.

As soon as a wren opened the door for them, it was obvious that these particular visitors obviously weren't from another all-male nest.

Everet hid his surprise well. Kane didn't. He stalled less than a foot into the room. Placing a firm, guiding hand on the small of Kane's back, Everet tried to nudge him subtly forward.

Nothing. Kane seemed to be welded in place.

"Kane?" Everet asked softly.

Ori had moved forward without them and now stood at Raynard's side. The guests were so busy greeting him, they didn't seem to have noticed the little scene in the doorway, but Everet knew that situation wouldn't last forever.

Kane didn't reply to his prompt. He didn't move. His eyes remained fixed on something on the other side of the room. Everet followed his gaze. A woman hung off an older man's arm. Her skirt was short, her heels high, and her jewellery clearly expensive. Everything about her screamed trophy wife, or perhaps a straightforward mistress.

Everet frowned. Kane couldn't be *that* shocked by the sight of a woman in the nest, not even by one who seemed to be glued to the side of a man at least twice her age.

Suddenly Hamilton turned the full force of his scrutiny toward them.

"I'd like to introduce you to our recently promoted Head of Internal Security at the nest—Everet, a raven of excellent standing in our community."

Everet blinked, never having heard the formal title that he'd apparently acquired, along with his mountain of paperwork. He'd never heard Hamilton speak so highly of him either.

The eagle's attention moved to Kane. His expression morphed into one of complete distaste. "And, I believe at least one of you already knows the magpie, Kane."

Everet slid his arm a little farther around Kane, doing his best to offer very general reassurance until he knew enough to offer something more specific.

"Come here, Kane," Hamilton ordered.

Kane remained exactly where he was. As far as Everet could

work out, it had nothing to do with disobedience, and everything to do with temporary paralysis.

"Kane!" Hamilton snapped.

"Hello, darling," the woman said, her tone full of joy at seeing Kane. If the emotion hadn't been brittle and obviously fake, she might have gone up in Everet's estimation.

Her words rather than Hamilton's order seemed to finally convince Kane to take a step forward. He walked across the room in slow even strides. Everet kept close to his side.

"Hello, Crystal."

"You know each other?" Raynard asked from the other side of the group.

"Yes," Kane said, his tone emotionless, as if he'd gone completely numb. "She's my sister."

Chapter Thirteen

Everyone looked shocked, except Hamilton.

Everet's eyes narrowed as he studied the elderly eagle. "That's why you invited them here, isn't it?"

Hamilton peered over his glasses at him. "I don't believe I need your permission to entertain whomever I wish in *my* nest."

He obviously intended to intimidate Everet with the reminder of their respective ranks. All he did was make Everet even more determined to protect Kane from whatever the hell the sanctimonious bastard was plotting against him.

"If you're trying to fob him off onto us," Crystal said. "Don't bother. My Harold doesn't swing both ways, do you, darling?"

The old man she'd been fawning over ever since they'd entered the room laughed. Crystal joined in.

Everet glanced down at Kane. He didn't laugh. The light that shone so brightly in his eyes while they were in the silver room was gone. As Everet watched, the last traces of expression faded from Kane's face.

"Thanks, *sis*, but I've never needed your help to catch a meal-ticket."

Crystal looked them both up and down. Tossing her hair back with a hand laden with huge, flashy rings, she laughed. "Oh, darling, from what I can see, you need all the help you can get."

The differences in the two siblings' clothes, or in the amount of precious metals that decorated their bodies, couldn't have been more different. The clothes Everet had bought for Kane were of the same quality as those he wore himself, but their styling was simple, and no jewellery had been added to Kane's outfit.

The smudges of polish probably didn't help in her eyes either. Everet had no idea what Kane thought of them, but for himself, he loved them. Signs of hard work and diligence weren't to be sneered at. Lack of vanity could only be a good thing.

"*Dating* some cop or other might be worthwhile if you find yourself in a jam, but you should know better than to think one could be useful in the long run," Crystal said, her words sharper and more vicious by the moment. "He'll never be able to look after you the way Harold takes care of me. Will he, Harold, darling?" She tittered as if it was a joke. Harold obviously didn't care if everyone knew his lover was bought and paid for. He chuckled along with her as if she were the funniest comic ever to stand up before a mic.

Kane remained perfectly serious.

Everet moved his hand up to rest on Kane's shoulder. The woman was Kane's sister. Everet had no idea how Kane would react if anyone pointed out that she was doing a bloody good impression of a complete arsehole. He forced himself to remain silent, restricting himself to observing until a clearer course of action presented itself.

The man with Crystal, Harold, lifted a champagne glass to his lips. On the inside of his wrist, Everet made out his species mark. A pheasant. Not the brightest of birds at the best of times. Far too amenable to be sensible—any magpie who hadn't been taught the difference between right and wrong could easily run rings around one.

Hamilton waved a hand toward a little group of chairs and sofas set around a low table. Gilding and dark green upholstery covered everything within view. "Please, do take a seat, everyone. After you, sire."

Tension radiated off every fibre of Kane's body. He'd come so far in the last few weeks. Everet couldn't risk forcing him to remain in his sister's company. "Thank you, sir," he began. "But—"

Before he could finish, Kane stepped forward and stood at one end of a fancy sofa that no one had laid claim to. Everet quickly took his place next to him, ready to occupy the other end of the sofa when it was their turn to sit down.

Ori quickly took his seat, then the birds of prey settled themselves into their chairs, followed by the guests at the nest. Of those present, Kane and Everet were the lowest avians in the pecking order.

For the first time, Everet's spine stiffened at having to wait while the order of precedence made itself felt throughout the group. Kane was barely holding himself together as it was—Everet could sense how nervous he was, how close to the cliff-edge he stood.

Waiting around like idiots couldn't help.

"We don't have to stay here if you don't want to," Everet whispered to Kane, as it finally became their turn to lower themselves into their seats and he had the chance to dip his head and whisper in his ear.

Kane didn't even glance toward him. If his attention had been fixed on his sister, that would have been understandable, but it wasn't. He stared directly ahead, gazing blindly at the wall opposite him.

Everet followed Kane's line of sight, but nothing special hung on the wall there. There was no mirror, no portrait, just the same ancient decoration that covered the rest of the walls.

Everet set his hand on Kane's leg, determined to let him know that, whatever was about to happen, he wouldn't have to face it alone. If Kane took any reassurance from his presence, he didn't let on.

"I'm sure you'll be happy to hear that Kane is making a good home for himself in our nest," Ori suddenly said to their guests. "He's becoming a great credit to us."

Everet could have kissed Ori for his kindness—if he hadn't been sure Raynard and Kane would both have killed him for it on the spot if he'd tried anything of the sort.

Crystal laughed as if the swan's words couldn't be anything other than a joke. Hamilton's lips twisted, as if he was amused, too.

Kane didn't smile. He sat so still, Everet had to study him for what felt like an age to be sure that he was breathing.

"Perhaps you'd be kind enough to tell us a little bit about your brother's life before he came to the nest," Hamilton drawled, twirling the stem of his glass between his fingers. "I'm sure we'd all find that quite fascinating."

Everet jerked his attention away from Kane. "With all due respect, sir. Surely it's the way Kane acts *now* that's important. Everything else—"

"When I want your opinion, I'll ask for it," Hamilton snapped.

"Oh, dear." Crystal smirked. "It looks like someone's afraid he'll be embarrassed by your indiscretions, Kane. You should have chosen your protector more carefully. If he can't deal with—"

"I am not ashamed of Kane," Everet cut in. Politeness and nest politics could both be damned. He made no attempt to mask his

202

anger. "Nothing you can tell me will change that."

"You're so sure?" she asked, sitting back in her chair and crossing very long, tanned legs.

"Yes," Everet bit out.

"Then you can hardly object to hearing a few highlights, can you?"

Everet glared across the room at her. She'd outmanoeuvred him, and they both bloody well knew it.

Taking one step toward the door would ensure that everyone there thought he was ashamed of Kane. Worse, it might make Kane think that, too. Everet scrolled through every curse word he knew.

He couldn't fix this. Neither could Raynard and Ori, from the other side of the little seating area. Everet turned to Kane. He still hadn't moved his gaze from the point he'd selected on the wall when they first sat down.

"It's up to you," Everet said.

Kane took a slow breath. "I'll stay."

Everet waited for more, but that really seemed to be it. He didn't ask Everet to stay with him. All Everet could do was hope that was because it didn't even occur to Kane that his master would leave him there on his own.

"So glad we have your permission to continue," Hamilton spat.

"Well, let me see," Crystal mused, twisting a lock of long, blonde hair around her fingers. "There are so many stories to tell…"

Everet gritted his teeth so hard he risked shattering his molars.

"Kane started young," Crystal said with obvious relish. "*Really* young. He found his first sugar-daddy almost an entire decade before he completed his first shift."

"As if I had a choice," Kane snapped. He finally looked toward his sister, his anger flaring so quickly, Everet had no time to step in and try to check it.

"You will be silent," Hamilton commanded.

Everet shifted forward in his seat. "Sir!"

"You will *both* be silent. If you can't keep your peace, Everet, Kane will stay, and you will leave. I don't want to hear another word from you."

Everything Everet wanted to say to the eagle died unsaid. He couldn't risk being thrown out, couldn't take the chance that Kane would be left there on his own. He realised then that he'd never truly hated another man—not until that moment.

"Mr. Hamilton, if I am permitted to speak."

Ori!

Everet turned his gaze toward the swan. So did everyone else in the room.

"All I've asked for is a true account of Kane's history, sire," Hamilton told Ori, his tone suddenly all civility. "It's a perfectly reasonable request, if he wishes to become part of this nest."

"Will Kane be allowed to present his version of events, too, sir?" Ori asked.

"Certainly, sire. When his sister has finished, we'll all hear his side. I have no interest in being unfair."

Bollocks—the only thing he was interested in was proving that he'd been right when he said Kane would be a disgrace to the nest and there was no point trying to reform him. The only thing Hamilton had been interested in for months was proving that he was still the best man to run the nest—that neither Raynard nor Ori would do a better job. That fairness and kindness were weaknesses rather than strengths.

Everet glanced at Kane, hoping that Ori's intervention provided him at least a little relief, but apparently not. He'd gone back to staring at that spot on the wall.

"Crystal, if you'll continue?" Hamilton requested.

"Of course," she trilled. "I've got plenty of stories about Kane. Do you know he once managed to run five different men at one time, getting each one of them to pay through the nose for him? He took the money and spent it all on drugs."

She and her companion laughed.

"You should have seen their faces when they found out they'd all been played. You should have seen Kane's face when they'd cut him back down to size, too—I've never seen anyone so messed up!"

For some reason, they found that funny, too.

Kane would have his chance to tell his side soon. Everet repeated that fact over and over again inside his head as he listened to Crystal prattle on and on, and Hamilton encouraging her every step of the way.

Everet kept his hand on Kane's knee, hoping his touch somehow helped Kane feel less alone under the onslaught, but she seemed to go on for hours. It was torture for Everet, he could only imagine how much worse it was for Kane.

Kane's a whore. Kane's stupid. Kane's a thief. Kane can't be trusted. Not one word she said was in any way complimentary about her brother.

Halfway through it, Everet became convinced that Kane had blocked out the world, and everything she said flew straight over his head. But Everet couldn't afford to do that himself, not if he wanted to be a good master to Kane. He listened to every word. More than that, he really thought about what they meant when they were all joined together.

Kane's used to being used. He's used to being treated like a whore. He's used to being beaten black and blue and having to steal to survive. What she described wasn't a life where a man might receive any hint of kindness and compassion from the men who screwed him—or even a life where he could find some sort of discipline and consistency.

Kane had lived exactly the kind of life he'd been born to expect and Everet's heart wept for him.

"Thank you, Crystal. I think that gives us a very complete impression of Kane's character," Hamilton said, smugly.

"May I ask a few questions, sir?" Everet said.

Hamilton frowned over his glasses at him.

"That only seems fair," Raynard said. "Everet is Kane's master after all."

Hamilton glanced at Raynard, then at Ori. "Very well," he said, with obvious distaste.

"You said that Kane was involved in prostitution," Everet said.

"Very involved," she corrected—as if she hadn't dug a big enough hole for Kane already.

"Are you involved in it, too?"

She raised one heavily plucked eyebrow at him. "I know better than to give away for free what men will pay good money for, if that's what you mean."

"I'll take that as a yes," Everet said. "Your parents, they earned their money likewise?"

"I fail to see your point," she snapped.

"My point is—"

Suddenly, Kane leapt out of his chair. Twisting away from

Everet, he raced across the room.

Everet had been so focused on working the best way to show everyone what kind of man Kane really was, it took him far too long to react. Kane was out through the door before Everet even turned around.

Everet jumped up. He ran after Kane as fast as he could, but Kane already had a good head start. Hamilton called out for him to stop, but Everet only cared about closing the gap between himself and Kane as quickly as possible.

Kane could be bloody quick when he wanted to be. This time, there wasn't the shock of an alarm connected to an apartment door to slow him down. As Everet turned the corner at the end of the hallway that lead away from the nest's best reception room, he found the corridor ahead of him empty.

Letting out a curse, he slammed his hand against the expensive wallpaper that stretched all the way up to the richly decorated ceilings above. There were far too many corridors leading off this one, and no way of knowing which to race along.

Which direction would Kane have taken?

Kane didn't know this part of the building. Everet only know it because he'd have to be a bloody incompetent security officer not to be able to navigate every part of his territory. This wasn't the part of the nest they lived in. It wasn't even a part of the nest where they often worked.

Everet's eyes darted toward the various passageways.

What were Kane's options? Where would he go?

Everet pushed a hand through his hair and rubbed at the back of his neck.

Their apartment? The silver room? Somewhere else? Maybe he wanted to jump head first off the wagon and was heading down to the busiest part of the nest hoping to find someone who would help him get high. It was possible—even understandable, after his sister threw him to the birds of prey that way. And all because Hamilton wanted to prove that he was a better judge of character than Ori and Raynard.

Everet cursed. Standing around hating Hamilton wouldn't do any good. Two places seemed more probable destinations than anywhere else. Everet flipped a mental coin and headed toward their apartment.

Every man in the nest seemed to crowd the corridors and be

determined to get in the way. Desperate to get to his flat, Everet pushed his way roughly through the mob.

Kane would be there, he told himself. It was the obvious place for him to go. Everet would open the door, and Kane would be right there, as defiant and as in need of guidance as ever. Or maybe Kane would have hidden himself away in the bedroom, seeking solace and reassurance in the sex they could have there.

That would be even better. They could cheer each other up straight away. That would prove to Kane that nothing had changed between them faster than any words could.

Everet pushed open the door leading into his flat. "Kane?"

His gaze darted into every corner of the living room. Nothing. He rushed to the bathroom door and pushed it open, praying for angry words that demanded Kane should have the right to take a leak in private. No one stood in the small tiled space.

Everet raced across the living room and jerked the bedroom door open. Empty.

Everet shook his head at himself. He was an idiot. It should have been obvious that Kane would head straight for the safety and reassurance of the silver room. Everet raced out of his apartment and along the corridors leading down to the vault-like room hidden away in the servants' quarters, where no bird of prey ever ventured. Yes. The silver room. That's where Kane would be.

Everet raced down the stairs, taking them three or four at a time. He didn't care if he fell—if that got him to the bottom of the stairs more quickly, all the better, but his balance held out. He made it all the way to the corridor leading to the silver room without tripping once.

As Everet threw himself around the corner and hurtled toward him, the guard stationed at the silver room's door dropped the magazine he'd been idly flicking through.

The guy's eyes opened very wide. "I only glanced at—"

Everet grabbed him by his shirt and pushed him back against the wall alongside the door.

"Is Kane in there?"

"I swear, I've been—"

"I don't care!" Everet shouted. "Read whatever the hell you like. Jack off to porn right here in the corridor for all I care." He pulled the guy away from the wall and slammed him against it again. "Is Kane in there?"

The guard shook his head.

Everet's heart rate doubled. It wasn't as if Kane could have snuck in, no matter how interested in his magazine the guard might have been, but Everet was past the point of caring about logic.

"Open the door."

His hands were shaking with so much fear he dropped the keys twice, but eventually the guard obeyed. Everet strode into the middle of the silver room and turned a complete three-hundred and sixty degrees. It wasn't as if Kane could have hidden in one of the vases or goblets that filled so many of the glass cases, but Everet had no idea where else to look.

He closed his eyes for a moment, deep in thought. He pinched the bridge of his nose as he bowed his head, desperate to do the right thing.

He could order all the other men in the security flock to search the nest for Kane. That would let him look in dozens of different places at once.

No. As tempting as it was, Everet shook his head. That would make it seem like Kane was a criminal who had to be hunted down, and he wasn't.

Everet wasn't a security guard right then, he wasn't in charge of anything in the nest. He was just a man who wanted to find his lover, wrap his arms around him, and tell him that everything would be fine.

Everet pushed his hand through his hair and turned around again, as if Kane might suddenly pop into existence behind him. No such luck.

There was no sign of Kane. There were no thoughts in Everet's head now, either. It was just a complete blank. Everet squared his shoulders and walked out of the silver room as calmly as he could, well aware that the security guy, whose name he couldn't remember, watched his every move and would no doubt report back to the others at the first opportunity. Bloody gossips, the lot of them.

"If Kane comes here, I'm to be informed immediately," Everet said.

"Yes, sir."

Everet made his way up to the main part of the nest. He walked more slowly now, trying to give himself time to think clearly and come up with a plan. He scanned the face of every man who passed him, hoping against hope that one of them would turn out to be Kane—that good fortune would be on his side, just once.

Everet wasn't the kind of man who ever relied on luck, but just this once he'd make an exception. He needed to find Kane, right now—and maybe not just for Kane's benefit.

* * * * *

Kane wrapped his arms around his knees and curled himself into an even tighter version of the foetal position. The room wasn't cold, but it didn't need to be. The chill that seeped into his bones came from deep down within himself.

It wouldn't have been so bad if stone-cold fury had filled him. If he'd been able to hate someone, to want to lash out at someone, it might have been easier. But no, the only person Kane hated was himself.

He frowned. He supposed he could lash out at himself. He could hurt himself. That might work. He could slash at his skin and slam his fists into his own body. He could make himself hurt so badly it blocked out everything else. Pain was hot, wasn't it? It might ease the chill inside him.

Quicksilver was hot, too. He'd never be allowed to see the inside of the silver room again, but he could make silver dance through his veins instead. There was no point staying away from the stuff anymore. He might as well shoot up.

He trailed his fingers over the inside of his elbow. The skin there had stopped itching weeks ago, but the very thought of getting high made the part of him that had loved quicksilver expand within his mind. Kane closed his eyes as he heard someone walk past, but he didn't open his eyes to see if they cast a shadow he might be able to identify. He didn't want to see anyone.

He wasn't going to see anyone ever again.

Kane couldn't control much. He couldn't change who he was. He couldn't change what he'd done with his life. It was too late for anything like that now. All he could do was lie there, with the cold freezing him from the inside out, and wait for it all to be over.

Another set of footsteps passed by the dank little space Kane had found for himself, down where he belonged, at the bottom of the barrel with the rest of the dregs. He closed his eyes tighter and tried not to think about what Crystal had said—about the man who'd heard her say it.

Kane had spent the best part of his life not thinking about anything at all. Surely it couldn't be that hard to regain the ability when he needed it most?

* * * * *

"Everet!"

Everet spun around. "Ambrose?"

The huge albatross lumbered to a stop alongside him. "What the hell happened?"

"Happened?" Everet repeated.

Kane! If something had happened anywhere in the nest, it was reasonable to assume that there could only be one man in the middle of it on any day. Today that was especially true.

"What's happened? Have you seen Kane? Where is he?"

Ambrose frowned down at Everet, out of breath from his sprint along the corridor. "You don't know?"

"Know what? Where is he?" Everet asked. His heart raced so fast, he wasn't sure he could stop it from exploding out of his chest if his friend didn't hurry the hell up and spit out what he knew.

Whatever it was, Everet had to know—now.

If something was broken, as Kane's master, he needed the information so he could fix it. If Kane was broken—

No. A shot of pure terror rushed through Everet's veins. Kane couldn't be broken, not in any way that couldn't be fixed, please, no…

Everet tried to shake Ambrose by the shoulders, but the other man was so big he couldn't move him an inch. All he could do was grab Ambrose's shirtsleeves and tug so hard he almost tore them at the seams.

"He's down in the cages and…"

That was all Everet heard. The "s" at the end of the word cages had barely hit the air before he started running.

For a few steps, Everet heard Ambrose hurrying along in his wake, but he was more narrowly built than the albatross, and far faster over the ground. And, when it came right down to it, Ambrose probably cared about whoever he knocked over and that slowed him down.

Everet had already run along almost every corridor in the nest, up and down a dozen different flights of stairs in his search for

Kane. His stamina held out until he was within sight of the guards' desk set in the anteroom leading to the cages, but getting there took every scrap of energy he had left to give. He half collapsed, bracing himself with his hands on the desk. His head spun. If he'd been a cartoon character, he was sure that pretty little stars would have circled his head.

He pulled in one deep breath and demanded that be enough. "Kane. Show me where he is. Now."

The man behind the desk didn't argue. He didn't ask questions. Grabbing his keys, he led the way down the hall. A man waving a loaded gun couldn't have achieved anyone's co-operation more quickly.

Almost at once, the small room opened up into a space higher than any other in the nest. On each side of the central guards' walkway, narrow cage bars ran from the ground all the way up to the ceiling; at least two-dozen yards above them.

Lines of metal filled the world. Everet had hated the cages the first time he set eyes on them. That was almost a year ago, when they'd first been brought back into use.

His opinion of them hadn't changed. Maybe some people thought they were more humane than a whipping, but he wasn't sure. The space closed in on him at the very thought of being trapped in one of the tall, narrow spaces.

He'd have walked more quickly if he could have, but it would have meant stepping into the back of the guard. And, even if he didn't want to admit it, rushing would have involved scraping together supplies of energy he didn't actually possess.

They passed the first pair of cages. One was empty. On their right-hand side, a man slept sprawled out on a narrow cot. A small slate board hung on the outside of his cage—*Crow. Drunk. Until sober.*

A few cages along, they passed by another occupied cage. *Seagull. Repeatedly disturbing the peace. Two days.*

Everet glanced past the metal railings. The gull was in his avian form, perched on a bar attached to the back wall of the cage. As their eyes met, it extended its wings and cawed at him.

"Bloody noisy things," the guard muttered under his breath.

They walked on. Everet found himself holding his breath. Right at the end of the row, he spotted another slate with something written on it. Everet turned his attention to the guard when the man stopped and started looking through a large ring holding keys. He selected the appropriate one.

Everet caught hold of the guard's arm and stopped him before he could reach for the heavy padlock that held the cage closed. He put out his free hand. The guard placed the correct key into it.

The guard took one look at Everet's expression, turned on his heel and walked away. He strode past the cage Kane occupied, and down a corridor that could have led straight to hell, for all Everet cared.

Everet stepped forward, but he didn't look beyond the bars. A bitter taste filled the back of his mouth. His stomach tightened into knots more complicated than any seagull had ever used. He had no idea what he'd see when he looked into the cage, but he couldn't let his fear keep him ignorant of the facts forever.

Summoning up every ounce of courage he could find, Everet lifted his gaze and peered into the cage.

Kane.

Kane was there. That was the main thing. They were together. Everything else could be worked out from there. Everet forced himself to take a deep, calming breath before he assessed the situation further.

Kane sat in the middle of a narrow bed, his legs drawn up close to his chest and his arms wrapped around his knees. His head was bowed so low, his forehead rested on his arm.

His face was blocked from view, as was much of his body. A hundred injuries could've been hidden from Everet's gaze. There was only one way to find out the full truth. A man couldn't call himself a good master if he didn't step up and deal with each and every scrape his submissive endured.

"Kane?"

Whatever caused his voice to sound calm and steady, Everet sent silent thanks for it up to a god he'd never believed in. Forget interrogating fools who'd caused trouble in the nest; *this* was when Everet really needed to be in complete control of himself.

Kane's head snapped up. His face was deathly pale, but there wasn't a mark on it.

Everet let out the breath he'd been holding, but his pulse didn't slow in the slightest. "What happened?"

Kane's Adam's apple bobbed as he swallowed several times

in quick succession. His eyes were red. He'd obviously been crying.

Kane shrugged, but Everet felt sure that his silence had nothing to do with him feeling incapable of speaking past his emotions.

Unwrapping one of his arms from around his body, Kane rubbed at his face with his shirtsleeve. His efforts did little to make his cheeks appear less tear-stained.

"Kane?" Everet prompted.

Kane turned his face away from him.

Forget taking it easy and not spooking Kane. Everet slid the key into the padlock on the cage door. The mechanism was well oiled. It turned over easily. The lock sprung open.

"You can't do that!" Kane straightened up in his seat on the bed. "You're not allowed in here. Guard!"

Everet jerked open the barred door, stepped inside, and pulled the cage door shut behind him. "I want an answer."

"And I want you to get the hell out of here." Kane launched himself to his feet. He used every ounce of momentum he had and pushed against Everet's chest. He hit against Everet's shoulders and neck in a frantic effort to shove him out of the cage, but he failed to move him a single inch.

Everet caught hold of Kane's wrists and tried to pull the smaller man into a tight embrace before he hurt himself with his flailing about. Kane allowed nothing. He kept pushing, kept struggling. "Get off me. You can't just come in here and do whatever the hell you want with me. You can't—"

"Yes, I can. I'm your master."

"Get off me."

What had made Kane freak out before? Fear of being disowned.

"You're mine," Everet tried. "That hasn't changed."

"Yes, it has. I quit." Kane looked up at Everet, but he didn't seem to be able to actually focus on anything. His eyes were wild. His movements were jerky. He was stronger than anyone his size should have been.

Everet's whole body tensed.

What have you taken?

He kept the words to himself. Asking Kane would have been pointless. He'd have lied.

Everet knew that if he'd fallen off the wagon, Kane wouldn't be able to do anything else: the drugs would call all the shots and every scrap of progress they'd made would have been wiped away as easily as a needle could pierce a man's vein.

Kane delivered a particularly vicious kick to Everet's shin. "I don't want to belong to you. Get off me!"

Everet stilled. Holding on to Kane's wrists, he simply stood there and let the other man rail against him, kicking and pushing at him with all his might. Kane cursed and shouted until his voice started to give out. He fought until he was so breathless he became unable to stand on his own.

Suddenly, he was completely reliant on Everet for support. Everet wasn't just holding him still now, he was holding him up.

"Tell me what happened after you left the meeting room," Everet ordered, when silence finally settled over the cage. Exhaustion filled every cell in his body, but he made sure it didn't seep into his words.

"None of your business." The words were barely muttered loud enough for anyone to hear. It was obvious that Kane's heart wasn't in it any more.

Everet had never seen a man look so defeated. He longed to wrap his arms around Kane, but he didn't dare let go of his wrists just yet. It wasn't beyond the realms of possibility that Kane merely wanted to lull him into a false sense of security.

Unable to ignore their surroundings, Everet looked at the bars around them. Knowing that Kane was once more safe with him, another question presented itself for his consideration. Who the hell would dare put his submissive in a cage without his permission—without even sending word of his submissive's location to him? It was tantamount to a challenge for ownership.

"Who brought you down here?" Everet demanded.

"I don't need to be *taken* places. I've got legs. I can go wherever I want without someone hovering over me warning me to look both ways before crossing the road." Kane stared at the floor, pouting like a child who realised he couldn't get his own way and so now intended to make life as annoying as possible for the man who refused to indulge him.

"You put yourself in here?" Everet asked.

Kane shrugged, but it was obviously the truth. It would have been too bizarre a lie for anyone to tell—even Kane, even if he was high as a red kite.

"Why would you do that?" Everet demanded.

Another shrug.

"Answer me!" For the first time, Everet let a little of the fear he'd felt as he raced around the nest out as anger.

Kane looked up. His expression made it clear he was just as scared and just as angry as Everet. A little of the fight he'd shown earlier came back. He straightened up, squaring his shoulders.

"Why?" Everet repeated.

"Isn't it obvious?" Kane demanded.

Chapter Fourteen

"If it was obvious, I wouldn't have to ask," Everet said, as calmly as he could, which given the circumstances wasn't as calmly as he would have liked. If it sounded like he spoke through gritted teeth, it was for a very good reason.

"Because this is where I belong!" Kane suddenly yelled.

Everet stared down at Kane for several seconds in complete silence. He had no answer to that. The statement was so bizarre, he wasn't sure an appropriate response existed. "No, you—"

"What would you know about it?" Kane demanded, before Everet could get a third word out. "You're not one of us. You don't know what magpies are really like."

"I know you," Everet said.

"No," Kane cut in. "*I* know me. And I'm just like her, like my parents, like every magpie that's ever lived—I'm like all of them!"

"No, you're—"

"Stop saying that," Kane demanded, completely ignoring the fact Everet hadn't actually managed to finish saying anything once, let alone repeat it. "You want to know what the rest of my family's like? We're all the same; thieves, whores, and gold diggers. Happy now?"

Everet had guessed what kind of example the rest of Kane's family had set for him. However, the arguments about nature and nurture that he'd intended to set out in front of the elders, and Crystal, seemed pointless now.

Kane fell silent. He stared down at the way Everet's hands still encircled his wrists as if he'd never seen skin pressed against skin before. "You can't cure a man of his species, Ev. You saw her up there. She's a whore. So am I. You can't change that—no one can."

Everet thought he'd felt angry before. It was nothing compared to what he felt now. He stepped forward, forcing Kane to retreat. Pushing him back against the bars of the cage, he held Kane there with both hands.

Kane's eyes opened very wide with shock, but his expression soon changed to one of acceptance. Of being beaten? Or worse? Everet didn't know, but every possibility that ran through his mind turned his stomach.

"I'm not going to hurt you," Everet growled.

"Too late." The words were barely louder than a whisper.

Everet immediately checked his grip and eased the pressure he put against Kane's body. Looking down, he started checking for any injuries he'd failed to notice before.

Kane laughed as he shook his head. The sound was so sad; it cut through Everet to the bone.

"You don't have a clue, do you?" Kane asked. "I don't care how tight you hold me. I'm used to having it rough. But, you're worse than any back alley trick, you know that? You made me think I could actually have something like that, with someone like you! You made me think I could have the job, and the guy, and the life, and..." He shook his head again. "You bastard..." The words were just on the edge of hearing.

Kane tried to push Everet away, but there was far less strength behind his struggles now. It was as if he knew Everet wasn't going to budge, that he had no choice but to submit to whatever the guy pinning him to the wall wanted to do to him next.

Whatever Kane might have expected, Everet was too surprised to do anything. For what seemed to be years, he just stood there, trapped in a bubble of shock. "I've never offered you anything you can't have," he finally managed to say.

Kane shook his head, keeping his gaze averted; peering at the bars of the cage he'd put himself in, rather than risk looking Everet in the eye.

"You haven't done anything wrong. You know that, don't you? All you've actually done today is listen to some vindictive little shit-stirrer babble on about things that are all in the past. Nothing she said has changed anything between us. It hasn't changed your position in the nest."

"You're right," Kane said. "It didn't change anything."

His tone was off. Everet tensed, knowing that there was more to come. He couldn't possibly have won that easily.

"It just reminded me of who I really am. It's been fun playing pretend with you. And the sex has been great—I'll give you that. But no one can play a part forever." He shrugged, still not looking Everet in the eye. "Sooner or later, I'll start acting like a magpie again. I'll screw up; you'll have enough and get rid of me. I'll end up in the cage one way or another. So, I'm not going through all that bull, I'm jumping straight to the last bit and—"

Everet released one of Kane's wrists and put his hand over Kane's mouth. Against all his expectations, Kane didn't bite him. He didn't even lift his gaze.

"I won't get rid of you," Everet promised, willing Kane to believe him with every fibre of his soul.

Kane closed his eyes as if in more pain than ever.

Everet ached to be able to ease his agony, but he had no idea how anyone even started to heal the years of pain Kane had endured.

Kane mumbled against his palm. Everet lowered his hand.

"You have no idea, do you?" Kane whispered.

"About what?"

"That would just make it worse."

It took all of Everet's self-control not to curse the sheer rate at which Kane seemed to change what he wanted from him. "How the hell could it make things worse?"

"You deserve better than me. If you did get all stubborn about it and decide to keep me no matter what, I'd still start screwing up. You'd end up getting whipped, or worse, just because of me. I can't…"

Everet blinked down at him. "Keep in mind exactly what you just said. And tell me, do you still think you're too much of a magpie to fight against your instincts and put someone else first?"

Kane frowned for a moment, then shook his head, tossing aside everything Everet said as if it amounted to nothing.

"You can't change your species, Kane," Everet said, damned if he'd back down now. "You can't change the fact you might always be tempted to do some things that are wrong. But you can change whether or not you give in to temptation."

He stared down at Kane as he ran the past couple of weeks over inside his head.

"Scratch that, you *have* changed whether or not you give in to temptation."

Against every instinct he possessed, Everet forced himself to take half a step back, allowing Kane a little more freedom; making it clear that he trusted Kane to make good use of whatever independence he chose to give him. Even so, he kept hold of Kane's wrists—he was still his, after all.

Kane's frown deepened.

"You have no idea how proud I am of you, do you?" Everet asked. "Every species is prone to certain weaknesses, but you've faced every one of yours head on, and you're controlling them. Kane—you're amazing."

And I love you all the more for it. Everet somehow managed to keep those words back, but only because he was sure Kane wasn't in any condition to take them in right then.

*

Everet wasn't the kind of man who told jokes on a regular basis, but a bad sense of humour was the only explanation Kane could come up with. He tugged, trying to pull his hands out of Everet's grip. No one was more shocked than him when he succeeded.

He stared down at his freed wrists. It really was true, then. No matter what he said, Everet had no interest in holding on to him anymore. Until that moment, some stupid little part of Kane had actually believed that Everet gave a damn about him.

He shook his head as he turned his back on Everet. He should have known better. No one could really care about a magpie. He'd known that all his life. Why should it change now?

"Kane?" Everet asked.

"Don't," Kane whispered to the bars.

"Don't what?"

"Whatever you're going to say, don't," Kane tilted up his chin and turned back to face Everet. "Don't make fun of me—not for this."

Everet frowned. Even then, Kane couldn't help but acknowledge that Everet looked hot when he was grumpy. There really was no limit to Kane's own stupidity.

"I'm not joking about anything."

"Really?" Kane demanded.

Well, that was fine. If he had to play the game, fine. "So, what are ravens' weaknesses?" he asked, folding his arms across his chest.

Everet smiled slightly.

It wasn't just while grumpy he looked sexy as Satan himself. In spite of everything, Kane's cock tried to rise.

"An inclination to try to control the whole world; to make rules and bully people into following them for their own good, regardless of whether they want to or not."

Kane turned away. "That's not a weakness," he snapped, as he reached the other side of the cage.

"It would be if I wanted to date a man who doesn't get some sort of benefit from his lover micro-managing his day and checking up on him all the time," Everet said. He sat down on the narrow cot, no longer making any attempt to block Kane's exit or his path across the cage.

Stepping into the middle of the small space, Kane glared down at Everet. "You're not making this easy."

Everet leaned back against the only side of the cage constructed out of masonry rather than steel bars. The stark white paint was cold, hard and uncomfortable. Everet made it look like luxury.

Kane stood uneasily with nothing to lean against, nothing to support him—nothing except Everet. He quickly looked away from the raven, but he couldn't change the facts. Everet had supported him ever since they'd met. He did it as if it was the job he'd been born to do.

Everet was there, and he looked after him, and made sure that he obeyed the right rules. No other species had managed to get Kane to obey one rule, let alone dozens of the damn things. It came so naturally to Everet. And—

Kane closed his eyes.

"I've never promised that anything I asked you to do would be easy," Everet said.

Kane pointedly ignored that. Everet hadn't told him it would be like crawling over broken glass on his hands and knees either.

"But it feels good when you know you've done the right thing, doesn't it?"

"To know that you'll be pleased with me," Kane corrected, unable to keep the words back. Doing the right thing be damned. It felt good to know that Everet was pleased with him—felt better than almost anything in the world, apart, perhaps, from being screwed by Everet over a table covered in silver.

"That's a start," Everet said.

Kane swallowed. His head was so full of confusion he wanted to reach inside his brain and pull out the muddle of thoughts. That was obviously going to be the only way he'd ever get them all unravelled.

He looked down as he scuffed his toe against the bare concrete floor. "You said you're proud of me." He offered no opinion on such a declaration.

"Yes. I am." Everet leaned forward. "That said, at some point, we're *really* going to have to work on your inclination to run away when you get scared. I can't run around the nest like a madman again. I don't think my heart would take it."

Kane said nothing. Working on things in the future, meant having a future together, didn't it?

"It must have been a shock seeing your sister there," Everet added.

Kane shrugged. He shuffled his feet again. Somehow, he ended up taking a step closer to Everet in the process.

"I'm guessing you two don't get on?"

"No."

Everet said nothing. The silence demanded to be filled.

Kane had no interest in talking about how she'd treated him when he was a fledgling. "I used to be just like her," he said, instead.

"Not anymore," Everet said. He sat so still, he might have been a statue.

Kane helplessly took another pace toward him. "You really don't want to get rid of me? You don't mind that I'm a magpie?"

"I've got far more respect for a man who battles his demons than one who gives in to them, or even one who didn't have any to begin with."

Another foot of distance disappeared from between them. If Everet could ignore his failings, then it hardly seemed right for Kane to keep harping on about them. He now stood right next to the cot. His knees were just about to bend and sit him down next to his lover and—

"When was the last time you stretched your wings?"

Kane took several very quick steps back. "What's that got to do with anything?" he demanded, any inclination to get up close and personal with Everet vanishing in an instant.

"I want to see the other side of you."

"No."

Everet remained silent.

It would have been far easier to argue with the man if he'd co-operate and argue back. Silence was hard to disagree with. Kane glared down at Everet until inspiration struck.

"I haven't seen your avian side either." Ha! He grinned with glee, knowing he'd won.

"Fair point," Everet said. "We'll both shift together. Maybe that will convince you I have no objection to your species once and for all."

All Kane's triumph drained away. Everet had adopted that stubborn tone of voice now—the one that meant nothing anyone could do, or say, would change his mind.

Everet got to his feet. Reaching for the hem of his T-shirt, he began to undress. He obviously intended to put his plan into action without any delay.

Kane half turned away and obstinately refused to follow his lead. He made a brief attempt to look at the bars and not even watch Everet strip. It was no good, the prospect of seeing Everet's naked body was far too much temptation for him.

Kane soon stared straight at Everet, taking in every gorgeous line of muscle that came into view. Within moments, Kane was as turned on as he had ever been in his life.

Everet smiled; his movements full of confidence as he folded the last item of clothing and placed it neatly on top of the little pile he'd created on the floor at his feet. He moved forward to stand directly in front of Kane. Dipping his head, he brushed their lips together.

"Just remember this, sweetheart, there's far more than one way to get high. And there's at least one way that I completely approve of."

The kiss was so sweet, and Kane had been so sure he'd never feel their mouths meet again, and—

Everet stepped back. Without any warning, he extended his arms and pulled his knees up toward his chest as he leaped high into the air. Shifting mid-jump, his human form vanished, to be replaced by a flash of feathers that quickly morphed into the sleek black wings of a raven.

Using the momentum from his leap to gain more height, he rapidly flapped his wings and overcame the last few tendrils of gravity. Within a few seconds, he rose up the narrow column of air that made up ninety percent of the cage's volume.

No!

Kane didn't think—he followed.

His body automatically began to shift—determined to shadow his master's movements by whatever means necessary. In hindsight, his body failed to invite his brain in on the decision-making process.

Kane's clothing fell around him, trapping his wings and covering his beak.

He struggled against what seemed to have become yards of thick fabric with a mind of its own. Kane cawed and pecked at it, but his head remained covered. Wings were no use at all. His claws only managed to scratch at the denim beneath him.

All at once, light appeared overhead. The fabric moved away entirely of its own volition.

No. As Kane peeked his head above the neckline of his T-shirt, he realised the edge of the fabric was held in a raven's beak. Squirming out of the clinging material, Kane hopped onto a clear patch of floor and shook out his wings, encouraging his feathers to settle around him in a far more attractive way.

Through avian eyes Everet was…Kane let out a sound as close to a huff as a bird's throat could produce. Everet looked just as he always had. Sleek black feathers replaced sleek black hair. He was still big and strong; his movements were still confident. He still had that look in his eye that hinted he was keeping a perpetual watch over the whole world and was ready to pounce on the first man to break the rules.

And Kane loved him for that as much as for any of the other things that made Everet who he was.

Kane was reasonably sure he couldn't blush in his avian form, but he wasn't going to risk Everet seeing any hint of embarrassment in him. Everet would be bound to want to know what he felt, and why, and a million other things that were none of his business.

Stretching out his wings, Kane hopped up onto the edge of the cot. It was strange being back in this form after so many years spent as a human. His pulse was so fast, his limbs so different. Controlling wings wasn't easy when part of him clung to the belief they were still arms.

Taking no more than a moment to bunch his muscles and ready himself, Kane took flight. It would have been much easier out in the open, where he could have taken a long straight course and got his wings properly under his control.

Frantic flapping wasn't the most elegant way to take to the air, but Kane determinedly did whatever it took to gain height—to get high. As loath as Kane was to admit it, something about flying gave him the same rush of adrenaline and pleasure that the quicksilver had provided. Although, he still wasn't sure *anything* could match that table in the silver room.

He rose higher as he sensed Everet join him on the wing.

Cleaning might have made him improve a few human muscle groups. It had done nothing to make his wings stronger. A perch soon called to Kane.

He landed, wrapping his claws around the welcome resting point and clinging to it with all the fear of a shifter who wasn't sure big human feet could balance on such a narrow bit of wood. He looked up just in time to see Everet catch up. Everet didn't hesitate to join him on the thick wooden pole extending a yard out from the side of the cage.

Kane turned his head and glared at the raven, as if he wasn't completely thrilled to be perched next to his master. Everet dipped his head and let the top of it rub against the side of Kane's neck.

Kane hadn't been in his avian form for years—not since he took up residence in the human world and discovered quicksilver made shifting impossible. Even when he had flown, it was only with other magpies.

Kane looked down. He never remembered receiving such a gentle, flirtatious touch from anyone while in his avian form. Unsure how he was expected to respond, not wanting to let his master down, Kane hesitatingly copied the gesture.

Everet made a noise that sounded approving. That was good enough for Kane. He'd have grinned, if his beak had been willing to co-operate.

Several other perches were set around the edges of his cage.

Kane hopped off his current resting place and swooped down to a lower one. Everet followed. Kane rubbed the top of his head against the other man's feathers, before quickly leaving that perch for another—this time higher up on the bars.

Everet followed. No, Kane knew that was wrong.

Everet wasn't the type to follow. If he was on a man's heels, it was because he chased him.

Predator and prey. Dominant and submissive. Cop and criminal.

Raven and magpie.

Maybe one really would be lost without the other...

As he dipped and weaved, flapped and swerved around the cage, Kane's soul sang out in wonder. Why had he never realised before just how bloody wonderful flying could feel? Even in this stupid cage, it was pure ecstasy.

It would be even better out there in the real world, where he'd be able to see all the way to the horizon and nothing could stop him claiming the whole sky as his own.

Kane paused on a perch for a moment, sudden fear making him less than inclined to spread his wings again.

A flutter of feathers behind him made him look over his shoulder. The whole time he'd been on the wing, Everet had never been more than half a yard behind him.

The sky would never belong to Kane alone. Everet would never let him leave the nest and fly all on his own. The world might stretch all the way to the horizon line, but Kane knew that Everet would only let him loose out there once he'd made him recite all the rules and limitations he placed on him a million and one times.

Everet hopped along the perch until he was close enough to dip his head and straighten a few of Kane's wing feathers that had slid askew by his awkward landing.

Nothing could frighten Kane while another man cared about him that much. He took flight again. He had no idea how many times they circled the cage; their journeys short but quick as they dashed from one perch to another, spreading their wings and resting by turn.

Each time he took to the wing, more and more adrenaline and endorphins rushed through Kane's avian form, until he suddenly reached a point where his magpie form was too small to contain it.

His decent was rapid. The air rushed past as he sped toward the base of the cage, racing against his own desires. He was aware of Everet swooping down after him, but in the raven's case, it was probably by choice rather than necessity.

Kane barely managed to reach the cot before he began to shift back into his human form. The raven landed on the cot just a second after Kane crashed down on it. The moment he touched the rough canvas, Everet began to morph.

His hands had barely changed from wings into fingers before they wrapped around Kane's wrists, pinning him down against the hard mattress. Their mouths met the second their beaks deserted them.

Kane tipped back his head, thinking of nothing other than offering the other man his complete submission. There were no games to be played now. It was too soon after his change for him to be anything other than the man he was and to react the way his nature dictated.

Everet was bigger and stronger than him, but more to the point, he was good and strict, and Kane really did love him more than he'd ever believed a magpie was capable of loving anyone other than himself.

Everet growled deep in the back of his throat. Kane moaned in response and squirmed in an effort to spread his legs and offer his body to him.

"Mine," Everet snarled against Kane's lips.

Kane was too busy kissing to talk. Lifting his head off the mattress, he brought their lips together again. Everet pulled away, swiftly taking his mouth out of kissing range and glared down at him. He was as stubborn as ever. Nothing would be granted to Kane until he did what was required. Another shot of adrenaline shot through his body.

Perfect.

"Yours." There was no hint of doubt in his voice.

Everet rocked his hips, rubbing their crotches together. Hard flesh slid against a mirror image of itself; teasing, tempting, and slicking skin with pre-cum. There was no controlling themselves, no way that they could actually have sex.

Fingers which still half-thought they were wings weren't suited to applying lube. Humping each other like teenagers in heat was all they could manage—it was all they needed.

Kane gasped, moving even more quickly as he revelled in the lack of control he sensed in Everet's movements.

Masters absorb something of their submissives too.

Ori had been right. Even as he lay there, Kane sensed some of Everet's self-control give way to a little of his own brand of impulsiveness.

Everet was his master just as much as Kane was Everet's

submissive.

Kane squirmed and writhed beneath the heat and strength of Everet's body, glorying in both the mental and physical hold that Everet had over him, that they had over each other.

He bucked. Arching his back, he came; spilling between their bodies, slicking their movements even further.

Everet didn't pause for a moment. If anything, his thrusts became more determined, more resolute. Blinking rapidly, Kane managed to focus on Everet's face. His control gradually returned as his human side moved to the fore, but he still wasn't the ice man he'd been when they first met.

Kane stared up at his master, completely enthralled by Everet's every movement as he determinedly thrust his way to orgasm.

Pleasure flashed across Everet's face as he came. He was beautiful; it was a strong, hard, masculine kind of beautiful, but none the less perfect because of that. He was glorious—a man anyone in his right mind would fall in love with the moment he set eyes on him.

Everet collapsed against Kane as all his energy seemed to desert him. Their bodies fitted together as if they'd been designed specifically for that purpose.

The cot was built for one. There was no room for them to move farther apart. Someone had to lie on top of the other. Everet had to pin him to the bed. Kane smiled as his eyes fell closed and sleep rushed to claim his mind.

Positioned as they were, Everet didn't need to have a lock on the cage door, or put an alarm on it, either. There was no way Kane could get up, move, or even breathe without his master knowing about it. He'd never felt safer in his life.

Chapter Fifteen

"So, this is where you two have been hiding yourselves away."

Everet lifted his head. It was the only part of his body he could move without waking Kane. The magpie lay half on top of him and half wrapped around him, in a complicated arrangement of limbs that barely allowed Everet to take a deep breath. Wriggling was out of the question.

Raynard stood just outside the cage looking more than a little amused. "Hamilton's ordered the entire nest to be searched for you. Apparently, your fellow guards completely failed to notice your presence here..."

Everet said nothing. It seemed unlikely that Raynard would allow anyone to be disciplined for hiding his whereabouts, but it wasn't his place to risk other men's backs on it.

"You really ruffled Hamilton's feathers by rushing off the way you did." Raynard couldn't have sounded less concerned by that fact if he'd tried. "And after he put all that effort into getting her here so he could prove Kane is a lost cause."

"He's not a lost cause!"

Kane made a disapproving noise in the back of his throat and snuggled into Everet's side, as if he sensed his fury but, while asleep at least, couldn't comprehend that it wasn't directed at him. Everet automatically held him more firmly and stroked his hand down his spine in an effort to soothe him.

Everet knew that Raynard observed it all. He wasn't one to miss a thing, but when their eyes met, Raynard merely nodded his approval.

"Ori and I agree with your assessment. I wouldn't have believed it if I hadn't seen it with my own eyes, but he's turned out passably well."

From a man like Raynard, and directed at someone other than Ori, it was high praise indeed. Everet was too shocked to think of thanking him for it.

"Our visitors have left," Raynard went on. "Ori will talk Hamilton down off the ledge—he's proven to have quite a talent for it. So, it's quite safe for you both to come out of your cage. Neither of you will be punished."

"I'm glad you both think well of Kane, sir," Everet said. "I have a favour to ask." He studied Raynard's expression very carefully as he rushed out the request.

The hawk raised an eyebrow at him. "Oh?"

Everet took a deep breath. If it had just been for himself, he'd have bid a rapid retreat. Raynard and Ori had done so much for him already. Asking for anything from them was the most ungrateful insult he could have stumbled upon, but this wasn't for him.

Sometimes being a good master involved putting your submissive first and doing whatever needed to be done—even if it meant going down on bended knee and begging a favour, even if it meant admitting that he wasn't able to make everything right in Kane's world all by himself.

* * * * *

Kane arched his back, stretching his spine as he stirred. He lay against a warm, strong body. That was always a good way to wake up. A calm, content feeling filled every corner of his mind. That was even better. It meant the body he rested half on top of was Everet's. No one else had ever made him feel that way.

He opened his eyes and lifted his head.

Everet was already wide awake. Their eyes met.

Kane smiled as a wonderful idea rushed to the front of his mind. Morning sex!

He blinked and rubbed at his eyes then, as his surroundings nudged at the edge of his senses, hinting that they weren't in Everet's bedroom.

Metal bars. Narrow cot. Cell. Cage. Damn!

Kane pushed against Everet's chest as he tried to sit up and re-process everything that happened just before he fell asleep. He failed on both counts.

Everet's arms wrapped around him, making it impossible for him to rise. As for his memories, Kane was sure they would never make sense.

"Anything special you want to say?" Everet asked.

Giving up on doing anything except leaning against Everet's chest for the moment, Kane shook his head.

"Raynard dropped by while you were asleep," Everet mentioned, almost casually.

Kane's instincts for self-preservation instantly went onto high alert. "Why? What did he want? Am I—?"

Everet put a hand over Kane's mouth.

Bite? Kiss? Caught between two options, Kane finally settled for doing nothing.

"We're expected in the elders' meeting room. Now."

Kane pulled his head back, taking his lips away from Everet's hand.

"No." Everet's tone of voice didn't invite disobedience at the best of times, but it seemed to be especially true then.

Kane was caught so off guard, he forgot what he'd been about to say.

"Don't talk. Just do as you're told." Everet released Kane from his embrace. "Get up. Get dressed."

Within seconds, Everet was on his feet and he already had half his clothes on. A strange kind of tension filled his body. Kane saw it in every movement Everet made. Something was wrong. Everet was hiding something from him.

Kane frowned as he hesitantly followed Everet's example and picked up his trousers. Cum stains decorated both their bodies. Kane toyed with the idea of suggesting they head up to the apartment to take a shower—after all, it would probably be disrespectful to turn up in front of the elders unless they were nice and clean. And, once he got Everet up to the flat, he could probably convince him to—

No. Kane stopped himself short before a single word left his lips. Everet deserved better from him than that sort of behaviour. That probably applied even when Everet was keeping secrets from him.

Kane dressed. His T-shirt had torn as he'd shifted while still wearing it. There was a rip in one leg of his jeans too. It made him think back to the first clothes Everet had given him. Everet had given him so much, even if it wasn't all quite as shiny as Kane would have preferred. He followed Everet to the cage door.

As he stepped outside, Kane spotted the slate and saw what was written on it for the first time. His stomach knotted up as he read it.

Species: Magpie. Crime: Being a magpie. Duration: Until he stops being a magpie.

"Me and the guard who wrote that are going to have a long talk later on," Everet promised.

"I said it," Kane blurted out.

Everet turned to face him.

"He asked why I had to go in a cage." Kane met Everet's gaze for a moment.

Everet wiped everything off the slate with his fingertips. "Well, we've already talked, so you already know better now. Don't you?"

Kane nodded. There was no need for them to have a long talk.

Everet stepped back, but Kane lingered in the entrance to the cage. There was a strange sort of safety to be found behind the bars. There were no temptations there. It was impossible for him to do the wrong thing.

"Come on."

Everet's order pulled Kane away from the cage, offering him a different kind of security—one that put all his temptations directly in front of him and demanded he learn how to resist them.

The guards said nothing as Everet walked past them with no more than a nod. Kane hurried to keep up with him, feeling as if they'd just enacted the least subtle jailbreak in the entire history of the cage.

Up in the main part of the nest, Kane tensed even further. People were staring at them, turning their heads to watch them pass—and it probably wasn't because they both smelled like sex. Something was up. Kane had been in the cage for less than a day, but something had changed while he'd been there.

Kane sped up, walking closer to Everet's side. For once in his life, he wasn't interested in being the centre of attention.

Everet glanced toward him. His expression changed slightly. The seriousness in his eyes didn't disappear, but it softened a little. Reaching out, he took hold of Kane's hand—not his wrist, his hand.

It shouldn't have felt either reassuring or strangely romantic. It was either criminally soppy or a blatant precaution against any attempt to run away on Kane's part. Somehow, Kane still found he liked it. Being connected to his master that way felt good. Not as good as being screwed into the silverware, but very nice nonetheless.

Bolstered by Everet's touch, Kane didn't hesitate, not even when a servant opened the door leading to the elders' meeting room and they made their way inside.

They walked forward, side by side, until they stood directly in front of the long oak table. On the other side of it sat Raynard, Ori and Hamilton. None of the other elders were present. Kane wasn't sure if that was a good sign or not.

His mind rushed back to the day he'd first arrived at the nest. It felt like a lifetime ago, and, at the same time, as if it were just yesterday.

A few extra elders had sat on the other side of the table then. Other things were different, too. Kane wasn't the same man. How he felt about the guy next to him had changed beyond all recognition. The circle had completed itself. He was back where he started.

The amount of self-control it took to stand in front of the elders and neither throw a temper tantrum nor run and hide, was almost more than Kane could manage. It was only Everet's grip on his hand that kept him there. It was only his desire to be good for his master that made him try his best to keep his chin up and his heart from leaping out of his chest.

Everet squeezed his fingers.

Kane turned his head and glanced up at him.

The smile Everet gave him was worth whatever effort Kane needed to expend in order to meet a raven's expectations.

Finally, Hamilton finished shuffling his papers around. He glared up at them over his glasses.

"Last time you stood before us, you convinced the council of elders to grant you permission to undertake an experiment." Distaste dipped off his every syllable. "The experiment is over."

No! Kane tensed. He swayed forward, more than a little tempted to grab hold of Hamilton's lapels and shake him until he changed his mind.

"It is the opinion of the elders that Kane has proven that he can maintain the level of conduct required of him in order to be accepted into the nest as a free avian." Hamilton couldn't have sounded less pleased with the pronouncement if he'd spoken his own death sentence. "From this moment, Kane is a free avian, with all the rights and freedoms that entails. He does not belong to Everet and is no longer under any kind of supervision."

Hamilton stood up, turned on his heel and strode out of the room. The door in the far wall slammed in his wake.

Kane stood perfectly still. He was quite sure the death sentence Hamilton had announced was his own rather than the eagle's. A life without Everet was...

"Kane, I know you're scared right now, but you're not going to run away." Everet turned so they faced each other. His hand tightened around Kane's fingers as if to make sure of that. His other hand came to rest on Kane's shoulder. "This isn't where it ends."

"Yes, it is," Kane whispered. "Hamilton said..." He looked up at Everet and forced himself to meet his gaze. "Hamilton can really do that? He can just wipe away everything we've...?"

"Some things," Everet corrected. "Not everything."

Kane swallowed. "What do I have left?" By supreme force of will, he kept his voice level and the majority of his emotions in check.

"The experiment is over," Everet said. "The elders' interest in our relationship is over too...if you want it to be."

Kane frowned. What he wanted mattered?

Someone cleared their throat.

Kane jerked his attention away from Everet. He'd almost forgotten that Ori and Raynard still sat on the other side of the table.

He turned back to Everet. It didn't matter who was there, he had to sort things out with Everet. If other people heard him, that couldn't be helped.

He looked up into Everet's eyes. "I love you." Kane mentally cursed. He hadn't intended to just blurt it out that way, but the words had been right there in the front of his head and he hadn't been able to stop them escaping—not even if they made him look like the biggest idiot alive.

"I love you, too," Everet said, very calmly, as if that should have been obvious.

"As I was about to say," Raynard cut in. "As far as the elders are concerned, there's no reason why the two of you can't enter into a properly ratified contract, if that's what you both want?"

Everet didn't even glance in his direction and, as important as Raynard's words felt, Kane couldn't look away from Everet for long enough to blink, let alone peer across the room at another man.

"Hamilton was right about one thing," Everet said, his voice suddenly turning gruff. "I can't speak for you anymore. You're a free avian. You have a choice." He paused for several seconds, as if to allow Kane time to process that. Finally, he spoke again. "Do you want to belong to me?"

As confident as Everet sounded, something in his eyes hinted he wasn't as at ease as he might wish he was. Everet was scared.

That couldn't go on. Kane needed him too much for Everet to be scared by anything. He loved him too much to let him feel any sort of pain.

Kane had to fix this! "Yes," he rushed out. "To everything."

As easily as that, Everet's expression cleared. He might not grin often, but when he did, it was certainly worth the wait. Kane beamed back at him, success and relief mixing in his veins and making him dizzy.

"I'll arrange for someone to visit you tomorrow and draw up a contact that you both find suitable," Raynard offered. "I suspect you've both had enough excitement for today."

"Thank you, sir." Everet turned toward Raynard as he spoke.

"Kane?" That was Ori's voice. Kane turned toward him.

"Everet has asked us to make sure that the contract is binding, that there be no way for either of you to leave it, except for the most serious of possible reasons. It's the kind of contract that's intended to last for life. Is that what you want?"

Kane turned back to Everet. "You asked them?"

Everet nodded, just once.

This was what Everet really wanted. Kane's mind reeled with the knowledge. Everet hadn't been landed with him. He hadn't stepped in to rescue him from the cage. He hadn't taken him on at the spur of the moment. Everet had planned this. He wanted him.

"Kane?" Ori prompted gently.

"Yes." Kane nodded rapidly, as he glanced toward the swan. "That's what I want."

Ori smiled. His fingers twitched, and Kane noticed that Ori had hooked them into the band of leather he wore around his neck, the way he'd seen him do so many times in the silver room.

"You've got the same kind of contract, haven't you?" he asked.

Ori nodded. His grip on his collar tightened. He didn't need words to explain what they'd chosen to commemorate their understanding.

Kane tugged on Everet's hand. "I want a collar."

Raynard chuckled. "So there is still a bit of the magpie left in him."

Kane ignored him. So did Everet. The raven's attention remained all on him. "I'll get you one," he promised.

Raynard and Ori walked around the table. Hands were shaken. Raynard babbled on about something, and no doubt Everet listened to him very politely, but Kane's mind was all on the prospect of getting the collar he wanted. Lifting one hand, he touched his neck, working out exactly where it would lay against his skin.

Yes, he'd have a collar—but not a boring black leather one like Ori wore...

Finally, Everet turned and walked toward the door. Apparently, there'd been enough talking. They were free to go. Kane was more than happy to leave, his hand still held within Everet's grip.

The heavy wood had barely closed behind them before Everet turned to him.

"Yes."

Kane looked warily up at him "Yes?" he asked.

"Yes, you can have a silver collar," Everet said. Lifting his left hand, he traced a fingertip along the same line Kane had followed around the front of his throat. "And it will glitter and sparkle beautifully. I promise."

"You made me another promise yesterday," Kane reminded him with a grin.

"I did?"

Kane nodded very seriously.

Everet's eyes narrowed. "And what was it?"

"You said that, after we went to the meeting with the elders, we could go back to the silver room and get laid."

"Did I?" Everet asked, far more relaxed now. His tone of voice completely off.

Kane shook his head sadly. "You're a good master. But you're a really bad liar."

Everet blinked, doing his best to look innocent and uncomprehending.

Kane pushed his free hand against Everet's chest. "Don't tease! You know what I'm talking about."

Everet hadn't even swayed when Kane pushed him, but his

hand automatically came up to rest on Kane's back, keeping him steady and safe as naturally as any other man might breathe.

Kane leaned forward, rose up on his toes and whispered into Everet's ear. "If you want me to get down on my knees, right here in front of everyone in the corridor and, very loudly, beg you to do everything you've ever done to me in the silver room all over again, in precise and graphic terms, I'm more than happy to do that."

"Still trying to blackmail me, after all this time?" Everet asked. If he attempted to fake a stern tone of voice, he failed spectacularly. He was clearly as high on life and love as Kane felt.

"Nope. I'm just trying to hurry you the hell up. I want my daily dose of silver. And my daily dose of you, too."

Everet laughed, looped his arm around Kane's shoulders and turned them both toward the silver room. "Only one dose of me a day?"

Kane frowned. "My morning dose," he corrected. "Which is very different to the afternoon dose, or the evening dose, or the happen to catch you in the shower dose, or the—"

"I get the idea," Everet cut in, with another chuckle.

Kane grinned. Making Everet laugh felt good. Wearing a piece of silver Everet had given him around his neck would feel brilliant, too.

As they turned a corner, Kane slid his arm around the other man's waist in return. For once, it didn't even occur to him to try to pick his lover's pocket, not even when this perfect opportunity presented itself to him.

He didn't need to bother with that kind of stuff anymore. There was no need for him to think about stealing a damn thing. Not when he already had everything he'd ever wanted.

Also in the Avian Shifter Series

Duck!

Raised among humans, Ori Jones only discovered he was an avian shifter six months ago. Unable to complete a full shift until he reaches his avian maturity, he still can't be sure of his exact species.

But with species comes rank, and rank is everything to the avians. When a partial shift allows the elders to announce that they believe Ori to be a rather ugly little duckling, he drops straight to the bottom rung of their hierarchy.

Life isn't easy for Ori until he comes to the attention of a high ranking hawk shifter. Then the only question is, is Ori really a duck—and what will his new master think when the truth eventually comes out?

Also in the Avian Shifter Series

Celebrate

It's not easy learning how to be a swan, but Ori Jones has worked hard to embrace a role that still doesn't come entirely naturally to him. Now, almost a year after his first full shift, he finally feels as if he is making a difference at the Anderson nest.

Ori's happier than he'd ever been, until a few words from his master, Raynard, suddenly bring all of Ori's old fears rushing back to the surface.

The nest's elders want to have a party for Ori's birthday, but Ori can't see any reason to celebrate in it being a year since he reached his avian maturity. After all, what's the use in learning to be a good swan when Raynard never wanted a swan in the first place?

Other books by Kim Dare

Series

Werewolves & Dragons
The Avian Shifters
Kinky Cupid
FIT Guys
Thrown to the Lions
Rawlings Men
Sex Sells
Sun, Sea and Submission
The Whole A-Z
Pack Discipline
G-A-Y Lust Bites
Perfect Timing
Collared
Pushing the Envelope
Kinky Quickies

Kim Dare has also written a number of free short stories.
You can find these on her website.

About the Author

Kim is a bisexual submissive from Wales (UK). First published in 2008, she has since released over 100 BDSM erotic romance titles ranging from short stories to full length novels. Having worked with a host of fantastic e-publishers, she moved into self publishing in 2013.

While she occasionally enjoys writing other pairings, most of Kim's stories focus on Male/Male relationships. But, no matter what the pairing, from paranormal to contemporary, and from the sweet to the intense, everything she writes will always feature three things - Kink, Love and a Happy Ending.

You can find out more about Kim's books on her website, follow her on twitter, catch up with her blog, and email her directly using the links below.

Website: **www.kimdare.com**
Twitter: **www.twitter.com/KimDareAuthor**
Facebook: **www.facebook.com/kimdareauthor**
Blog: **www.kimdare.wordpress.com**
E-mail: **kim@kimdare.com**

CPSIA information can be obtained
at www.ICGtesting.com
Printed in the USA
FSHW020953150819
61077FS